LUCKY LARRY

Pat Feehan

For Jennifer and Kevin

Chapter 1

Larry made a beeline for the back door as soon as Casper went out for his breakfast. He wedged the door open with a bit of wood he kept for the purpose and looked out onto the narrow lane. It was used for rubbish and for some deliveries so it gave him a bit of a cover story. If Casper came back early, he would say he was taking stuff out to the bins. He quickly lit up and inhaled greedily.

Casper went out every morning about ten to grab a coffee and a roll and sausage in the Ritz café next door and that was Larry's cue to nip out for a fag. But today things had been busier than usual and Larry's thoughts had kept drifting to the packet of Marlboro in his jacket pocket. He'd been trying to check the time without being spotted but it felt like there were eyes everywhere.

He wasn't allowed to smoke in the shop and Casper didn't even like him lighting up at the back door; said it was bad for the animals and put the customers off. Larry suspected the real reason was that Casper had stopped smoking a year ago and hated to see anybody else enjoying a fag.

In any case, he thought, the smoke masked the stink from the animals. The stench had hit him on his first day in the place. Like somebody had soaked a bundle of old clothes in dirty water and left them steaming over a low heat. He couldn't decide which of the wee buggers smelt worst.

He wasn't an animal lover and, based on the number of times he'd been bitten or nipped, it seemed the feeling was mutual. He was only here because he'd no other options. He'd lost his last job, in the whisky warehouse, due to a 'misunderstanding' over a few cases of ten-year old malt. Sharon had been furious, and threatened, not for the first time, to throw him out or even divorce him. She said that, with his police record, she'd get full custody of the kids. Larry was sure she was exaggerating; he'd only ever done small stuff. But he couldn't take the risk. He had to keep in her good books.

After making him suffer for a week or so, she'd persuaded her brother, Casper, to give Larry a job in his pet shop. The two of them acted like they were doing Larry this big favour. But spending his working life feeding animals their weird food and cleaning up their shit wasn't his idea of fun. Not to mention that Casper gave Sharon regular reports about what Larry got up to.

He watched the smoke curling into the cold air and glanced back inside the shop. Dozens of eyes were staring at him. They were probably just wanting fed, but it felt like he was being watched from every angle.

The lane was shared by all the shops on the block. Next door there was the café, then the bookies and further along there was a tattoo parlour and a second-hand book shop. Occasionally you'd get someone cutting through as a shortcut, or the odd drunk sneaking in, caught short on their way home, but at this time of the morning it was quiet. He covered his nose as a gust of wind carried the rancid smells from the bins. Christ, he didn't know what smelt worse, the shop or the lane.

His thoughts were interrupted by the sound of voices. There was nobody in sight but they seemed to be coming from a few doors down. He leaned further out into the lane and saw the back door to Tony the bookies was open. He listened for a minute. Definitely an argument. One of the voices was Tony's but he didn't recognise the other one. He was intrigued but, despite his natural curiosity, he stayed where he was. Experience had taught him to mind his own business, not get involved.

He leaned back against the doorframe, drawing deep on his cigarette when, out of the corner of his eye, he saw a long-eared rabbit go hopping out the door. It paused and turned to look at him before setting off down the lane in a bid for freedom. He paid as little attention as possible to the animals but he recognised this one. It had a distinctive white coat, the only one of its kind in the shop. As it hopped down the lane, Larry saw the black patch on its left rear foot, the only blemish on its otherwise pure white fur. He swore; he must have left its cage door open when he was cleaning it. Casper would kill him. He sucked the last of the smoke into his lungs, flung the stub over the wall and went chasing after the rabbit. It was headed straight for Tony's door.

Every time he bent to pick the rabbit up it dodged in the other direction. By the time he finally caught up with the animal, it was just about to go through the back door of the bookies. He crouched down and grabbed it just in time. As he did so, he caught sight of Tony, pinned against the wall of the shop by two vicious-looking guys. A third man was holding a knife to Tony's cheek. Larry had seen him before, couldn't remember where, but he was obviously bad news. The guy had a ragged scar down his left cheek and some sort of weird tattoo on his neck. Larry crouched there, holding the rabbit, desperate to get away but afraid to move in case he made a noise and they spotted him.

Suddenly the one with the knife dragged it down Tony's cheek and surveyed the damage while Tony screamed blue murder. He butted him on the nose and Tony slumped to the floor with blood spurting from his face. The three men laid into him with vicious kicks. The grunts of the men and the groans from Tony echoed along the deserted lane, giving Larry his chance to slip away unnoticed.

He tightened his grip on the rabbit, softly got to his feet and tip-toed back to the shop. He closed the door behind him, carried the rabbit over to the sink and gave it a quick wipe with a damp cloth. As he locked the animal back in its cage he released the breath he hadn't realised he was holding in.

Chapter 2

He'd just started to check that the rest of the cages were locked when the door crashed open and the three thugs from the bookies came into the shop. Larry felt his heart drop into his stomach. They must have spotted him in the lane after all. He glanced towards the back door assessing his chances of escape and took a half step in that direction.

'Thinking of going somewhere?' Scarface said. The guy sounded like he gargled with gravel every morning.

'No,' Larry said, 'I thought I heard the back door.' He looked towards the front door, hoping somebody would come into the shop. Where was Casper when he needed him? 'I thought maybe it was a delivery.'

The man gave Larry a look that made his stomach turn over. 'Is that right?'

The question was put quietly, almost gently. But Larry knew the type, the sort who would switch from quiet calm to violence without missing a heartbeat. Larry's eyes were drawn to the guy's scar.

'The fuck you staring at?' the man said.

Larry realised he was shaking. 'Nothing. Sorry. No offence.' He dragged his gaze away to look at the other two but they just stared at him with dead eyes. One was well over six feet and huge, a mountain, the other was shorter, wiry and evil-looking, like a rat that had escaped from its cage and was out for revenge on its captor. Both of them were wearing scuffed leather jackets, denims and some sort of heavy desert boots. The boots were spotted with red streaks that Larry realised must be Tony's blood.

The boss signalled to the mountain. 'Take a look and see if there's anybody out there.'

The man lumbered over to the back door, opened it and looked out. 'Nothing,' he said, closing the door behind him and moved back into position beside rat face.

The boss took a step towards Larry, then stopped, leaned towards him and sniffed. 'Something stinks in here. Have you shat yourself?'

He looked at his henchmen and they laughed on cue. He turned back to Larry. 'Where's Casper?'

'He's not here.'

Scarface grabbed Larry's left ear and twisted it. 'You trying to be funny?'

Larry rubbed his ear. 'No.'

The man slowly looked round the shop. 'I can see he's not here.'

'He's away out for his breakfast, a coffee and a roll,' Larry said, aware that his voice was squeaking.

'What do they call you?'

'Larry.'

'Larry? I'll remember that. I used to have a dog called Larry, a greyhound, a wee scrawny thing. He was useless. Had to get rid of him.'

Rat face sniggered.

Scarface pointed both index fingers at Larry, like a two-gun cowboy. 'We'll be back,' he said. He paused and gave Larry a cold look. 'Tell the wee bastard not to go too far, I want a quiet word with him.'

'Who will I say was asking?' Larry said, but they were gone. He watched them through the window as they crossed the street, got into a Range Rover and headed off towards Glasgow Cross.

Heart racing, he slumped into the nearest chair. What the fuck was that about? It looked like they hadn't spotted him in the lane. If that was what they did just because you didn't answer their questions the right way, what would they do if they knew you'd seen them kicking the shit out of somebody? He didn't want to find out. After a couple of minutes he hauled himself to his feet and went into the wee kitchen at the back of the shop to make a cup of tea.

While he waited for Casper to return, Larry tried to decide how much he would tell him. He didn't want his boss to know he'd been smoking at the back door or that he'd let a rabbit escape. That could lose him his job and that was all Sharon needed. It seemed the thugs hadn't spotted him so nobody needed to know anything about that. He'd tell Casper somebody had been in looking for him, but that was all.

Casper came back about ten minutes later, whistling and full of the joys for a change. But when Larry described the three guys who had been looking for him, his mood changed, lightning fast. 'Eddie Black and his two Rottweillers, that's all I fucking need.'

As soon as Casper said the name, Eddie Black, Larry joined the dots. He'd heard it mentioned in The Ship and other pubs. The guy was seriously bad news. Whenever people talked about him it was never in a good way. It was the sort of name that people whispered to each other, shaking their head and looking over their shoulder.

'Eddie Black?' he said to Casper. 'What does he want with you?'

Casper tapped his finger against his lips. 'You don't need to know and you don't want to know. And you don't say anything to anyone. That includes Sharon. Right?' With that he headed for the back shop, pulling out his mobile as he went and closing the door behind him.

Larry was relieved that Casper didn't ask any more questions. He'd been right not to mention what he'd seen in the lane. If he told Casper about it, then the whole story would come out. Larry might not love his job but he needed the money and Casper was just looking for an excuse to get shot of him. Larry maybe wasn't all that bright, but he wasn't daft either.

Chapter 3

He made a quick detour to The Ship for a pint and got home just after six. Kelly and wee Joe were getting ready for their swimming club and he gave them both a hug and made up a funny story about the hamsters to make them laugh. But his good mood was quickly shattered when Sharon went on the rampage.

'The washing machine's finally packed in. You said you were going to get your pal, Tosh, to fix it.' She pointed to a large laundry bag in the corner. 'You'll need to go to the launderette on the corner.'

'What about my tea?'

'You can grab a bag of chips once the washing's in the machine.'

He thought about protesting but knew it was no use. She'd made her mind up. In any case, she was right. The machine had been playing up over the last two weeks and he'd promised to call wee Tosh. But, with one thing and another, it had slipped his mind.

So much for Friday night, he thought. He liked to have a few drinks with his mates after his dinner. Maybe he could still fit a quick pint in after he'd taken care of the washing. While Sharon was getting ready to leave, he asked the kids how they were getting on in school. They both seemed to be happy with their teachers and had plenty of friends so that was one bright spot in Larry's life. He told them to enjoy their swimming and gave them a thumbs-up as they headed out the door.

The woman in the launderette kept getting up to check her machine and then moved a little bit further away from him each time she sat down. Larry assumed she could smell the pet shop from him. People talked about a face like a bulldog chewing a wasp but that didn't even cover this one.

She scowled and he wondered if she could read his thoughts. She heaved herself off her seat again and waddled over to her machine. Larry looked at his own machine. He knew they were both thinking the same thing. There was only one tumble dryer working so whose machine would finish first?

They were the only customers in the place. The attendant had nipped out the back for a quick fag before closing up for the night. Larry stared at his washing going round and round. The water was turning a pale shade of pink. He shouldn't have added that red tee-shirt at the last minute. Sharon would kill him.

His machine shuddered to a halt. He transferred his washing into a basket and carried it over to the dryer. The woman was standing in front of it as if she hadn't noticed he was going to use it. Eventually she moved aside, giving him a dirty look. As he transferred his washing into the machine he could feel her eyes drilling into his back.

'I'll be wanting that dryer soon,' she said.

He nodded. 'I'll not be long.'

She grunted and lumbered back to the bench.

He went over to the drinks machine and studied the options on offer. Half of the names were scored out; some had been over-written in red pen. He searched through his pockets and found a pound coin. He slipped it into the slot, pressed the button for coffee and was presented with a cup of something that definitely wasn't coffee. He sniffed it then took a cautious sip. Oxtail soup. He hated oxtail soup. There was a handwritten sign blu-tacked above the desk:

The management are NOT responsible for the drinks machine.

Typical. He wondered if bulldog features might want it. She looked at the cup as if he was trying to poison her.

'I haven't touched it', he said. 'I wanted coffee, but the machine gave me oxtail soup.'

'Oxtail soup? Are you at it?'

Larry wondered what her problem was. He was just offering her a cup of soup; it wasn't as if he was asking her to pay for it. He realised he was staring at her.

'What are you looking at?' she said. 'Are you trying to pick me up or something?' She sniffed and shifted further down the bench.

He looked at her. She was built like a scaled-down Sumo wrestler and had a chin like Desperate Dan with the six-day stubble to match.

'No hen. I'm not trying to pick you up.' He placed the cup of soup on a table. 'I don't fancy

11

giving myself a hernia,' he said, and smiled at his own wit.

It took her a moment to work this out, then she turned even uglier. She was working out her reply but just then the door of the launderette opened and a man came in. He was roughly the same shape as the woman but with a few inches extra in every direction. He had a face like a bag of spanners.

'Haw Billy,' she shouted. 'This bastard's been trying to pick me up. And when I gave him a knock-back he called me all sorts of names.'

The man looked puzzled, maybe struggling with the idea that Larry would want to make a move on his woman. Apart from anything else, she was about twice as heavy as him. But honour had to be satisfied. Before Larry could say anything the man grabbed him by the collar, yanked him to his feet and marched him towards the door of the launderette.

'I'll be back in a minute, doll,' he said over his shoulder and hustled Larry out of the door.

Larry looked around him in the hope that help might be on hand but the street was deserted. He started to explain but the guy head-butted him and Larry went down hard, landing in a puddle next to a lamp post.

The man moved towards Larry and drew his foot back. 'I just offered her a cup of soup,' Larry shouted. 'Oxtail,' he added.

'She fucking hates oxtail, you dick.' The guy landed a vicious kick in Larry's groin followed by one to his face. 'Try it on again and I'll kill you, you wee shite.'

Larry lay curled up on the ground in agony, bleeding all over the pavement. The man sauntered back to the launderette, job done. A minute later the door opened again and Larry watched the woman emerge carrying a big laundry bag. She walked over to the edge of the pavement, looked down at Larry and turned the bag upside down emptying his washing into the gutter. He could see the faded red tee-shirt on the top of the bundle. She scowled at him. 'Don't give yourself a hernia picking up your washing.' She gave him the old two-finger salute, tucked the bag under her arm and went back in dusting her hands together as she went.

Larry wondered if he'd passed out because it seemed just a moment later that she reappeared. Billy followed behind, laundry bag slung over his shoulder. He was sipping at the cup of oxtail soup and he held it out towards Larry in a silent 'cheers' gesture. Larry struggled to his knees and watched them waddle along the pavement.

He heard a noise behind him. An Alsatian dog cocked its leg at the lamp post, the stream bounced off and sprayed over him. He scrambled to his feet cursing and grabbing at the clothes, trying to save as much of it as he could. He trudged back to the launderette, hoping to run it though the machine again. The door was locked, the attendant was busy switching off the lights and she ignored his knocking.

He leaned his head against the window of the launderette for a moment then he took off his jacket and bundled the washing up in it as best he could. As he made his way home to face Sharon, it started to rain.

Chapter 4

As he turned into Battlefield Road, he saw Sammy sitting in front of the close, like the lord of the manor. The cat followed him in and weaved in and out of his legs as he made his way up the stairs.

'Get out the road, you daft wee bugger,' he said.

He hadn't seen the car outside the close so Sharon was probably still at the swimming with the kids. He opened the door cautiously, just in case, and listened for voices. He was in luck, the house was empty. The cat slipped into the house ahead of him and was standing looking at him by the time Larry reached the kitchen.

He examined the washing to assess the damage. Some of it didn't look too bad but others had black and red stains on them. He hung it out on the clothes horse, on radiators and on chairs, making sure that he put the worst-looking stuff at the back and mentally crossed his fingers.

The cat wrinkled its nose and yawned disdainfully, clearly not impressed by his feeble efforts. He pushed it out of the way with his foot, but didn't go as far as actually kicking it. It was Sharon's pet and he had no time for the creature. In any case, he got more than his fill of animals at the pet shop.

He cleaned himself up and changed his clothes. He was checking the fridge for something to eat when he heard the door opening. The kids were excited, as usual after the swimming, and they came running in to see him. When Sharon appeared a minute later she immediately clocked the washing draped everywhere.

'What in God's name happened? Did you not put the clothes into the tumble dryer?'

Larry did his best to explain but Sharon just stood there shaking her head and giving him one of her looks.

'How come you always manage to get into bother wherever you go?'

He spread his arms wide. 'It wasn't my fault.'

She examined the washing, peering at the clothes hanging at the back. 'For God's sake, look at all these dirty marks, and some of it looks red. It'll all need to be washed again.'

The cat strolled over and rubbed itself against her legs. Larry wanted to strangle the animal but he tried to remain calm.

'I told you what happened. They were a pair of nutters. Vicious as well.'

She was having none of it. 'Christ, I ask you to do a simple thing. Anyway, you wouldn't have had to do it if you'd got the washing machine sorted.'

He was tempted to reply in kind. She never took his side, always wanted to blame him for everything. And it wasn't as if she was perfect. But out of the corner of his eye he saw Kelly and Joe standing in the doorway, watching them. He hated arguing in front of the kids so he bit his tongue.

'Right, I'm away for a pint.'

He winked at Kelly and Joe and gave them both a hug. As he passed Sharon, he thought about saying something, some further word of apology, to keep the peace. But the words stuck in his throat. With everything that had happened in the shop and the launderette, he couldn't take any more. He shook his head in defeat, grabbed his jacket from the hook and slammed the door behind him.

It was well after midnight when he fumbled his way in through the front door. His first stop was an urgent visit to the toilet then it was into the kitchen for tea and a couple of slice of toasted cheese. He quietly hummed 'The Galway Girl' to himself and did a vague attempt at an Irish jig as he waited for the toast. He thought he had been quiet, but, a minute later, while he was standing, half-bent-over, watching the bread under the grill he heard Sharon's voice behind him.

'For God's sake, you're going to wake the kids. Look at the state of you. You're covered in mud and stinking of drink and God knows what else. I'll deal with you in the morning.'

She turned to head back to bed but she paused at the kitchen door. 'By the way,' she said, 'if you want that bread to toast, you better switch the grill on.'

As she walked away Larry made a strangling gesture behind her back.

'One of these days,' he muttered, 'one of these bloody days.'

17

Chapter 5

When Larry woke up on Saturday morning, he was feeling rough. The symptoms were all too familiar, mouth like the bottom of a budgie's cage, head pounding and a nagging feeling that he'd done something he'd be paying for later. Sharon was snoring away contentedly. He thought about nudging her with his elbow but decided against it.

He levered himself out of bed and shambled into the kitchen. He switched the telly on low so as not to disturb the kids and made himself tea and a bowl of Cheerios. He poured a second cup and had a slice of bread with a nice, thick coating of strawberry jam. He tasted it and nodded to himself, that was better, the extra sugar rush was what he needed this morning. He chewed away at it, washing it down with mouthfuls of tea while he watched the news. It always seemed to be bad news these days. Murders, drugs, organised crime. He was no angel himself but things were getting out of hand. He got up and walked over to the window and pulled the net curtain to one side. About a mile to the south, the White Cart River glinted in the cold morning air.

He slumped back into his seat and downed the last of his tea. The thought of going into work made him want to crawl back into bed. The place was bad enough at the best of times but being cooped up with all those animals while suffering from a hangover was enough to make you throw up. For the briefest of moments he toyed with the idea of phoning in sick but it was a non-starter. Sharon knew he'd been out drinking and she would give him hell if he tried it on, plus she would tell Casper. At that moment he heard her moving about in their bedroom and he roused himself and nipped in for a shower before she could start on him.

An hour or so later, Larry was leaning on the counter of the pet shop, staring at a sheet of paper. The words and the numbers were dancing in front of his eyes. A price list for bird seed. Casper had told him to check it over before sticking it up in the shop window. Bird seed, for Christ's sake. Who gave a shit? To add to his misery, the smell from the animals was worse than usual today. He couldn't understand why anyone would want a rabbit or a gerbil as a pet. Even worse, why would you want to open a pet shop and be surrounded by the wee bastards all day long?

How long could he stick it here? Out of all the places he'd worked, this had to be the worst. He'd had lots of jobs since leaving school with no qualifications. His favourite had been a wee Italian restaurant, near George Square, working in the kitchen, helping prepare the food. But he'd lost that when he'd had a fight with his boss about the tips. The thieving bastard had been taking more than his fair share and even though everybody knew what was going on, only Larry had spoken out. Next thing he knew, he was out the door. Maybe he could get back into that line of work. He enjoyed cooking and Sharon had loved the leftovers he sometimes sneaked out.

Casper had made a few sarcastic comments about last night's launderette fiasco when Larry had arrived at the shop. So Sharon had obviously been on the phone to him last night. Larry hadn't risen to the bait, there was nothing he could say that would make it better anyway.

Shortly after that, Casper had gone out somewhere, a wee bit of business, he'd said. Larry wasn't interested, he was just trying to somehow get through the day. He was there in body only, his mind occupied in a pleasant daydream. He was on holiday in Tenerife with Sharon and the kids and they were all having a great time. He'd won money on the lottery and he was in Sharon's good books for once.

He was snapped out of it when someone banged on the counter. He hadn't heard the bell on the door. He opened his eyes to see the menacing face of Eddie Black two inches from his own. The rasping voice chased away the last traces of Larry's daydream and he felt himself go tense.

'Where's that wee shite, Casper?'

Larry straightened up and noticed the two henchmen standing behind Black. Their eyes were drilling into Larry. He pulled his attention back to their boss. 'He's away out. A bit of business, that's what he said.'

'Business? What the hell sort of business would he be doing? I thought this was his business.'

Larry didn't know if he expected an answer but Black was moving on. 'Is that his office back there?' He headed for the back shop.

Before he had time to think about it Larry had reacted. 'I don't think he'd want you to go back there. It's private.'

Black stopped dead, turned and gave Larry a look that chilled him to the heart. 'Is that right?' He took a step forward and leaned in so that his face was inches from Larry's. 'You get allowed one mistake like that, challenging me. Do it again and you'll be sorry. Clear?'

Larry swallowed hard and nodded. He managed a 'yes', trying to be matter-of-fact but he knew it came out as a squeak and he felt the sweat break out all over his back.

'You stay right there and have a nice chat with the boys.'

Larry looked at Black's henchmen, hoping in vain for some clue as to why they were here. It couldn't be about what Larry had seen them doing to Tony the day before. If they knew he'd seen them, they'd have dealt with him at the time. So, what then?

Black had told him to have a chat with the boys. He tried the casual, friendly approach. 'You must get out and about a lot, in your line of work.'

The bigger of the two, the mountain, just smiled then leaned forward and belched into Larry's face. The other one, his face deadpan, hissed softly. 'What line of work is that, then?'

Larry stammered. 'You know, going to see people. Helping Mr Black with his business and that.' He knew he was babbling.

'What do you know about Mr Black's business, you wee prick?'

He tried desperately to think of a reply but they both laughed and turned away, dismissing him. He fidgeted with some fliers for the pet shop to try and calm himself. A few minutes later Black reappeared and leaned into Larry's face. 'Did you give Casper my message yesterday?'

Larry felt his throat tighten. 'Definitely. I told him as soon as he came back into the shop.'

'So how come he's not here when I want to see him?'

Larry could only shrug his shoulders.

'Next time I come in here I expect to see him. Right?' He clamped his hand over Larry's face and squeezed hard. 'Otherwise I'll make sure he gets the message some other way.'

Black gave Larry's face a final slap before turning away. He nodded to his two henchmen and they left.

Chapter 6

Casper appeared half an hour later, looking quite pleased with himself. Larry knew better than to ask what he'd been up to.

'Anything exciting happen while I was away?' Casper asked as he headed for the back shop.

Larry hesitated before answering. 'Well, Eddie Black was in again, with his two pals. He wasn't too happy at missing you twice in a row. '

'What did you tell him?'

'Just what you said, that you were out on some bit of business.'

Casper shook his head as if he couldn't believe what he was hearing. 'What the fuck did you tell him that for?'

'What else was I supposed to say?'

'Anything else. I don't want that big bastard knowing what I'm up to.' He must have noticed Larry's expression. 'What?' he hissed.

'Well, he was nosing about in your office.'

'He what?' Casper's face turned red, then white. 'How did you not stop him?'

Larry laughed. 'You're kidding, right?'

Casper stared at him for a minute, shook his head and hurried to the back shop. Larry could hear him opening drawers in his desk and in the filing cabinet, probably checking to see if anything was missing. After a few minutes Casper closed the office door presumably to make some phone calls. Sure enough, a few minutes later, Larry could hear him having a conversation and he didn't sound too happy. Larry thought about trying to hear what was being said but just then the bell on the front door sounded as a customer came in.

The woman was looking for a suitable pet for her ten-year old niece. Larry suggested a tortoise or a budgie. She asked him some questions about food and cleaning and so on and he surprised himself by answering quite knowledgeably. After a few minutes browsing, she made her choice, a budgie. Larry recommended a cage he said was suitable and good value. She looked dubious, presumably looking for a cheaper option. Casper was always telling him to get the most out of every sale so he offered her a discount if she bought a few accessories. After a few minutes she agreed and said her husband would call later to collect everything.

The rest of the day passed in similar vein. The usual varied series of customers. Some were regulars, in for food or other supplies for their pets. Others were looking for a different sort of birthday present for a child or elderly relative.

Larry just wished they'd leave him in peace. His hangover wasn't any better despite stoking up with a bridie and chips for lunch from the Ritz. Fortunately there was no further sign of Black or his two gorillas. Larry laughed to himself. Gorillas in a pet shop. Not that there was anything to laugh about with those three. Casper spent most of the day in his office and from time to time Larry could hear him on the phone, voice raised, whether in anger or anxiety he couldn't tell.

When he got home, about half six, the hangover had gone but, with all the stress of the last two days, he was knackered and all he wanted to do was lie down and sleep. Sharon was getting ready to go out, a few drinks with her pals, followed by bingo, then a few more drinks. She seemed happy, last night apparently forgotten, but Larry was in no mood to join in. It seemed she was going out more and more these days. Always moaning to him about money being tight, but she always found enough to go out with her pals or the people from work.

Anyway, it meant he'd get a bit of peace from her moaning, and he'd be able to spend time with Kelly and Joe. His dinner was on the table, between two plates, gammon salad. Sharon sent Joe out to get him a bag of chips from the shop on the corner. Kelly was watching some reality nonsense on the telly.

Sharon barked orders at him while he sat eating his dinner. He'd had enough hassle in the shop without coming home to this so he tuned her out.

She could obviously read his body language. 'Don't ignore me when I'm trying to talk to you,' she said.

The kids obviously sensed the tension and he saw them glancing at him to see how he would react. He hated them getting caught up in this sort of stuff so, with an effort, he swallowed what he really wanted to say and muttered an apology.

Once Sharon had left, the atmosphere changed. Larry finished his dinner and asked the kids if they fancied a wee game of cards. They both nodded enthusiastically, wee Joe ran over and got the cards out of the drawer in the unit, Kelly got a pen and paper and the three of them sat up at the table. They drew cards to decide who would pick the first game. Joe got an ace and picked Hearts, his favourite. Larry watched their faces as they played their hands, both of them trying to appear cool and professional but loving every minute of it. When they'd had three rounds of Hearts, Kelly picked the next game, Rummy. He watched them biting their lips as they concentrated and tried to remember the run of the cards. When it was Larry's turn, he told them he was going to teach them a new one, Twenty-fives, an Irish game his dad had taught him years ago. The rules were a bit confusing and they laughed every time they made a mistake but after a while they got the hang of it and Joe said he would teach it to his pals next time he saw them. Larry felt the worries of the day drift away as he enjoyed this simple time with his children.

They finished off the night with Match of the Day, then it was time for the kids to get to bed. They both gave him a hug.

'Thanks Dad,' Kelly said, 'that was absolutely brilliant. We should do that every weekend.'

Wee Joe dropped into a boxing stance and pretended to aim a punch at him and Larry feigned being knocked down and dropped into his chair. He felt a warm buzz in his stomach as he watched them heading for their rooms. Life could sometimes be good. His kids were the most important thing in his life. No matter how he felt about his job, he had to make sure he kept it and stayed in Sharon's good books.

Things used to be good between them, they used to have laughs, enjoy each other's company. But over the last couple of years the marriage had got more and more stressful. He checked the time, half past eleven and still no sign of her. He decided to wait up for her. He had a few episodes of 'The Wire' he wanted to catch up on so he settled down with a couple of beers and a bag of Tortilla chips.

When he woke up the telly was off, the room was cold and almost in darkness, just one lamp in the corner breaking the gloom. For a moment he was disoriented, he didn't remember switching off the telly. He checked the time, one o'clock. He got up and wandered through to the bedroom, Sharon was tucked up, snoring gently. He went back to the living-room, quickly tidied away his beer glass and the empty bottles and put the lamp out. Then he tiptoed back to the bedroom and slipped in beside Sharon.

Chapter 7

Larry was woken the next morning by Joe and Kelly arguing over the television. He glanced at Sharon, she was dead to the world. He eased himself out of bed and tiptoed into the living room, closing the door behind him.

'What's going on?' he asked.

'She wants to watch 'I'm a Celebrity' but it's my turn to pick.'

Kelly made a face. 'He wants to see that stupid programme about alligators.'

'Is it his turn though?'

Reluctantly Kelly nodded her head. Out of the corner of his eye Larry saw Joe punching the air.

'You pick the next programme, Kelly. But before you sit down, have you had breakfast yet?'

They both shook their heads.

'Right, we'll get some cereal and we'll watch the alligators together.'

Sharon surfaced a couple of hours later, looking the worse for wear. She slumped into the couch holding a hand to her head. Larry was still angry at her for all the nagging but he knew how it felt to have a hangover and he made her a cup of tea and gave her a couple of paracetamol.

'Good night?' he asked.

'Not bad. Maggie won a hundred quid on the last house. So we all went for a drink to celebrate.'

Larry nodded. It would have been useful if it had been Sharon who had won the money. 'What are we having for dinner?' he asked.

Sharon sighed and shook her head as if she was dealing with an idiot. 'I told you. We're going to Casper's for dinner tonight.'

He didn't remember her telling him anything about that but he let it go. He could do without seeing Casper, he got enough of him at work, especially this week. But the decision had obviously been made. Anyway, the kids loved going there. Casper's wife, Christine, always spoiled them.

'Right,' he said, 'I'll take the kids down the park for an hour or so, let you have a wee bit of peace and quiet.'

Sharon looked at him suspiciously. 'Why are you being so nice to me?'

Larry shrugged his shoulders. 'It's Sunday. I like spending time with my kids.' He did an attempt at imitating the meerkat from Coronation Street, 'Simples.'

As he walked along Battlefield Road and up the hill towards Queen's Park Larry tried to decide if he was happy. He'd never been particularly lucky with the jobs he'd had. Casper wasn't an easy boss to deal with and he kept Sharon informed about how Larry was getting on. As for Sharon, there was no pleasing her. She always compared him unfavourably to Casper and things had got worse since Larry had started working in the pet shop.

On the plus side, he had two brilliant children and they made everything worthwhile. He couldn't always give them what they wanted in terms of presents but they all got on really well together. Long may that continue, he thought, as he watched them running up the hill together. Joe was nine and Kelly was coming up for twelve. She'd soon be getting to that difficult stage when children sometimes rebel and start to give cheek to their parents. He couldn't imagine that happening with Kelly and he'd do his best to make sure it didn't.

Every time Larry saw Casper's house it made him realise how well his brother-in-law had done compared to him. A detached house with double garage, in one of the better areas of Glasgow. He'd heard that a few of Glasgow's criminal fraternity, including Eddie Black, lived fairly nearby. Obviously crime paid, for some people.

He watched Sharon admiring the house and knew what she was thinking. Why was she still living three up in an old tenement when her brother had this place? And he knew what answer she would give herself. She was married to a loser. In fact Larry couldn't see how the pet shop was doing well enough to finance this place. What did he know? He shrugged his shoulders and followed Sharon and the kids into the brightly-lit hallway.

Christine showed them into the living-room. 'Charlie's on the phone, business I think, but he won't be long,' she said as she invited them to take a seat.

She was the only one who called Casper by his real name. Almost as if she was making a point. Even Sharon called him Casper and she had grown up with him being called Charlie. The nickname had taken hold years ago when the new film version of Casper the Ghost had come out. Somebody made the connection with 'ghost' and Casper's surname 'White' and that was it. Even the kids called him 'Uncle Casper'.

Larry wondered who Casper would be on the phone to on a Sunday night. Christine had said it was to do with business but surely the gerbils and the goldfish could wait until Monday. Casper appeared a few minutes later, looking a bit agitated. He nodded to Larry, and gave Sharon and the kids a hug.

'Everything ok, darling?' Christine asked.

Casper glared at her. 'Of course, why wouldn't it be?' Before his wife could respond he went on. 'Have you not offered these good people a drink?'

As drinks were served and the small talk started, Larry wondered why Casper seemed so on edge. Maybe it was something to do with Eddie Black's visits. The man was obviously after something but Casper was keeping quiet about it.

Casper and Christine didn't have any children so they always made a fuss of Kelly and Joe. They sat at the table but were allowed to go and play as soon as they'd finished their meal. Once they'd left, the adults moved on to the usual topics of conversation. Larry noticed that Casper gave very little away about the shop and he was happy to follow his lead.

Christine was enjoying showing off her new tableware to Sharon and Larry could see his wife taking it all in and making a mental tally of everything they had and that she didn't. He knew this would be ammunition for Sharon the next time they argued.

'Did you enjoy your meal, Larry?' Christine asked. '

'Aye, it was great, thanks.' In truth, although Larry didn't get on with his brother-in-law and thought Christine was a bit of a snob, he always appreciated the meals they served. They'd had a starter of bruschetta, which was simple but tasty and the kids loved it. The main course was lasagne which Christine made with her special sauce; she'd got the recipe from an Italian neighbour. Dessert was crème brûlée. Larry enjoyed cooking and sometimes liked to try out new recipes but he hardly ever seemed to find the time. Maybe if his kitchen was as big as Christine's and stocked with all those modern gadgets, he'd make more of an effort.

Casper's phone rang and he mouthed an apology to Christine as he went out to the hall to answer it. Larry took advantage of the interruption to go to the toilet. As he moved down the hall he could hear a muffled conversation. It seemed to start off mildly but almost immediately he heard Casper's voice getting louder, and angrier. Shortly after that Casper must have closed the door of the room he was in because Larry couldn't hear anything further. By the time Larry returned to the dining room Casper was back in his seat but it was obvious he was in a foul temper and had no intention of explaining who had phoned or what it was about.

With Casper clearly in no mood for small talk and the kids needing to get to bed for school the next day, it was time to call it a night. As they said their goodbyes in the hall, Sharon said she'd need to return the favour, once they got themselves sorted but Larry wouldn't be holding his breath for that happening.

Anyway, he had to admit, it had been a great meal. It was maybe just about worth having to put up with Casper at the weekend and having to listen to Christine going on about her latest and most expensive piece of furniture to get a dinner like that. The other downside, though, was the lecture he could expect, later, from Sharon, about how poor their house was in comparison.

Sure enough, as soon as the kids had gone to bed, Sharon started on about how well her brother had done compared to her husband. Larry had heard it all before and he tried to go into 'sleep mode' and make his mind a blank. At that moment he even found himself looking forward to getting to work the next day. The chat from the parrots and the mynah bird would be preferable to Sharon's nagging.

Chapter 8

On Monday morning Sharon was still going on about how fantastic Christine and Casper's house was. She also let Larry know in various subtle, and not so subtle, ways, that she still hadn't forgiven him for the business at the launderette on Friday. His drinking bout on Friday night was also on the list of offences. All the good parts of the weekend had been forgotten.

She was in the kitchen with the kids, having breakfast. Larry had taken himself off to the living-room to escape her nagging. He was flicking between his Daily Record and the telly while he enjoyed a cup of tea and a roll and potato scone and fried egg.

He was sitting in his favourite armchair, the tea balanced on the arm, another thing that Sharon was always telling him off for. He couldn't see why it mattered. The thing was covered in all sorts of stains anyway. They'd had the suite for years, though that was another one of her complaints.

The kids came in to say cheerio and a minute later he heard the door slam behind them. He turned back to the telly and his interest perked up when the image on the screen showed the street where the pet shop was. He quickly turned the volume up but nearly choked on his roll at what the presenter said. 'A Glasgow bookmaker was found dead this morning, when cleaning staff arrived at the shop in the centre of the city. Police have not yet named the dead man.'

Larry turned the volume up even higher. He recognised Tony's shop from the picture on the screen. Casper's shop was clearly visible in the background.

'Police are appealing for witnesses who may have seen anything suspicious on Saturday or Sunday,' the presenter continued. Larry sat there in shock, tea and food forgotten. Images of Friday morning, with Eddie Black and his thugs laying into Tony, replayed in his mind. But Tony must have been okay because Larry had seen the shop open later on Friday and even on Saturday. So what had happened? They hadn't said that anybody had killed him but they were appealing for witnesses. Did that mean him? Was he a witness?

There was a knock at the front door. For some reason he immediately thought it was the police. Could they be here already? That was daft, how could they even know what he'd seen? He got up to answer the door but heard Sharon's footsteps crossing the hall and the sound of the front door opening. He turned the volume down to try and hear who it was. The conversation was brief but he recognised the visitor's voice. He breathed a sigh of relief, not the police after all. Sure enough, a minute later Casper came into the room.

'Have you heard the news?' Casper said, getting straight to it and clearly agitated.

Larry nodded. 'I was just watching it on the telly.'

Casper picked up the handset and turned the volume up even further, then pressed the rewind button. He dropped onto the seat that Larry had been sitting in. Larry was about to say something but decided it wasn't worth the hassle. They both watched in silence while the news item was replayed.

'What do you make of it?' Casper said. He stared at the screen instead of looking at Larry. 'Who the hell would want to kill Tony?'

'I've no idea.' Larry was about to sit down but he paused. 'Do you want a cup of tea?'

'No, I'm going to need something stronger this morning.'

'Sorry, I've nothing in,' Larry said. 'I finished the last of the beer on Saturday. He lifted the Daily Record out of the way and sat on the couch. 'What do you think happened? A robbery? Must be plenty of money in a bookies.'

Casper shrugged his shoulders. 'I haven't got a clue.'

At that moment, Sharon appeared. She looked at Larry, then at the television. 'Casper's just told me what happened. Do they know any more yet?'

Larry shook his head. 'Still early days.'

'Do they have any idea when it happened?'

Casper shrugged. 'Must have been Saturday night, if they found him this morning. We'll probably find out later today.'

Sharon nodded. 'I never met the guy, but it's still a shock, the fact that both of you knew him. Okay, well, I need to get to work,' she said. 'Let me know what happens.'

When Sharon had left, Casper looked thoughtful. 'The cops are bound to be coming round at some point asking questions.'

'Right enough,' Larry said. 'What are you going to tell them?'

'What do you mean? I'll just tell them what I know. What are you getting at?'

'Nothing.' Larry took a drink of tea. 'When did you last see him?'

'Saturday afternoon. What about you?'

The memory of Eddie Black laying into Tony on Friday morning was sharp in Larry's mind but he wasn't going to mention that to Casper. 'I think I saw him on Friday at some point, not really sure when.' Larry glanced at Casper to see if there was any reaction to this but he was staring at the telly where a police spokesman was voicing the usual appeal for witnesses.

'Do you think it was somebody with a grudge against him?' Larry said. 'Maybe a punter that he wouldn't pay?'

Casper seemed to consider this. 'I suppose it's possible. Why would he not pay them?'

'Some of these accumulator bets can mount up. A wee place like Tony's could go bankrupt. Sometimes the bookie tries to get out of it.'

Casper turned to look at Larry for a moment, then shook his head and turned back to the television. 'I can't see Tony doing that, but who knows?' he finally said, as he flicked through the channels to see if he could see any more about Tony.

Larry had only been working in Casper's shop for a couple of months and he realised he didn't really know that much about Tony. Certainly not as much as Casper apparently did. 'Was he into anything dodgy?'

'Dodgy? Like what?' Casper said, appearing to get angry. 'The guy's dead and you're slagging him off. You hardly knew him.'

'He always struck me as a bit of a chancer.'

'Look, you don't know what you're talking about. Anyway, it's better not to start rumours.'

Larry decided to say no more. Casper was right. After all, he didn't really know why Black and his men had given Tony a doing. He debated with himself whether to tell Casper about what he'd seen on the Friday morning but decided against it. Who knew where that would lead? They sat watching the telly in silence for a few more minutes in case anything else about Tony came on. But the news had finished and some chat show was on. After a minute, Casper stood to leave.

'Did he have family?' Larry asked.

'He had a wife, Maggie, no kids. She's away on a hen do in Marbella. I think she left on Friday morning.' Casper walked over to the window and looked out as if he might see Tony's wife standing there. He turned back to Larry. 'That'll be how she didn't report him missing. Christ, he told me he was getting hassle from some heavy mob but I don't think he was expecting anything like this.'

'Do you mean from the same guys that were looking for you the other day?'

'How the fuck would I know? And by the way, you don't want to start throwing Eddie Black's name about.'

'Who would I mention it to? What did they want with you anyway?'

'Don't ask, right. I told you, the less you know the better.' He looked pale. 'Right, I need to get out of here, get some time to think. I'm away for a pint.'

'At this time of the day?'

Casper glared at him. 'I need a drink, if you're sure that's okay with you.' He headed for the living-room door but stopped before he got there.

'I nearly forgot. This is why I came round. Here's the spare keys for the shop. You'll need to open up today. You're as well having a set anyway. I've got stuff to sort out.'

'Are we opening the shop today?' Larry asked.

'Of course we are. Or at least you are. Why wouldn't we?' Casper said.

'I don't know, maybe as a mark of respect for Tony?' Larry said.

Casper gave him one of his scathing looks and shook his head. 'You're forgetting about the animals, aren't you? They'll need fed and watered. Unless you want them to die of thirst.'

Larry hadn't thought about that. In fact, he would have been quite happy for the animals to die of thirst. 'I suppose so,' he finally said.

Casper glared at him. 'There's no suppose about it.' He turned for the door but paused. 'And if you're worried about showing respect get the hamsters to do a minute's silence.'

Larry was a bit taken aback. He hadn't realised Casper had this cold streak in him. 'What if the cops come round or those guys come back?'

'Just tell them I'll be in tomorrow. Anything else?'

Larry shook his head. He wasn't happy about the prospect of trying to fob off the cops or Eddie Black but he said nothing.

Kelly and Joe would be full of questions about what had happened. They'd be worried at their dad being so close to a murder, if that's what it was. He'd explain things to them as calmly as he could. There was no point trying to hide it from them, they would hear about it in school and there was so much violence out there anyway. He had another quick drink of tea then headed out the door to catch the bus.

Chapter 9

It took him ages to travel the few miles to the shop. At every stop it seemed there was someone who needed to ask the driver a question about their ticket. Larry felt his frustration mounting. He was desperate to get there, see if he could learn more about what had happened to Tony. At the same time he was anxious about what he might find. What if it was Black and his gang who had killed Tony? Would the police find out what Larry had seen?

Then there was Casper's reaction. He was being very tight-lipped about it all. Did he know something? Eddie Black had paid more than one visit to the shop and each time he seemed angrier than before. As for Casper, he seemed more and more troubled each day. Even this morning, turning up at the house like that with the keys, then almost forgetting to give them to Larry.

When he arrived at the corner of the street there was a crowd of spectators blocking the way. As he edged forward he recognised a couple of television reporters talking away to the cameras. He had to push and squeeze his way through the onlookers to the front.

Eventually he was right up against the police tape and got a glimpse of the activity going on behind the cordon. People were trying to get access to the street but the police were being selective, taking names and details and presumably only allowing through anyone who had a legitimate reason for being there.

When it was Larry's turn he started to explain his position to the police officer. The cop, a huge lump of a man, put a hand up to silence him. The officer was talking on his radio and at first didn't even look in his direction. After a few minutes he ended the call and turned to Larry.

'And you are?'

'Larry McAllister.'

The guy spread his hands to let Larry know that the name meant nothing to him. 'Only residents and those on urgent business are getting through.'

'I work in the pet shop.' Larry pointed vaguely towards the shop but the cop just stared at him. 'I need to get in to give the animals water and food, otherwise they'll die.'

The cop grunted then spoke into his phone. After a minute he ended the call. 'Have you got any ID?'

Larry looked blank. 'Like what?'

'Passport, driving licence.'

'I didn't think you needed a passport to go from one side of Glasgow to the other.'

The cop glowered at Larry, not appreciating the sarcasm.

'Sorry, I came in on the bus,' Larry added quickly. He fumbled in his pocket. 'I've got the keys for the shop.'

The policeman thought for a minute. 'Right. You can go in but you stay in the shop and you don't go wandering about. Somebody will be in to see you later.'

Larry gave him a nod and ducked under the tape. When he reached the door of the shop he saw more police tape round the bookie's door and as he fumbled with the padlocks on the shutters he saw uniformed police guarding the entrance while others, in their white forensic suits, no doubt detectives and forensic officers, went silently about their business. Some wore unreadable expressions, one or two looked shocked by whatever grim scene lay inside.

He realised there would be no customers to deal with because people couldn't get through the police cordon. So he enjoyed the relative calm and decided to treat himself to a cup of tea and ten minutes reading The Daily Record. He was tempted to put his feet up and relax but he wouldn't put it past Casper to come in to check on him. In any case, he would ask Larry to account for his time, especially since there were no customers. So, he cleaned the cages and tanks and topped up all the food and water as needed. He looked round the shop to make sure there nothing else needed attention. The shop wasn't as bad without the customers. If he could just get rid of the animals as well then this job might be okay.

About ten o'clock he went to the back door for a quick cigarette. As soon as he opened it and leaned out, a thunderous voice told him to get back inside the shop. He looked round and saw two cops standing guard outside the back door to the bookies. God almighty, could he not even get a quick fag? He slipped back into the shop but left the door open a crack and quickly had his cigarette.

Why were they guarding the back door to the bookies? Was Tony killed in the lane? On the television news they'd said his body had been found in the shop but maybe that wasn't right. Or was it in the back shop, where Larry had seen Black beating him up? He didn't even know how he had been killed.

Would the police find signs that Larry had walked along the lane on Friday and been at the back door of the bookies? He knew, from watching CSI and Unforgotten and the like, what they could do with a tiny piece of evidence. Christ, that was all he needed. He thought back to Friday, trying to retrace exactly what he'd done. The cops on the telly were always doing clever stuff with cigarette stubs. He was sure he'd chucked his over the wall on Friday.

As far as he could see, the most likely thing was that Eddie Black and his henchmen had killed Tony. After all, they'd given him a severe doing on Friday morning. It sounded like Tony had been killed on Saturday evening, presumably around closing time since he'd been found in the shop. Friday was probably just a warning. Had Tony not done what Black wanted, or not given him what he wanted and so they'd come back to finish the job?

Of course he could have been killed on Sunday, but Larry didn't see why Tony would have been in his shop on a Sunday. Bookies were allowed to open on a Sunday these days but, according to Casper, Tony had never done that.

If it was Black who had done it, what was it all about? Larry had heard the rumours about the man. A ruthless bastard who had all sorts of stuff on the go. Not the sort you messed with. What had Tony done to get on the wrong side of him? Black seemed to have business with Casper as well. So did that mean Casper was in trouble as well?

He finished his cigarette and closed the door. He shredded the butt and rinsed it down the sink. He spent the next hour checking the stock and generally tidying things up. Then it was time for another cuppa. He was sitting with his feet up on a crate of feed when Tina from the Ritz popped in.

Tina was always full of the joys so he was pleased to see her. He laughed when he saw her latest hairdo. It was piled up so high it added a few inches to her height. Even then, she was still well under five feet.

'How did you get past the Gestapo?' he said. 'They told me not to leave the shop.'

She laughed. 'I managed to sweet talk them.' She fluttered her long, dark eyelashes in mock innocence. 'I made them tea and gave them a couple of biscuits. When I told them I worked in the café, their eyes lit up. I think that's how they let me through in the first place.'

No doubt her exotic good looks had helped as well, Larry thought. Despite the carefree attitude, Tina always took great care over how she looked. She was a lot younger than Larry but sometimes

45

she would regale him with tales of her latest romantic entanglements, which, she had let him know early on, were exclusively female.

He got up to get her a chair. Every time he saw her, she seemed to have a new tattoo and today was no exception. On her left shoulder she had one of an apple with a bite taken out of it.

'That's brilliant,' Larry said, pointing to it. 'Is it not sore getting them done?'

Tina laughed and shrugged her shoulders. 'A bit, but I like them. I get them done in the wee place along the road.'

Larry smiled. Tina was one of those people who radiated positive energy and didn't take life too seriously. She was a bit of a gossip, but she was good company.

She took her seat and produced a paper bag with a magician's flourish. 'There you go,' she said as she placed it on the counter. She tore the bag open to reveal a couple of doughnuts and two little sponge cakes covered in jam and coconut.

'Brilliant,' Larry said as he poured her a cup of tea. 'I've not had an Eiffel Tower for years.'

Tina laughed. 'That's what my mum calls them as well. I told Rosa, but she insists on calling them coconut madeleines.'

They passed fifteen minutes sipping their tea and munching their cakes. The conversation inevitably centred on Tony and speculation about who might have killed him. Tina had all sorts of theories and Larry was interested to see that none of them included any reference to Eddie Black, at least not by name.

'I'm sure he was having an affair,' she said. 'Maybe it was some woman's husband that did him in. What do you think?'

Larry had no intention of telling her what he really thought, especially with Tina being well known as a gossip. The last thing he needed was for her to go blabbing to Casper or the cops about what he'd seen. 'I suppose it's possible,' he said. 'Though he didn't strike me as the type that women would find attractive.'

Tina shrugged as she took another bite of her doughnut. 'It takes all sorts,' she said, speaking through a mouthful of crumbs. 'And he must have had plenty of money, being a bookie. So that's always a factor.'

Larry tried to look as if he was considering this as a serious possibility. All the while he kept seeing Tony lying on the ground, getting the shit kicked out of him. On the other hand, that hadn't killed Tony. Casper had seen him on the Saturday afternoon.

'You might be right but maybe it was just a robbery. There must have been plenty of money in the bookies.'

Tina looked dubious. 'I'm not so sure. A lot of people use accounts or cards these days. I suppose it could have been some gang, after protection money, there's been some dodgy types hanging about. But they wouldn't want to kill him.'

Larry wondered if she was testing him, looking for a reaction but he said nothing.

She took another mouthful of tea and seemed to weigh up the options. 'No,' she finally said, 'I

47

think it was somebody's husband. Anyway that's what I told the cops when they spoke to me earlier.'

Larry snapped out of his daydreaming. 'They've already interviewed you? When was that?'

'Earlier this morning. About an hour ago. They came into the café, two of them. They spoke to Rosa and then to me separately.' She shrugged her shoulders. 'It was quite interesting.'

Larry knew the cops would be doing the rounds but hearing that it was actually happening was a different story. 'What were they like? Do you know how he was killed, or when?' He was aware that his voice sounded anxious.

Tina laughed. 'Calm yourself. Anyway, I don't know if I'd call it an interview. They just want basic information from the likes of us. Did I know Tony? How well? What did I think of him? When did I last see him? How was he? Did he have any enemies that I knew of?'

She took a mouthful of cake and a sip of tea. 'All that sort of stuff. We've not got anything to worry about.' She finished her doughnut and took another drink of her tea. 'Mind you, they did ask us both where we had been from Saturday evening through to Monday morning. So, they'll probably ask you and Casper the same thing.'

Larry did a quick mental review of his movements over the weekend. 'So they're obviously keeping their options open.'

Tina nodded. 'They were right nasty looking, especially the big one. I wouldn't fancy being interrogated by him if I did have something to hide. And no, they didn't tell me anything about how he was killed or when. They would keep that to themselves. Just like on the telly. I assume he was killed late on Saturday, after he'd closed up. So,' she said, changing tack, 'when did you last see Tony?'

Tina's comment about having something to hide had started Larry's nerves jangling again. He tried to calm himself and he gave Tina the same vague answer he'd given to Casper, hoping she would be happy with that. He didn't have to worry. Tina was nodding before he finished, desperate to give her own story.

'He usually pops into the café every day at some point. But I never saw him on Friday so, on Saturday, I went in to see if he wanted anything.' She paused for dramatic effect. 'And guess what?'

Larry shrugged his shoulders, though he suspected he knew what was coming.

'His face was cut and bruised, quite bad. Somebody had obviously beaten him up.' She raised her eyebrows as if she had somehow solved the case, inviting Larry to comment.

'Did he tell you who had done it?'

She took another mouthful of tea and shook her head. 'No. Said he'd tripped going down the stairs in his house.' She made a face to show what she thought of that.

Larry considered this. So, Tony had clearly been keeping quiet about Black beating him up. Probably because he'd been scared. And no wonder. 'Maybe that's what did happen,' Larry said.

49

Tina gave him a scornful look. 'Come off it. His wife's away for a few days to Spain somewhere on a hen do. I think he's taken the chance to have a fly wee session with somebody, the woman's husband's caught them, and gave him a doing. In any case,' she paused for effect, 'he told me a while back that he lived in a bungalow.' She spread her hands wide, and looked at Larry, the eyebrows again shot up to the top of the forehead.

Larry was puzzled. 'A bungalow? What's that got to do with anything?'

She leaned in closer as if she was about to tell him a great secret. She knocked her fist against Larry's forehead. 'Hello, is there anybody in? There's no stairs in a bungalow,' she said triumphantly and spread her hands as if to say 'case closed'.

Larry shook his head and had to laugh at the simplicity of her approach but she was also pretty astute, so, he'd need to be careful about what he said to her. 'In any case,' he said, 'if Tony was walking about alive on Saturday then that wasn't what killed him. Was it?'

Tina looked disgruntled at her theory being so easily challenged. 'No, I suppose so. But there's no smoke without fire. Right? The first doing was a warning. Then he decides to see the woman again, or maybe even another woman, he gets caught and the guy swings for him.'

Larry didn't quite know how to answer that so he just nodded as if in agreement.

She seemed satisfied with this and she stood up. 'Right, I better get back to the café, see if they cops want any more tea. You take it easy. Let me know how you get on with them. Where's Casper, by the way?'

'Away out on business. You know, this and that.'

She nodded, seemingly satisfied with this vague answer. As he watched her leave, Larry realised that he himself had no idea what Casper got up to on these frequent business meetings away from the shop. But the place seemed to trundle along quietly as normal in his absence.

He wondered if Tina could possibly be on the right lines with her theory. After all, it was Friday when Larry had seen Black beating Tony up, and Tina and Casper had both seen Tony alive and kicking on Saturday. So, unless Tony had died of some delayed effect of the beating he received on Friday, then somebody had had another go at him on Saturday. Was that Black, or the angry husband from Tina's theory, or some thief looking for cash?

He sat there for a few more minutes trying to put the events and his ideas into some sort of order. There were too many gaps. In any case, it was up to the cops to solve the murder. His priority was that nobody should know about what he'd seen on Friday morning.

He felt sorry for Tony, of course he did. Black was a nasty piece of work but Larry had no proof that Black had killed Tony. He certainly hadn't killed him on Friday. So what was the point of telling anyone? If he did, and Black heard about it, that would mean big trouble for Larry. He'd

51

already had a taste of his methods. Then there was Casper's involvement with Black which, as Casper had warned him, was better left alone. Larry nodded to himself, satisfied with his thinking.

Finally, he roused himself, deciding he better do a wee bit more work to earn his keep. Even though there were no customers, Casper would expect him to keep busy. He spent an hour or so giving the place a clean and then he was at a loose end again. Most days he couldn't be bothered with the customers but at least they would have broken the monotony. He looked outside and saw that the police still had the cordon in place. How long would it be there? He tried to remember what they did on the programmes on the telly.

By the time it reached one o'clock he was thinking of shutting the shop. He'd give it another hour and that was his lot. Casper obviously wasn't going to turn up. Larry briefly considered cleaning the spare cages but he just couldn't be bothered. Eventually he parked himself in a seat, perched his feet on a bag of birdseed and read his paper. If Casper could take himself off for a couple of pints, then he was entitled to a wee break as well.

He finished reading the paper and got up to have a look at the parrots and mynah birds. They were about the only things in the shop that remotely interested him. He remembered his granddad's mynah. The old guy had been in the merchant navy and had brought the bird back from Calcutta or somewhere like that. It was an amazing creature and a brilliant mimic. It was quite scary the way it could imitate voices so convincingly. Larry had tried to get the birds in the shop to say the odd word and about a week ago he'd managed to get one of the mynahs to say 'my name's Larry'. But he'd not managed to repeat that success. He hoisted himself up on to the counter and started to talk to them.

'Hello, my name's Larry,' he said. Most of the birds just stared at him. There was one who didn't even look at him. It hopped down off its perch and turned its back to him. He went through a whole catalogue of phrases trying to get at least one of the birds to repeat what he said. Nothing. 'Shower of useless bastards,' he muttered.

He jumped down from the counter and turned his attention to the rabbits. He approached the one with the white fur and the black foot, the one that had escaped from its cage on Friday.

He made his hand into a gun shape, pointed it at the rabbit and pretended to shoot it. 'You,' he said poking his finger through the wire, 'you could have landed me in trouble. If the cops find out...' But he was interrupted by the tinkle of the bell over the door.

Chapter 10

Larry moved towards the front of the shop. Two men were standing just inside the door. Larry would know that look anywhere. Cops. One was over six feet tall, mid-forties, face like a pile of concrete. Solid built. The sort you don't mess with. His colleague was younger and a couple of inches shorter. They were looking round the shop, taking it all in.

The big one waved his hand in front of his face. 'Christ, what a smell.'

Larry was struck by his voice. It wasn't that different from Black's, hard, cold, and with a hint of menace. But this guy seemed more in control.

'Mr Charles White?' he said, moving forward into the shop. 'I'm Detective Sergeant McNally and this is my colleague Detective Constable Wallace. We'd like a few words.'

'No.'

'No?'

'Casper's not here,' Larry said. 'He'll be in tomorrow.'

'Casper?'

'That's what we call him. Casper the ghost. Because of his name, White.'

The cop shook his head and looked at his colleague. 'Christ, the wit and wisdom of the Glaswegian.' He turned back to Larry. 'And you are?'

'I work here.'

'Your name, sir?'

'Larry.'

The man raised an eyebrow. 'Do you have a surname at all?'

'McAllister, Larry McAllister.' Larry noticed the younger one, Wallace, had produced a notebook and pencil.

'Ok, Mr McAllister we need to talk to you anyway. I assume you know why we're here'.

For a brief moment Larry panicked. Could they somehow know what he'd seen on Friday? He realised they were staring at him waiting for an answer. He nodded in the vague direction of the bookies. 'I assume it's about Tony,' he finally said. No response. 'I saw it on the telly.'

'Must have been a shock for you.'

'You're not kidding,' Larry replied.

'Did you know Mr Hamilton well?'

Larry shrugged. 'Not really. Just to pass the time of day, you know.'

'When did you last see him?'

'I'm not sure,' Larry said, trying not to see the image of Eddie Black dragging the knife down Tony's face and head-butting him.

Wallace stopped writing and looked at McNally. McNally looked at Larry. He swallowed uncomfortably.

'This is a murder enquiry, sir,' McNally said.

'I know, I know.' Larry made a show of trying to remember. 'I'm pretty sure it was Friday.' He felt comfortable as he said this. If Tina had seen Tony on Saturday then whatever Larry had seen on

Friday, no matter how bad it was, couldn't be that important.

'You never saw him on Saturday? You didn't go in and put a bet on the football or the racing?'

'No, I'm not into the gambling, just an occasional lottery ticket.'

McNally nodded. 'So, Friday then. What time would that have been?'

'It was some time in the morning.'

McNally tapped his fingers on the counter and waited, giving Larry the sort of look Sharon gave him when he came back late from the pub.

'I think it was about ten o'clock,' Larry said eventually.

'Right, now we're getting somewhere. Where did you see him?'

'In his shop, the bookies.'

'So, you did go into the shop on Friday?'

'No, I saw him from outside the shop.'

'Outside the shop?' McNally looked puzzled. 'Just wait there a minute.' He went out to the street and Larry could see him looking towards the bookies. He came back a minute later. This time he stood a lot closer to Larry, right up in his face. Larry could smell stale beer and whisky on his breath. He recoiled slightly and McNally seemed to enjoy the reaction.

'You can't see into the bookies from the street,' he said, eyeballing Larry.

Larry could feel the sweat starting to trickle under his armpits.

'It was out in the back lane. I nipped out for a quick smoke and I saw him out there.'

'So he wasn't actually in his shop?'

'No, he was in his shop. The back door was open and I saw him.'

'From your back door?'

'No, I had walked along the lane a bit. Just to stretch the old legs you know?' He could feel the tension in his throat and hear his voice rising with each answer.

'Did you speak to him?'

Larry shook his head. 'He looked like he was busy.' Busy, he thought, that was one way of putting it. Busy getting his head battered in.

'Busy?'

'With paperwork.' Larry realised the conversation was already sliding out of his control and he'd no idea where it was heading.

'Paperwork? You could see that from where you were standing, could you?'

Why the fuck had he said paperwork? 'He was sitting at the table, he seemed to be looking down at something.' Larry realised he was staring up into space. He looked back at McNally. 'I just assumed it would be paperwork.'

McNally nodded. 'His accounts, that sort of thing?'

Larry nodded. 'Exactly.'

'Couldn't he just have been reading a newspaper? Studying that day's racing?'

Larry felt himself nodding frantically. 'Aye, I suppose so. In fact that's probably what it was.'

'So why did you assume it was his paperwork?'

He knew there was no sensible answer he could give. 'It was just, just, you know, a guess.'

McNally seemed to be peering right into Larry's brain and not liking what he saw there. 'Was there anybody else in the shop?'

Larry felt his face going red. 'No.' He said.

'How do you know?'

Oh Christ, his throat felt like it was closing up. 'What, what do you mean?'

'If you didn't go into the shop, how do you know there was no-one else in there?'

'Right, right, okay, right, I see what you're getting at.' He nodded his head frantically. 'Well what I mean is, I didn't see anybody.' Larry felt the sweat reach the small of his back.

'So there could have been somebody in there with him then?'

He floundered about for some other answer but eventually all he could offer was, 'I suppose so.'

McNally glanced at his colleague before turning back to Larry. 'So let's get this straight. About ten o'clock you went out the back door for a smoke, you walked along to Mr Hamilton's back door to stretch your legs, you saw him apparently doing paperwork,' McNally paused, 'or reading the paper. You didn't speak to him because you didn't want to disturb him. Then you walked back along the lane and back here into the shop. Is that right?'

He said all this with a deadpan expression and Larry could tell the man wasn't impressed with his story. He nodded.

'Does Mr White not mind you nipping out during working hours?'

'Well, he doesn't really know about it, if you know what I mean.'

'No, I don't know.' McNally gave a cold smile. 'Why don't you explain it to me?'

'He doesn't like me smoking in the shop or anywhere near it, so, when he goes out, I take the chance to grab a quick fag.'

'So he wasn't here when you took your little stroll. Where was he all this time?'

'He was in the café next door, the Ritz. He usually has a coffee and a roll about ten every morning. You don't need to mention to him that I was out the back do you?'

'That depends, Mr McAllister. As long as we think you're being straight with us then there's no problem. But if we think you've been telling us a story, then we'll need to check it with Mr White. So, is there anything else you think you should be telling us?'

Larry shook his head and furrowed his brow, trying for a look of concentration. 'No, no I don't think so.'

McNally paused, staring at Larry, his eyes drilling into him as if trying to see what he was hiding. As Tina had predicted, he asked Larry where he'd been and what he'd done over the weekend. The detective listened, asking a few follow-up questions, while Wallace made notes. Eventually he nodded, slowly, like he was still weighing up what Larry had told them. 'We'll be in touch, Mr McAllister. Don't go wandering off anywhere. Let Mr White know we'll be in to see him tomorrow. Tell him to make sure he's here.'

Larry held his breath as they turned to leave. What did that mean about not wandering off anywhere? Anyway, the worst was over. Even if they hadn't seemed completely convinced, they couldn't prove he'd been hiding anything. He held his breath as they turned the handle. Wallace had just opened the door when, at that exact moment, the mynah bird decided to break its vow of silence. In a voice that sounded scarily like Larry's and that reverberated around the whole shop, it screeched.

'My name's Larry. Me in trouble if the cops find out.' The bird paused, then, in an even louder voice, it added: 'useless bastards.'

Larry's guts did a somersault. The trickle of sweat was now a torrent and it had made its way into his underpants. The two detectives remained still for a moment, then Wallace quietly closed the door again, McNally turned the sign to read *'Closed'* and the two men turned and walked back towards Larry.

Chapter 11

They looked completely relaxed, almost amused, as they strolled towards him but Larry braced himself for the storm.

McNally's tone was almost gentle. 'Right then, Mr McAllister let's see if I can make this as simple as possible,' he said, smiling. 'Do you watch a lot of telly?'

'Telly? A fair bit,' Larry said, wondering where this was going.

'Taggart, Rebus, that sort of thing?' McNally sounded genuinely interested.

'CSI and Unforgotten are my favourites'. Larry smiled, maybe this would be ok.

'You've probably seen the bit where some lowlife has been lying through his teeth and the cop loses patience and says we can do this the hard way or the easy way. Ring a bell?'

McNally's eyes were boring into him. He wasn't smiling any more.

Larry wasn't sure if he should reply. He was soaked in sweat, his left leg was shaking and he felt an urgent need to get to the toilet. He let go a nervous fart, as smelly as it was loud.

'I'll take that as a yes, okay?' McNally said, taking a step back and waving his hand in front of his nose.

Larry gave a nod and another fart escaped.

'So, unless you want to be taken in for accessory to murder, you better start telling us the truth. And cut down on the farts before you kill every canary in the shop.'

They moved in, one either side of him, and Wallace took out his notebook and pencil again. McNally nodded to him. 'Ok, let's start all over, right from the beginning.'

Piece by piece, they unearthed what had happened on Friday morning. McNally asked the questions while Wallace took copious notes, punctuating his writing with the occasional grunt or raised eyebrow. When Larry described how the white rabbit had escaped, Wallace gave a nod of approval towards the animal.

As the questioning continued, Larry tried to pick his words carefully and divulge the bare minimum, but they pressed and probed until they had uncovered the whole dangerous story of Black and his thugs battering Tony.

'What did Mr White say when you told him about this?'

'I never told him. The only thing I said was that some guys were in looking for him.'

'And you didn't know these men?'

Larry shook his head.

'Would you recognise them again?'

His left leg started shaking again. 'No, they were only in here for a minute, less than that even.'

'For your sake, I hope you're not lying again. You're already guilty of wasting police time, and you're a key witness in a murder enquiry.'

Larry's mouth was dry. 'He was still alive after that, so what I saw was nothing to with the murder, was it?'

McNally didn't bother to respond to this. He gave him a curt nod and headed for the door. 'You'll need to come into the station later today to speak to a police artist and help us work up a photofit of these guys.'

'I told you, I didn't get a good look at them.'

'Be at London Road police station at four-thirty,' McNally said, ignoring Larry's feeble protest. 'Don't have us come looking for you. You wouldn't like that.'

Wallace smirked at Larry as he closed his notebook and followed his boss out of the shop.

As the door finally closed behind them Larry locked it and walked back to the rabbit. 'This is all your fault, you wee, long-eared bastard,' he said putting his face close up against the cage.

The mynah bird chirped up from its cage 'wee, long-eared bastard'.

'You as well, you fucking grass.' The mynah opened its beak as if to protest its innocence. 'Don't even start,' Larry said, putting his face close up to the cage, 'or I'll feed you to the cat from next door.'

He was in trouble, so he had to think about damage limitation The cops would be talking to Casper soon and Larry wanted to speak to his boss and get his story in first.

63

Chapter 12

The cops probably wouldn't see Casper until the next day so that gave Larry time to think. He'd need to tell Sharon something as well, at least an edited version of events. She'd go mental that he'd got mixed up in a murder enquiry. It wouldn't matter that it wasn't his fault. She'd still blame him and who knew where that would lead.

He looked around the shop. There was really nothing else he could do here. He took a few minutes to tidy things up and then locked up. As he made his way back through the police cordon the officer checked his name off against a list and made sure that his colleagues had spoken to him.

He checked the time, he was in no rush. He'd get himself a pint and a bite to eat before heading to the police station, fortify himself for the ordeal.

Lots of new bars had sprung up in Glasgow's revitalised Merchant City. The city's old cheese market had been completely refurbished with bars and restaurants along the perimeter and an exhibition space in the centre. Larry liked the feel of the square and he'd brought the kids here on a couple of occasions. For him, the bars were overpriced but it was Casper's current preferred watering-hole. Larry preferred places like The Horseshoe and Sloan's where you could hear the conversation and be guaranteed a decent pint.

As well as its closeness to the shop, Casper said he liked the modern décor and the clientele that went with. Larry had been in with his brother-in-law a couple of times and he'd noticed him looking around to see who was in and who had noticed him. See and be seen, that seemed to be the point of it. As Larry went into the place, he paused to survey the crowd. At this time of day it wasn't all that busy but the customers were as Larry remembered, dressed to impress and more interested in what people were wearing rather than the drink. There was plenty of new money in here.

The guy behind the bar looked barely old enough to be in a pub. 'What can I get you, sir?' he asked Larry.

'Pint of Tennents, a pie and a packet of cheese and onion.'

'We don't do pies, or crisps,' he said. 'I can give you a plate of olives.'

Larry shook his head in disgust. 'Just the pint. Have you seen Casper today? He told me he'd be in here.' He described him for the guy's benefit and saw the glimmer of recognition.

'He was in earlier but I think he left a couple of hours ago.'

'Did he say where he was going?'

The guy looked Larry up and down, clearly not happy at discussing a regular customer with someone he didn't know. 'Sorry, I've no idea.' He placed the pint on the counter. 'That's five pounds please.'

'Five pounds? You're kidding. I've changed my mind.' He turned for the door.

'What about this pint?' the guy protested.

'You drink it, if you're old enough.'

Maybe it was just as well he hadn't found Casper. He took his phone out to call him but then thought better of it. A text would be safer. He didn't want to get into any details about the visit from the cops. No way did he want Casper to know that he had to go to the station for a photofit session. He sent him a simple text saying he'd taken care of the animals and the shop and that he'd closed early because there were no customers. Surely he couldn't find fault with that. He sent a similar message to Sharon. Job done.

Relieved at getting that out of the way, he went into The Horseshoe for a pint and a pub lunch. This was more to his taste, a good pub with no nonsense. It was one of Glasgow's favourite bars. Upstairs, the lounge was famous for its karaoke evenings but Larry preferred the downstairs bar. The actual bar counter was rumoured to be the longest in Europe and a plaque above the gantry said it was on a list of protected architectural heritage. But he wasn't here to admire the architecture. By the time he'd finished his second pint he was feeling less worried about his visit to the police. He had a quick whisky for good measure and, suitably refreshed, caught a bus for London Road.

He paused outside the long, three-storey building to finish his cigarette. As the smoke filled his lungs, he thought back to previous occasions when he'd been inside a police station. Never anything particularly serious, minor offences, but it had always stressed him out because you just never knew how it would turn out. He tried to console himself that this time he wasn't a suspect and wasn't under arrest, he was just a witness.

He knew he was kidding himself. He didn't want to be here at all. If you were a witness against the likes of Eddie Black, you were asking for trouble. The thought of it set his heart thumping and sweat broke out on his body. The image of Black dragging the knife down Tony's cheek was etched into his brain.

His children's faces came into his mind. What if..? He gave himself a shake. This was just a photofit, wasn't it? He could always say he couldn't remember the faces, or deliberately get it wrong, couldn't he? He took a final draw of the cigarette and dropped the stub into the gutter. His hands were damp with sweat, he wiped them on his trousers, took a deep breath and climbed the short flight of steps.

Chapter 13

'Thanks for coming in at short notice, Mr McAllister,' McNally said as he led Larry into a small room. Wallace was already there, installed at the computer, scrolling through a series of images on the screen.

He turned round as Larry came in. 'Mr McAllister, not lost any more rabbits I hope?'

Larry grunted.

'Good of you to come in and help us with this.'

Larry glared at him. 'I didn't really have much choice, did I?'

McNally gave a humourless smile. 'No, you're right. And you better remember that.' He leaned forward until his face was just inches away and Larry noticed the same smell of stale alcohol. He wondered if the detective noticed he himself had been drinking. His question was soon answered.

'I see you've had a wee refreshment or two.' McNally laughed. 'A bit of Dutch courage maybe? Don't worry, we're well used to the smell of beer. Anyway, this should be pretty straightforward. It'll all be over before you know it. Just like the dentist.' He winked at Wallace who laughed appreciatively at his colleague's humour while Larry glowered at him.

McNally paused and focused his gaze on Larry to signal that the banter was over. 'Ok, let's get some things straight. This is a murder enquiry.

You were less than honest with us earlier. 'He waved down Larry's attempt at protest. 'We expect complete openness and cooperation. You don't want to be charged with obstruction of justice, do you?'

'Or wasting police time,' Wallace added, obviously feeling the need to get his tuppenceworth in. McNally gave him a look that suggested he wasn't completely happy with the interruption.

Larry held his hands up in a surrender gesture. 'Ok, ok, I get the message. I've already told you everything I know, so that's cooperation, isn't it.' He tried to convince himself that he had, in fact, been completely open with them. 'Right then, where's this photofit guy that I need to speak to?'

McNally perched on the desk in front of Larry. 'We actually call them e-fits these days. We've gone all modern,' he said. 'But we can maybe save ourselves some time.' He pointed to the computer that Wallace was sitting at. 'We've got some lovely wee photos we'd like you to have a look at. See if you recognise any of the faces.'

Larry swallowed hard. 'Photos? I thought it was a photofit, not photos.'

'Let's see how we get on,' McNally said. He pulled back a seat, inviting Larry to sit. 'Make yourself comfortable. Can I get you anything? Soft drink, popcorn?'

Larry was about to reply when he realised McNally was winding him up. 'Very funny,' he said. He sat down and tried to prepare himself. Ok they were going to show him some pictures. He could still get through this without too much damage. If Black and his thugs come up, just don't recognise them, that's all. He realised he was nodding to himself. Had he been talking out loud? He glanced at McNally but there was no reaction.

'We're going to show you photos of some of Glasgow's finest upstanding gentlemen,' Wallace said, 'otherwise known as the scum of the earth.' He glanced at Larry for a moment, then continued. 'Let us know if any of these guys are the ones you saw on Friday.'

Larry tensed as the first picture flashed up on the screen but it wasn't anyone he knew and he shook his head in response to Wallace's question. As each new picture appeared Larry braced himself, Wallace gave him a questioning look, Larry responded with a shake of the head and released his breath.

He was starting to relax when the image he had been dreading appeared on the screen. His insides did a somersault. Eddie Black, looking his most evil. Larry looked at the face staring out from the screen. A face only a blind mother could love. The eyes were dark and cold, boring straight through the camera, the mouth twisted in a sneer. He remembered the grinding voice and the air of absolute menace. He started to sweat. He tried not to give anything away but it was no use, these guys were experts in reading people's expressions.

'Well, I think we've got a result,' Wallace said.

'Mr Eddie Black, lovely character, isn't he?' McNally said, looking over Larry's shoulder. 'So you can confirm that he was one of the men you saw assaulting Tony Hamilton?'

Larry tried to play for time. 'I'm not sure. I mean it's hard to tell just from that one photograph.'

'Not a problem,' Wallace said. He clicked the mouse and several other images of Black filed the screen.

McNally leaned in so that Larry could feel his breath on his face. 'Please don't try and mess us about, Mr McAllister. Was this one of the guys you saw?'

Larry hesitated, then nodded.

'Sorry, what was that?' McNally said.

'Aye, he was there,' Larry mumbled.

'What part did he play in the assault?'

Larry knew he was at the start of a dangerous journey but he couldn't think of any way to stop it. 'He had the knife.'

'So this was the guy you saw butting Tony Hamilton in the face and dragging a knife down his cheek?'

Larry nodded and mumbled a 'yes'.

Wallace made a note on his pad. 'Ok, good stuff. Moving on,' he said as he continued to scroll through the mug shots.

Larry tried to concentrate as the photos rolled across the screen, tried to keep calm, but his mind was racing and he kept seeing images of Tony lying on the ground, blood streaming from his face. Was that what Larry had to look forward to? What about his family? As the pages of images scrolled past, from time to time he saw a face that he recognised, somebody he'd seen in the streets around Glasgow Cross or in The Ship or some other pub. Thankfully none of them were the guys that had been with Black.

As Wallace continued to bring up new pictures, he would occasionally glance at Larry to see if there was any reaction. McNally had sat down opposite Larry and was studying his reactions to the images on the screen. Larry stared at him for a minute. The face was empty of any sympathy for Larry's predicament.

The next batch of photos came up and Larry felt himself jerk back from the screen. It was the mountain, no question. He tried to put on his poker face but it was no use. He'd always been crap at poker.

'I see we've got another winner,' McNally said. He stood up and came round to look at the screen. 'Well, there's a surprise. Shug Dunbar, a right nasty bastard.'

Wallace sat with his pen poised. 'Is this one of the men you saw with Eddie Black?'

Larry looked to right and left as if he might try and make a run for it. He was trapped and he knew it. Eventually he gave a slight nod.

McNally cupped a hand to his ear. 'Sorry, I can't hear you.'

Larry glared at him, in no mood for the feeble attempt at humour. 'Aye.'

A few minutes later Larry's day was complete when he picked out the other thug.

'And that's the hat trick. Well done Mr McAllister. I would say that's a definite result. He turned to look at Wallace. 'If I'm not mistaken, that is your friend and mine, Vinny Stuart.' McNally clapped him on the back. 'That wasn't too bad, was it?'

'Maybe not for you. What happens when they find out I've shopped them.'

'We won't be saying anything about you, don't worry. We don't want our star witness coming to any harm.'

'Star witness?' Larry looked at him. 'What the hell are you talking about? I'm not going into any witness stand, not with Eddie fucking Black standing across from me, giving me the death stare.'

'It's just a figure of speech. Anyway, as I say, we'll be looking after you.'

Is that meant to make me feel better?'

McNally looked as if he was about to ignore this, then he said, 'Would you prefer if we just abandoned you to these scumbags?' When Larry didn't answer, he went on, 'Right, we just need to get this all down in a witness statement and you'll be good to go. Get home in time for your tea.'

Larry felt his heart lurch. 'Witness statement? You never said anything about a witness statement.' He shook his head. 'There's no way I'm going into court and testify about this.'

'Don't worry, it won't come to that.' McNally turned to Wallace. 'Isn't that right, DC Wallace?'

'Definitely. It's just so we can show it to our boss, DCI Flint. Let her see that we do everything by the book. She likes everything done right.'

Larry wasn't convinced. 'Aye, right. You must think I button up the back.'

'Look,' McNally said. 'You remember what I said about wasting police time? Well if you don't sign a statement confirming what you've just told us then you really would be just taking the piss.' His voice dripped the words like acid. 'I mean, we don't want to go down that road, but if you force our hand…'

Larry knew he was cornered. 'You lot are a bunch of bastards. I don't know who's worse. You, or Eddie Black and his lot.'

McNally placed his hand on Larry's shoulder, he let it rest there for a moment and then he dug his fingers into the muscle. Larry yelped and tried to twist out of the vice-like grip but the detective seemed not to notice. 'Believe me, we're much, much worse.' He loosened his grip and clapped Larry on the back. 'I'm only kidding. Look, the sooner we get this over the better. It'll never get used in court. You've got my word on that.'

Larry knew it was rubbish but he just wanted to get out of there. Wallace clicked the mouse several times, clattered the keyboard and after a minute a blank statement form appeared on the screen. He typed away furiously for some time, pausing occasionally to consult his notes or to check a point with McNally. Only twice did he ask Larry a question. Eventually he was done. He presented Larry with the draft statement and got him to check and sign it.

'We'll be in touch,' McNally said, an hour later as he opened the door. You've been a great help. DCI Flint will be impressed.'

Wallace escorted Larry to the main entrance, thanked him for his cooperation and that was that.

Chapter 14

Larry stood outside for a minute, numbed by how quickly everything had happened. Now the cops knew everything, how long would it be before they confronted Black and told him what Larry had seen, maybe even arrest him? Then what? He rubbed his cheek as he remembered, yet again, that knife being dragged down Tony's face.

All his plans not to give the police any information had been a waste of time. He felt like an idiot. Why did everything in his life go wrong? He suddenly realised he was standing in full view outside the police station where anyone could spot him. He ran down the short flight of steps and walked as fast as he could for a couple of blocks.

When he felt he'd put enough distance between himself and the station he paused and took out his phone. Brilliant, he thought, six missed calls from Casper and Sharon. He'd need to decide how much he was going to tell them. Should he call Casper now or wait till tomorrow morning to tell him what had happened? He couldn't see a good ending to the conversation either way.

He'd reached The Templeton Building at Glasgow Green and was staring at his phone trying to decide whether to call Casper when the ringtone made him jump. He was so wound up that he dropped it. By the time he picked it up it had stopped ringing. He glanced at the display.

Casper. It rang again. He thought about rejecting the call but he might as well get it over with.

'Where the fuck have you been?' Casper wasn't a great one for preambles. The voice rasped in Larry's ear. 'I've been trying to get hold of you for the last two hours. Sharon had no idea where you were. Your message said you'd closed the shop early. What the hell have you been up to?'

He decided he'd keep his answer vague. 'The cops came into the shop, like we thought they would. They were asking all sorts of questions.'

'What kind of questions?'

'Did I know Tony? When did I last see him? Was anyone with him? All that sort of stuff.'

'What did you tell them?'

'I told them I knew him, obviously, and that I had seen him at some point on Friday.'

Casper didn't speak for a moment. Larry could hear other voices in the background. 'Did they let you away with being that vague?'

Larry knew he was starting to tie himself up in knots. 'I think so. I mean, Tina said she saw him on Saturday and so did you, so he was still alive and well then.'

'Tina?'

'She came into the shop earlier.'

'Anything else?'

'They asked me what I'd done and where I'd been from Saturday evening through to Monday morning. '

There was another silence. Larry glanced around him, he was approaching the bridge over The Clyde.

Casper spoke again. 'Aye, I suppose they'll ask all of us the same thing. Did you tell them you were at my place on Sunday?'

'Aye, but I assume they'll double check that with you.'

'When I saw Tony on Saturday, he wasn't looking too clever,' Casper said. 'Did they say when they thought he was killed?'

'No, but they're hardly going to tell me that, are they?'

Casper was silent again. 'So that was that then? And they seemed happy with your story?'

'It wasn't a story, it was just what happened.' As he said this, Larry realised he was starting to forget what was the truth and what was a story.

Casper sighed. 'You know what I mean.'

Larry nodded even though Casper couldn't see him. 'Aye, they seemed to be okay with it.' Larry remembered himself signing the witness statement and tried to bury the image. 'I can't see how it will be much use to them though.'

'Did they ask anything else about me?'

'Not really, only to ask me how long I'd been working in the shop and how I got the job. Obviously they said they'll be speaking to you sooner rather than later.'

'Fair enough. Where are you by the way?'

'Just going through Glasgow Green.' He could picture Casper's face and he braced himself for the reaction. Sure enough, the explosion was instantaneous.

'What in Christ's name are you doing in Glasgow Green?'

Larry thought hard. He had to get this right. He'd heard somewhere that the best lie was one that contained some truth. He took a deep breath. 'When they were leaving the shop they wanted me to nip in to the station to look at some photos they had. See if I recognised any of the faces and if I'd ever seen any of them with Tony.'

'What people?' Casper asked.

Larry shrugged. 'You know, gangsters and that. One of the photos they showed me was Eddie Black.'

'Christ on a fucking bike. You didn't say you knew him, did you? At least tell me you didn't say he'd been in the pet shop.'

Larry could feel Casper's tension crackling in his ear. He was on dangerous ground but, in a way, he was also starting to enjoy this. 'I gave them a wee half-truth. I thought they might expect me to know who Black was and so if I completely denied it they'd think I was lying.' Larry was quite pleased with how this sounded and was actually starting to believe it himself. 'So I told them I thought I'd seen his face somewhere but I didn't know his name and I'd never seen him with Tony or anywhere near the shop.'

Another brief silence from Casper while he presumably thought this through. 'Did they believe you?'

'I think so. They moved on to other pictures anyway.' Larry wondered how long this story would stand up. Presumably only until the cops spoke to Casper. Well, for the moment, he'd just have to take each day as it came.

'Who else did they show you? What about Black's cronies?'

Time for another half-truth. 'No, they never showed me their pictures or mentioned anything about them. I mean I recognised a few of the faces, some of Glasgow's finest, from the Cross and the pub. I told them the faces were familiar but I didn't know them.'

Casper seemed satisfied with this. 'Did they say when they want to see me?'

'Tomorrow. And I don't think they'll be happy if you're not there. They're talking to everyone in the shops. See if anybody can tell them anything. Tina said they'd spoken to her and Rosa as well.'

'For God's sake don't tell Tina anything, she's got a mouth the size of the Clyde Tunnel.'

'Don't worry, I know what she's like. Anyway, she's too caught up with her own theories about the murder.'

'Like what?'

He told Casper what Tina had suggested and there was silence while Casper apparently considered the possibility that a betrayed husband had killed Tony.

By this time he'd reached the other side of Glasgow Green. Once he crossed the bridge, it was only a ten minute walk to his tenement flat in

Battlefield. 'Look, I better go. I want to call Sharon before I get into the house.'

Casper laughed. 'It'll take more than a phone call to placate her. She was spitting blood about your disappearing act.' He paused before adding, 'Listen, I want you in the shop early tomorrow. I've got stuff to do.'

Larry was about to object but he realised that Casper had already ended the call. 'Aye, we'll see about that,' he muttered before calling Sharon.

He had intended to give Sharon a shortened version of what he'd told Casper but, as predicted, she was in no mood to be fobbed off. He gave her the gist of it and said he'd fill in the rest when he got home.

Chapter 15

DCI Helen Flint was on the phone when McNally and Wallace appeared at the half-open door. She waved them in, indicating that she was nearly finished.

'I'm sure you didn't, Councillor. Yes, of course, the police and local officials should maintain a good working relationship.' Flint looked at McNally and made a face to show what she thought of the conversation. 'Remember what I said. When I need a favour, I'll be giving you a call.'

She hung up and dusted her hands together as if glad to be done with it. 'Was that Councillor Scanlon by any chance?' McNally asked.

Flint nodded, her expression clear to read.

'So, we're not charging him, then?'

Flint shook her head. 'To be honest, we probably couldn't make a case stick. Other people at the party were snorting cocaine, and there was all sorts lying about, but the good councillor was just leaving as we got there.'

'So he gets completely away with it?'

'Maybe, but I told him that charges could still be brought, if new information comes to light. The line he's taking, no pun intended, is that the police and the local authorities need to be cooperating to tackle serious crime.'

McNally laughed. 'Just as long as we're not going after the local authorities themselves.'

'I know, but the point is, we couldn't actually make a case against him. So we're not letting him away with anything. But he doesn't know that so he now wants to be my best friend forever and I'm letting him think that. You never know when we might want the councillor to help us out in some small way.'

McNally raised an eyebrow. 'Nice one, boss.'

She closed the file on her desk and dropped it into her desk drawer. 'Anyway, I hope you've got something good for me, Tom. I'll be briefing the Super later on.'

McNally nodded sympathetically. Detective Superintendent Brian Murrie was not the easiest person to deal with. But then, McNally supposed, if he was, he wouldn't be a Superintendent.

'Well, we've just had the guy from the pet shop in, Larry McAllister.'

'That's the one who might have seen something but wasn't too keen to tell us about it?'

McNally nodded. 'That's him.'

'What's he like?'

McNally shrugged. 'A typical small-time chancer. Won't tell you the truth if he can avoid it.'

'I thought he looked a bit like one of Frodo's mates,' Wallace said.

McNally looked annoyed. 'Who the hell is Frodo?'

'Frodo from 'Lord of the Rings', he's a hobbit.'

'Christ on a bike.' McNally's expression said it all.

Flint raised an eyebrow. 'Hobbits are usually meant to be trustworthy.'

Wallace ventured one final comment. 'I mean he's obviously a fly guy, a bit of a chancer, as DS McNally said. But I don't think he's a bad person deep down.'

The DCI decided to cut this short before McNally exploded. 'So, did you have any luck with him?'

'We took him through the rogues' gallery,' McNally said, glancing at Wallace and shaking his head.

'And?'

'He identified Eddie Black as the guy who drew the knife down Tony Hamilton's face. Also, he picked out Shug Dunbar and Vinny Stuart as the two thugs who helped Black beat up Hamilton.'

Flint nodded. 'Good result. Black and his cronies? I haven't had the pleasure but I've heard so much about them from you, I feel I know them. A right bunch of charmers I'm sure.'

'We could arrest them for assault, boss.'

'I know, but would we be able to make any charges stick? The victim can no longer give evidence and it doesn't sound like this McAllister would make much of a witness in court.'

McNally shrugged. 'At least it would rattle their cages.'

'I know, Tom. But we're investigating a murder and if we're looking at Black as a likely suspect it might be better not to tip our hand on this for the moment.'

McNally nodded but said nothing.

Flint was silent for a moment. 'Right, we'll be paying a visit to Mr Black and his merry men.' She checked her watch. 'That will probably be tomorrow. I'll give the boss a quick update and then we'll have a proper debrief. I think he'll want me to make a short statement to the media later.'

Half an hour later Flint made her way back to her office and signalled for McNally and Wallace to join her.

'Have a seat, guys,' she said, as she dropped into her chair. 'I've just been updating Superintendent Murrie. He's keen for us to speak to Black but doesn't want us going off half-cocked.'

'Never hurry a Murrie, eh?' McNally said. He noticed Wallace's puzzled look and explained. 'It's from an old advert. You can Google it. Superintendent Murrie's famous for never rushing his decisions.'

Flint called things back to order. 'Rest assured, I let him know that's not how we operate. However, there's an element of good sense in what he's saying. With somebody like Black, who knows all the dodges, we need to be on our best game. So once we've worked out our plan of attack we'll pay him a visit. That'll be a treat for you and me tomorrow, Tom.'

McNally nodded. 'We'll get him at home first thing. If he's not there we'll try his known haunts. There's a casino down near Glasgow Green. Word is that he's in there at all hours of the day.

He probably owns a slice of it, but there's nothing on paper.'

'Sounds good. Something else I thought of. We've heard that Black's into people trafficking so I'm calling in my favour with Louise for letting her go on secondment to the organised crime unit.'

'If Black's into trafficking he might be employing some of the people himself,' Wallace said. 'He's got a carwash and an office cleaning business, both well known for employing off-record staff and illegals.'

'And he's got a tanning salon,' McNally added.

Flint held up a hand to stem the flow. 'You're right, you're both right. This is all good stuff. Let's make sure we've got a comprehensive list of what we know. There's a huge amount of intelligence already in the files. Tom, can you make sure someone has a full brief for us first thing tomorrow. There could be any number of reasons why a lowlife like Black would kill Tony Hamilton, but let's see if we can come up with the most likely motive. Once we're set, we'll head off to see the man himself.'

She was interrupted by a knock on the door and they all turned to see DS Louise Spencer.

'Well, well, we are honoured,' McNally said, doing a mock bow and winking at Wallace. 'It's so nice to know you haven't forgotten the little people, Louise.'

Spencer had no problem in deflecting the banter. 'In your case I have tried, Tom, believe me.' She smiled to show it was just a bit of kidding, then nodded to Wallace. 'Nice to see you again, Willie.'

Flint was always struck by the contrast between Spencer and McNally. They were opposites in almost every respect but they had always worked well as a team. 'I asked Louise to come in and share what she has on Eddie Black. Right, Louise, what have you got for us?'

Spencer spent half an hour giving them a rundown on what the organised crime unit had on Black and the team listened carefully, pitching in with questions from time to time.

Flint knew that Spencer couldn't be too free and easy with information that could be traced back to her. But her loyalty to her former boss still stood for something and the DCI knew the information would be reliable and up-to-date. Spencer finished her briefing and Flint gathered her thoughts.

'Okay, thanks very much, Louise. That gives us several further areas to think about. Obviously we won't raise with Black any of the stuff that is officially known only to your unit.' She looked round her team to make sure everyone understood the point.

'So, as we said earlier, Black has got so many varied illegal activities, that he could have had any one of a number of motives for murdering Tony Hamilton.'

She turned to Wallace. 'What's the latest on time of death, Willie?'

Wallace checked his notes. 'The best estimate at the moment is Sunday probably between six in the evening and midnight.'

'What was he doing there at that time on a Sunday evening?' Flint said.

'Good point, boss,' McNally said. 'Some bookies open on a Sunday but Hamilton didn't. We're still waiting for CCTV from the area near the shop.'

Flint nodded and made a note. 'What about forensics?'

'We should have a report late tomorrow morning.'

It wasn't perfect by any means, but Flint knew this was how it worked. The forensics and the CCTV often cracked a case for them but they had to wait for it. They'd see tomorrow morning what Eddie Black had to say for himself. In the meantime, as she had predicted, she was off to do a brief press conference.

Chapter 16

'That's me back,' Larry shouted, as he opened the door. He looked into the living-room. Sharon was sitting on the couch, feet curled up under her, watching a recording of 'Unforgotten' on the telly. She seemed calm enough but he could sense the underlying tension and knew she was just biding her time.

She glanced round then turned back to the television. 'Your tea's in the microwave and the kids are in their rooms.'

Larry nodded to the back of her head. 'Thanks. I'll nip in and see them in a minute.' As he turned for the door, her voice followed him. 'Once you've had your dinner we'll have a good talk about this, find out what you've been up to.'

He was expecting it but he still felt the shiver go down his spine. Sharon liked to be in control, needed to be in fact. She held the threat of access to the kids over him. As he headed into the kitchen he tried to put his thoughts in order. Would he tell her exactly the same story as he'd told Casper? He realised he had no choice. Casper might have already called her and given her the highlights. Her brother was a few years older than Sharon but they were very close. She had told Larry once that she and her brother had no secrets from each other. He doubted that was the case but, even so, it was safe to assume they would keep each other informed about what Larry got up to.

He opened the door of the microwave to discover that tonight's treat was cottage pie, one of his favourites. He had to admit, despite her faults, Sharon always did well with the meals. In the early days they liked to make the meals together, spend time picking out a recipe they hadn't tried before. But these days they usually went for something easy and quick. He stood there for a minute, staring at the food then gave himself a shake and went in to see the kids.

As usual, Kelly and Joe were full of stories about what had happened in school that day. The three of them sat together in Kelly's room chatting and laughing. Despite his problems and his many failings, Larry knew he'd been lucky with his kids. He loved spending time with them and they seemed to enjoy it too. Fingers crossed it stayed like that.

He sat in the armchair eating his dinner, the tray balanced on his lap. Sharon was watching the last few minutes of 'Unforgotten'. He usually liked the programme but all the talk of forensics and DNA, CCTV and mug shots unnerved him with its echoes of how he had spent his day and of what had happened to Tony at the weekend.

He tried to put it out of his mind by thinking back to his chat with Kelly and Joe. They were good kids, okay, he was biased, but it was still true. Kelly was starting to get a bit of an attitude but that was to be expected at her age and, by comparison to most of her pals, she was a gem. Wee Joe was a bit of a character, everybody liked him. The two of them were really close, which wasn't always the case with brothers and sisters.

He thought of his own sister, Mary. They had got on well as youngsters but had grown apart as they grew into teenagers. She had gone off to work in Newcastle for a big multi-national. A few years later she moved to the States, Cincinnati, with an American who worked for the company. They swapped cards at Christmas and did the occasional video call. She was always saying they should come over and visit, but Larry never took it seriously. There was no way they could go over there, it would cost a fortune.

The programme finished and Sharon switched the telly off. Larry nursed a faint hope that she might postpone the discussion and head for bed. No such luck.

She turned to face him. 'So, do you want to tell me what the hell you've been up to? You left a message saying you'd closed the shop early. Casper called me about six times, going absolutely mental. He had no idea where you were. Did you even go into the shop today?'

He realised that she hadn't spoken to Casper after his earlier phone call, otherwise she would know about the cops coming into the shop.

'Of course I was in the shop. You saw Casper here earlier when he asked me to go in and open up, to take care of the animals and that.'

'Just because he asked you, it doesn't mean you did it. We all know you can take liberties when it comes to work. God knows, you've done it often enough in the past.'

He decided not to rise to that and just told her, as calmly as he could, what had happened over the course of the day. Of course he didn't tell her everything, he gave her the same edited version he'd told Casper.

The interrogation went on for about half an hour but eventually Sharon decided she'd made him squirm enough or maybe she was just tired. She took herself off to bed, finally leaving him in peace.

Larry breathed a sigh of relief and stretched out in the armchair to review the day's events. All in all, it had been a hell of a day. The police had got the better of him, no doubt about that. They now knew what he'd seen on Friday and they'd got him to ID Eddie Black and his two henchmen. Could he trust the cops to keep his name out of it? No chance. They would say anything to get their result. In any case, he knew it wasn't necessarily in their control. So he'd just have to keep his fingers crossed.

In any case, there was nothing to say that Black and his thugs had killed Tony. They had assaulted him on Friday morning but Tony was alive and kicking on Saturday. So, it could have been Black but it could have been the angry husband from Tina's theory or simply a robbery gone wrong.

Maybe the fact that Larry had seen Black on Friday would come to nothing. He gave himself a reality check. Who was he kidding? If it wasn't

Black and his crew, who else would it be? He didn't really rate Tina's theory. Tony hadn't exactly been God's gift to women. No, it had to be Black and his gang. Which meant the cops would definitely keep hassling Larry because as far as he could see, Black was their number one suspect.

At least he'd managed to fob Casper and Sharon off with his story and avoiding hassle from them was always a plus. The cops would be in to talk to Casper tomorrow. Would they tell him what Larry had seen? No reason why they should do Larry any favours. On the other hand, they liked to play their cards close to their chest. Anyway, there was nothing he could do about it tonight.

He'd switched the telly back on when Sharon had gone to bed and left it on mute. Sometimes that helped him to think. A news item came up on the screen and he hit the volume button. A press conference outside the police station. A woman talking about Tony's murder, she wasn't local, sounded like a Newcastle accent. Based on information received, she said, they were following a definite lead in the case. Larry swore. Those bastards. So much for keeping him out of it. It wouldn't take a genius to work it out. He spends three hours in the station and now the cops have a definite lead. Obviously he was the one who had given them the information and the 'definite lead' had to mean Eddie Black. This was not good. Sharon might not pick up on it, but Casper would and these things had a way of getting out. How long before it reached Eddie Black's ears?

Chapter 17

It was Arthur Simpson's birthday and he decided to give himself a treat. He knew just what he wanted. He'd had treats before but his mum had always picked them. This time was different, his mum wasn't there anymore, so Arthur would decide, he was in charge. He had woken up that morning feeling excited, though he was also a bit scared. He'd been thinking about it ever since his mum's funeral last week and he'd decided today was the day.

He pulled the book from under his pillow and looked at the picture again, ran his fingers over it as if he could stroke the soft fur. He giggled and slipped the book back under the pillow. He'd always wanted a rabbit. Even when he was really young he'd wanted one, but his mother had always said no. She never gave him a reason, just gave him a clout on the head when he went on about it.

But his mother was dead now and he could get a rabbit if he wanted one. In fact he could do anything he liked. He didn't have to answer to her now or to anyone. The idea that she couldn't do anything about it made him feel excited and the sick feeling in his stomach became a sort of laugh. He remembered one of his mum's friends talking about a belly laugh and Arthur thought that must be what he felt.

He had his breakfast, his usual mug of tea, in his favourite Spiderman mug, with a toasted banana sandwich on Mother's Pride plain bread. His mother had always insisted on plain bread and it was Arthur's favourite too. His mother had a lot of other rules and Arthur knew them all by heart. He didn't understand them but he'd always had to live by them. Until now.

Since it was his birthday he treated himself to a Mars Bar along with a second mug of tea. Once he'd cleared up his dishes, he made sure he had money in his pocket, took one last look round the room and went out, double-locking the door behind him. A minute later he came back in, went into the kitchen and checked that the gas was turned off. He nodded to himself and set off for town.

His mum had never liked him going into town on his own. Said he might get into trouble. When she got sick and had to go into hospital, he'd decided that, quite soon, he would go in on his own. Mrs Ritchie, the nice neighbour across the landing, had told him how to do it, what bus to get and how to pay for his ticket. He'd kept the note she'd given him.

He was to get the number 67 bus and get off at the street called the Trongate. Mrs Ritchie had told him there was a pet shop nearby, in a street near The Saltmarket though she didn't know the exact address. The names of some of the streets sounded funny to Arthur but Mrs Ritchie had written down the street names and directions for him. When he got off the bus he'd try and find the pet shop. He was still a bit nervous about going into town on his own but it had to be done because he wanted his rabbit.

When he left the house, he immediately met his first problem. Danny Johnston, from upstairs, was at the front of the close talking to the blonde girl from two closes down. He'd have to squeeze by them to get out of the close. He thought about going round the back to avoid them but he remembered that he was trying to be brave today.

So, he went out the front way and did his best not to panic. As he approached them they stopped their conversation and looked straight at him. Arthur felt his face get hot and his heart was hammering. When he drew level with them, Danny said, 'Alright Arthur, how's it hanging?'

Arthur had no idea what this meant and didn't know what to say. He muttered 'thank you' and kept his eyes on the ground as he threaded his way between them. He was almost past them but at the last minute he allowed himself to glance up at the blonde girl. She caught him looking and she laughed.

'Off to town are we, Arthur?'

He didn't know what to say. He mumbled the word 'rabbit' but wasn't sure if they understood what he meant.

'Have a nice time then,' the blonde said. 'Don't do anything I wouldn't do,' and the two of them burst out laughing.

Arthur felt his face getting hotter and sweat broke out all over his body. How could Arthur know what somebody else might do? He kept walking and soon left them and their laughter behind.

He found his way to the bus stop and double-checked the number of bus he needed. A few minutes later, a number 67 came round the corner and Arthur put his hand out like his mother had always told him to do. He paid the driver and sat as near the front as he could. Everything was working out fine and he smiled to himself as the bus headed towards the city centre. He remembered some of the buildings from trips he had taken with his mum. Mrs Ritchie had told him to look out for the big clock with a blue face and to get off at the very first stop after that. The traffic was getting busier and Arthur thought he was getting close to his stop. But suddenly the bus stopped and everyone was getting off. Arthur could feel the panic building up inside him and knew he had to ask the driver.

'Excuse me, is this The Trongate?' he asked as politely as he could.

The driver was reading a paper and looked up impatiently. 'No this is the 67a. We don't go as far as The Trongate.'

Arthur almost burst into tears. 'But I need The Trongate.'

The driver didn't seem interested but he must have seen the look on Arthur's face. 'Look, you just need to walk for a few minutes and you'll be there. Where exactly do you want to go?'

'A pet shop, I'm going to buy a rabbit.'

'A rabbit? Good for you.' He turned back to his paper but then relented. He looked at Arthur again. 'Look, hang on a second.'

The driver signalled to a policeman who was passing and explained the situation. They exchanged looks and the policeman agreed to help out.

'I think I might know the place you're looking for,' the officer said.

Arthur was nervous about walking alongside a policeman. His mum had always said never to trust the cops but he had no choice and this man seemed nice. As they made their way along the busy streets, he could feel people staring at him as if he was in trouble. He was starting to panic.

Chapter 18

When Larry woke up, the house was quiet, no sound of Sharon or the kids. That meant it was either earlier than usual or later than usual. There was a lot of noise from the street so that wasn't a good sign. He fumbled for his phone to check the time. Half past nine. How the hell had that happened? Last night, he had deliberately set the alarm for an early rise, six o'clock. He checked the settings. There was an alarm set for six but he'd somehow set it for Mondays only, and this was Tuesday. Why had nobody woken him? He lay there for a minute trying to assess the extra grief this would give him. Next minute his phone rang. He knew who it was going to be.

'Where the hell are you?' Casper's voice came rasping down the line. 'I told you I needed you in early this morning.'

Larry got out of bed before he answered. 'Sorry. My alarm didn't go off.'

'Are you fucking at it?'

'No, straight up. I set it for six. I was going to be there before eight but somehow it didn't work and Sharon didn't wake me.'

'Don't try and put the blame on Sharon. You're a bloody adult. At least you're supposed to be. When will you be here?'

Larry thought for a minute. If he got dressed right away, forgot about a shower and took the car instead of the bus he could be there in about half an hour. 'Three quarters of an hour.'

'You've got half an hour or you can find yourself another job.' The line went dead.

Ten minutes later he was hurrying down the stairs, munching a slice of bread. He didn't like taking the car into town but he'd have to today. It was usually hard to find a parking space and, in any case, it was expensive to park for the whole day. Plus, the car was old and not that reliable, so it could be more bother than it was worth. Sometimes Casper let him use the delivery van for going to and from the shop but he always made it seem like he was doing Larry some massive favour. Just another way of keeping him in his place. The van had its own parking spot in the lane behind the shop and that was where Casper parked his car as well. There was just room for the two vehicles so Larry had to try and find a free spot somewhere or pay full whack for the day.

Luck was with him. Because of the time, the traffic was lighter than normal so he made good time and got into the city centre for ten to ten. He was about to head for the municipal open air car park five minutes from the shop when he saw an empty space near the railway arches. He pulled in. There was no parking meter and no lines or notices warning against parking there.

This sometimes happened when the council changed the parking restrictions. You could get a day's free parking right in the centre of town before they painted in the new lines and installed the meter. He got out and double-checked for parking notices. Nothing. There were another four cars parked there, all presumably taking the same chance as him. Safety in numbers he decided. He checked the time. Five to ten. He locked the car and hurried off to the shop. He would just make it.

The bookies was still cordoned off but both ends of the street were open so there was no hold-up there. He stepped through the door of the shop at a minute to ten. Maybe today would be okay after all.

The Green Rooms Casino wasn't open to the public at this time of day but, based on what Spencer had told them, Flint was confident they would find Black inside even this early in the morning.

She got out of the car and surveyed the building. Built about ten years ago across from Glasgow Green, it had proved popular with locals and tourists. With its many possibilities for moving cash in and out, it was also a favourite haunt of many of the city's criminals. Spencer had confirmed Flint's own information that Black had an interest in the casino but, not surprisingly, there was nothing on paper.

They approached the ornate entranceway and Flint tried the doors only to find they were locked. She pressed the intercom button and a moment later a metallic voice said 'We're closed.'

'Police.' Flint said, in her best no-nonsense tone. 'Here to see Mr Black.'

'What makes you think he's here at this time of the morning?'

'We saw him arriving earlier.' Flint had no compunction about offering the small lie. 'Open the door, now.'

A camera linked to the intercom flickered into life and a pale face appeared in the screen. 'I'll need to see some ID.'

Flint and McNally held their warrant cards up to the camera. There was a moment's pause then the voice said 'Come up to the first floor.' A moment later the door buzzed and they pushed it open.

Flint had not met Eddie Black before but she had read the file, seen the pictures and heard the stories from McNally and others. She knew the type from her years of dealing with criminals in Newcastle. These people were the same all over. Cold, calculating and menacing. Sociable and generous company when it suited them and if your face fitted but they would turn nasty in the blink of an eye and wouldn't skip a heartbeat at killing anyone who got in their way. However, even though she knew the type, she didn't know the individual. So she tried not to make too many assumptions about how this would go.

They heard the voice before they saw the man. 'Well, well, if it isn't my old pal, Mr McNally. I see you've brought your bird with you. Going in for the older woman now, are we?'

Flint let McNally know to keep silent for the moment. She still couldn't see Black but she quickly scanned the room and realised he was sitting in a booth near the window with his back to the officers. Obviously he had looked at them on the CCTV camera.

Flint walked over and sat directly opposite Black. She looked at the gangster, raised an eyebrow and gave a quiet laugh. She turned back to her sergeant. 'Are you sure we've got the right guy here, DS McNally? I was told Eddie Black was a clever man but this bloke obviously doesn't have a clue what's going on.'

She fixed Black with a stare. 'Would you get us a cup of tea, pet? And tell your boss we're here. We've got important stuff to talk about.'

Black glared at her while his two henchmen looked at each other in puzzlement. The silence continued for a minute then Black spoke. 'State your business, then fuck off.'

Flint pretended to look hurt. 'No tea then? Probably just as well. Never know what you might put in it.' She gave McNally a nod and he slipped into the seat beside Black, boxing him in. Flint surveyed the premises. 'Not bad at all. Is it yours?'

'A friend's,' Black growled.

'Got a lot of friends, have you?' Flint asked sweetly. She didn't wait for an answer. 'Tony Hamilton. He was one of your friends, wasn't he?'

Black scowled. 'Never heard of him.' He made a show of looking puzzled. He shrugged his shoulders and looked at his men who went through the same pantomime. 'No, can't help you there.'

'Really?' Flint looked disappointed. 'I must have heard it wrong. I was told you and him were best of buddies. That you were always popping in there to see him with your two pals here.'

'Why would I bother going into a bookies?' He made a gesture to include the casino. 'I can do any gambling I want right here.'

Flint smiled and nodded. 'Right enough. But who said anything about a bookies? I thought you said you'd never heard of Tony Hamilton.'

Black gave her a dead stare. 'I just remembered I read about him in the paper.'

'Reading newspapers now are we?' McNally spoke for the first time. 'Moved on from the colouring books, then.'

The remark earned them a scowl and Flint took up the questions again. 'So you've never been to Tony Hamilton's bookies in Saint Andrews Street?'

'I don't remember being in Saint Andrews Street recently,' Black said.

Flint made a show of consulting her notebook. 'Strange. I've heard otherwise. Well, our old friend CCTV might have a different story to tell.'

Black shrugged. 'I'm not saying I've never walked down the street. I might have, but just not realised it was, what did you call it, Saint Andrews Street? There's a lot of streets in Glasgow.'

Flint moved on. 'Where were you from Friday evening to Monday morning?'

'Me and the boys treated ourselves to a wee weekend away. A lovely spa in a hotel just about an hour's drive away, near Edinburgh. It's called 'Out of This World'. Beautiful wee place. Dead relaxing. I mean Glasgow's great. Lovely people,' he paused and glanced at McNally, 'for the most part. But sometimes it gets me down. The noise, the violence. So I like to get away whenever I can and that's the perfect place.' He nodded, as if agreeing with himself. 'You should try it sometime. A nice swim, a wee massage. Gets rid of the stress.' He looked at 'the boys' and they nodded enthusiastically.

Flint knew of the place. She had thought about going there for a long weekend with her husband once, but they'd had to cancel at the last minute when police business intervened. Well, she'd scratch that place off her list. Her expression showed she was unimpressed. 'What time did you head off?'

'We left here Friday about six o'clock and got back late Sunday.'

McNally grunted. 'What time on Sunday?'

Black shrugged. 'Can't really remember. Does it matter?'

'If I'm asking, then it matters.'

'I'd say we left the hotel about seven, took our time on the way back, stopped off for a drink on the way.'

'Where was this?' McNally asked.

'A wee place near Broxburn, The Fiddler's Rest.'

Flint picked up the questions again. 'So, when did you actually get back to Glasgow?'

Black glanced over at his men before answering. 'We probably got back to Glasgow about nine or ten. The boys dropped me off at my place and they headed off.'

Flint stared at him. 'No doubt you'll be able to prove that?'

Black gave her a warm smile but his eyes were two chips of ice. 'Definitely. I'm sure we can. Now, if there's nothing else, I'm a wee bit busy at the moment.'

Flint nodded to McNally and they got up to leave. As she headed for the door, she paused. 'We'll be checking out your alibi later today. You take care now, pet.' They were out the door before Black could muster a response.

'So what do you think, boss?' McNally asked as they emerged onto the street.

Flint glanced back at the casino. 'What do I think? I think he's a scumbag. Typical of the animals we have to deal with. Ego the size of the planet and he thinks he's smarter than everybody else. Believes he's untouchable.'

McNally nodded as he increased his pace to keep up with Flint. He'd seen her like this before; when she got worked up about a case and her mind was working overtime, it seemed to translate into her physical demeanour. 'Do you think he's behind the murder of Tony Hamilton?'

'I'm not sure about that. It seems so obvious that it would be stupid. Then again, we've both met lots of stupid villains. Obviously we'll check out his alibi. Even if he was there for some of the weekend, it would be easy enough to slip away and drive to Glasgow, kill Hamilton and drive back.'

'Of course, he might not have done it himself or even been there. He could have got one of his thugs to do the deed.'

Flint shrugged, acknowledging the point.

'What next?' McNally said.

'We'll get Willie on to the alibi. And we need to get a more exact fix on the time of Hamilton's death. Black said he was back in Glasgow around nine or ten on Sunday. Maybe it will turn out his alibi doesn't actually help him. In the meantime you chase up on any links between Black and Tony Hamilton. Black's clearly got an interest in that casino, even if not on paper. So maybe that ties in to Hamilton's bookies shop somehow. We'll need to check the records for the bookies as well as digging up everything we can about Black. I'll have another word with Louise, see if she can give us any more info now that we've got the initial response from Black.'

When they got into the car McNally said, 'So is it back to the station?'

'For you, yes, but drop me at the mortuary. I've got a date with the late Tony Hamilton.'

Eddie Black stood at the window as Flint and McNally made for their car. What had led them to ask him about Tony Hamilton? Were they just fishing? Or did they know more than they were letting on? Had they found out about his involvement with the man? If so, who had told them? These days there were eyes everywhere, and ears.

He turned to Shug Dunbar and Vinny Stuart. 'Have any of you been spouting off about my business dealings lately?'

The men looked offended. 'No way, boss,' Dunbar said.

Stuart shook his head in agreement. 'I mean, what would we do that for?'

Black was impassive. 'Don't try and flannel me. To impress a bird, or your pals. I know how you work. You know my rules, both of you and you know what happens to anybody who fucks me up.'

He held his hand up to cut short the protestations of innocence. 'Right. In that case, we'll pay a wee visit to Casper later today. The cops will have been talking to the people in the shops next to the bookies. One of them might have said something. I've got a few things to sort out first but be ready to leave in about half an hour.' He picked up his phone to signal that the discussion was over.

Chapter 19

Arthur took a moment to calm down. It had worked out fine after all. The policeman had found the place for him. He took in his surroundings. He liked this street. It felt safe and comfortable. He could smell food and it made his mouth water. He looked along the row of shops, there was a nice little café just along the road. He wandered along to have a look at the cakes in the window. He might go in there later and have a cup of tea and a cake but it was a bit busy just now. In any case, first things first, as his mum always said. He was here for a rabbit and right in front of him was the pet shop.

It looked a bit run down from the outside, he thought, but he liked that. It made him feel comfortable. A bell tinkled on the door as he went in. A damp, warm smell hit him as soon as he stepped into the shop. He wasn't sure if he liked it but he thought he did. The shop was fairly dark and he stood there for a minute, peering round him, to get his bearings. When he closed the door behind him the smell was stronger and he stepped forward towards the centre of the shop.

He was standing there wondering what to do next when he heard someone speaking but he couldn't see them. It sounded like they were on the phone. After a minute the voice stopped and a man appeared from a door at the back of the shop.

'Help you?' he said. He was older than Arthur, he was wearing a suit and tie and, even though this was the first time he'd been in a pet shop, Arthur thought that for some reason it looked a bit odd. The man's voice was like somebody off the TV, one of the men who ran the quiz shows. Arthur thought he looked a bit like him as well.

'I want a rabbit, please,' Arthur said, remembering to be polite. Good manners cost nothing, his mother always said.

'Well you've come to the right place,' the man said. 'We've got plenty of rabbits. Any particular type?'

Arthur just looked at him. He didn't know there were different types of rabbit. 'Just a rabbit,' he said.

'Right, if you'd like to come over here I'll show you the various rabbits that we have,' the man said, walking towards the back of the shop.

Arthur looked at the cages as he passed. There were hamsters and mice and other animals he didn't recognise. There were also fish with bright, shiny colours swimming around in a big glass tank. Arthur felt hypnotised by their swirling shapes and colours and he stopped in front of the tank.

The man noticed Arthur's reaction. 'They're fascinating to watch and make great conversation pieces, the tropical fish, almost as good as the telly.'

Arthur didn't know what to say, so he just nodded.

'Tropical fish, hamsters and rabbits are big sellers. We're not allowed to sell dogs and cats these days, most people get them from breeders or from the refuges.'

Arthur had no idea what the man was talking about so he just made a non-committal noise.

They passed more cages of hamsters and more tropical fish then Arthur gave a little skip as he saw the rabbits.

The man started to explain the different types of rabbits and their respective advantages and disadvantages. 'All rabbits aren't the same you know. A lot of people don't realise that. So it all depends what you're looking for.'

Arthur knew exactly what he was looking for but he didn't know how to explain it. In his head he had a memory of a rabbit. It wasn't a real rabbit. It had been in a book his teacher had shown him. She had told him that it was a Ladybird book. It had lots of pictures. 'One picture for every letter of the alphabet,' she'd said.

And at the letter R there was a picture of a beautiful rabbit. The picture was still clear in Arthur's mind after all these years and that was the rabbit he wanted. He had looked for that book at the library and in shops but he had never been able to find it. The closest he had got was a book about a rabbit called Peter. It wasn't the same but it was the best he had. If he'd known there were so many different types of rabbits he could have brought his book to show the man.

Arthur looked along the rabbit cages, there seemed to be so many. He saw one that seemed to be pure white, but he couldn't see his rabbit anywhere and the man's voice was confusing him, he was talking too much. Arthur was about to give up when the door opened again. The man excused himself telling Arthur to 'have a wee look round' and headed to the front of the shop.

Arthur heard him talking angrily to someone. He heard the words 'about bloody time' and a murmured response. Then Arthur heard nothing else because suddenly, in a cage at the very end of the row, he saw the rabbit from the Ladybird book, his rabbit. It was exactly like the one in his picture, light brown all over with a few darker patches on its fur, and Arthur knew he had to buy it. He had been right to come on this adventure after all, his mum had been wrong.

The man reappeared a few minutes later and before he could say anything Arthur pointed towards the rabbit and said 'this one, please.'

'A common domestic short-haired, a good choice,' the man said. 'Do you have everything you need for it?'

Arthur looked at him, not understanding.

'A hutch, a water bottle, food, all the rest,' the man said.

Arthur started to panic again. He hadn't thought about that. He did know that rabbits lived in little houses called hutches. In fact in the Ladybird book there had been a hutch in the picture behind the rabbit.

'Don't worry we'll get you sorted out,' the man said, giving Arthur a reassuring smile. 'Larry,' he shouted, 'come and help this gentleman with rabbit accessories.'

Arthur felt an excited sizzle in his stomach. He was getting his rabbit, and something called 'rabbit accessories' and the man had called him a gentleman. He would show his mother that he could manage without her.

The man called Larry came wandering over to where Arthur was standing. He was dressed differently from the other man, no suit or tie, he had denims and what Arthur thought of as a cowboy shirt. He was shorter than Arthur and he had a funny sort of face, it looked happy and sad at the same time. Arthur thought it was a face he could trust. The man nodded hello and said, 'Okay dokey, so we want a rabbit, do we?'

Arthur pointed to the cage so there would be no mistake. 'This rabbit, please.'

The man gave Arthur a funny look for a moment but then he smiled and helped Arthur pick out everything he needed. When Arthur couldn't decide about certain things the man decided for him. Eventually the man, Larry, said, 'Okay, that should do it. Let's go and see what the damage is.'

Arthur had no idea what might be damaged so he just nodded and followed Larry over to the counter. When Arthur heard the total he realised it was a lot more money than he had expected. But mum had always hidden lots of money around the house and Arthur knew the hiding places, so he didn't panic too much. It had been a hard morning but he was pleased with his shopping.

The man looked at the bundle of shopping and back at Arthur. 'Do you want to bring the car round to the door and I'll help you load up?' Larry asked.

Arthur looked at him.

'Where are you parked?' Larry asked him.

'Parked?' Arthur said.

'Where's your car?' Larry said.

'I came on the bus, the 67a. It was meant to be the 67 so I had to walk the last bit,' Arthur said.

The man called Larry looked up at the ceiling and sighed. 'How are you going to get this lot home then?' he asked.

Arthur had no idea what to do, but at that point the first man reappeared. 'What's the problem?' he said.

Once things were explained, the first man soon arranged everything. He got Arthur's details and said Larry would bring all the stuff to Arthur's house tonight on his way home. He said it wasn't much of a detour and they would only charge an extra tenner for the delivery. The man called Larry didn't look too happy about it but Arthur could tell that the man in the suit was the boss.

Arthur wasn't very confident with money, his mother had usually taken care of that. He counted out the money slowly on the counter and the boss nodded to show him he had the right amount. With his shopping paid for, Arthur bent down to the rabbit in its cage, told it he'd see it tonight..

He was about to open the door when it was banged wide on its hinges and three rough-looking men came swaggering in. One of them was huge and looked absolutely brutal. Another was a bit smaller but had a mean, angry look. Their faces were twisted in scowls and distorted by deep scars. The third man was a bit smaller but he was the one that scared Arthur most. Arthur had seen a programme on the telly once, about a shark. He had never forgotten how the creature had seemed almost bored as it devoured its prey, its lifeless eyes apparently looking elsewhere as it killed. This man's eyes were as cold and dead as the eyes of the shark. Arthur stood there gaping at him, rooted to the spot in terror.

'What the hell are you staring at, you prick?' Shark Face said to Arthur. 'You want a fucking picture? Or maybe you want a sore face, a scar like the one I've got?'

Remembering his manners as always, Arthur muttered, 'no thank you'.

Shark Face seemed about to take exception to what he presumably thought was sarcastic cheek but the man in the suit stepped forward.

'All right, Eddie, this customer was just leaving. What can I do for you?'

Shark Face leaned right into Arthur. 'I'll remember you, you fucking oddball,' he snarled, before moving to the back of the shop.

Arthur went out, closing the door quietly behind him. He knew he would remember the man as well.

Chapter 20

Eddie Black pushed his way past the cages and baskets and stopped in front of Casper. 'I don't like it when people aren't here when I come looking for them, Casper.' He tilted his head towards Larry. 'Did bawheid here not give you my message?'

Casper held his hands up in apology. 'Sorry about that. He did tell me you'd been in looking for me. Everything's all over the place with Tony getting killed. And there's always a lot of stuff to sort out with the shop.'

'Tony? Aye, shame about that. I see the boys in blue are still busy at the bookies.' Black looked around him. 'I don't see how this place can be taking up your time. You hardly ever see a customer in here. He nodded towards the back shop. 'We need to have a wee chat. But we'll get to that in a minute.'

Black turned to Vinny Stuart. 'Lock that door. I want a wee bit of privacy to talk to these two.' He perched on the counter and beckoned Casper and Larry. 'I had a visit from the cops earlier today, poking their noses into my business. And I don't like that. They were asking if I knew Tony Hamilton and where I was over the weekend.'

'Fuck.' Casper said.

Black nodded. 'Aye, fuck indeed. So I was wondering why they might connect me with

Hamilton, why they might think I knew anything about what happened to him.'

Casper spread his hands wide and gave a non-committal look. 'No idea, Eddie.'

Larry didn't think he sounded very convincing but he said nothing. In the silence that followed Casper's reply, Larry kept his eyes focused on the floor. When he finally looked up Black was staring at him. Larry shrugged.

'They've been talking to everybody who might have known Tony.' As soon as he said it Larry realised his mistake.

Black was straight in there, he took a step towards Larry, the voice growling with menace. 'Is that right? And why would they think I might know him?'

Larry was sweating. Somewhere inside his head a small, crazy voice was shouting, 'Because I told them you were in his shop on Friday, beating him up.' He tried to steady his nerves, managed to look Black in the eye and finally said, 'I don't know. They were in here yesterday asking if we knew anything.'

Black's gaze swivelled to Casper.

'I wasn't here. I've not spoken to them yet,' Casper said.

'What about you, bawjaws?' Black said, turning back to Larry.

Larry felt the trickles of sweat breaking out all over his body. 'They just asked me if I knew him, when I'd last seen him. The usual sort of stuff.'

Black smirked. 'The usual sort of stuff? Hear that boys? He fancies himself as an expert in murder enquiries.' He shook his head. 'Where do you get your expertise from? The telly?'

Larry shrugged, he knew whatever he said would be wrong.

'Who was it you spoke to?' Black said.

Larry made a show of trying to remember. 'I think one of them was called McNally. The other was maybe Wallace.' He felt the need to elaborate the story. 'A right couple of evil-looking bastards, they were.'

'Evil?' Black laughed. 'I don't think you know what that means.' He indicated his heavies.' But you might find out. Did you tell them anything about me?'

Larry stammered. He could see in his mind's eye, as clear as day, the photos of Black and his cronies that he had identified in the police station. 'You? No. I mean what could I tell them about you? What do I know?'

'Do you know what happens to people who fuck with me? Or who lie to me?'

Larry shook his head, not trusting himself to speak.

Black said nothing, just fixed Larry with eyes that seemed to look right into his heart. Eventually he nodded, apparently satisfied. He turned back to Casper, dismissing Larry.

'Make sure you watch what you're saying when they talk to you.'

'Casper nodded several times. 'Of course, Eddie, no bother, you don't need to worry about that.'

Black smiled his cold smile. 'No, but you do. So,' he said, changing the subject, 'have you got an answer for me yet, about that other business?' Black paused as he noticed Larry standing there watching and listening. 'Haw you, tosspot, why are you still here? Away and play with the buses.'

Before Larry could react, Casper gave him a fiver and said, 'go and get yourself a cup of tea and a roll.'

Larry grabbed the money and hurried out. As he walked the few yards to the café he wondered what the 'other business' was and what question Black needed an answer to. But he was mainly concerned with whether Black had been convinced by his answers. He'd already seen what Black and his men were capable of and he didn't want to be on the receiving end of that. So far, he'd managed to avoid giving the game away.

He'd need to let Sharon know that he'd be home a bit later tonight. Thanks to Casper, he needed to deliver that stuff to the guy who had been in to buy a rabbit. Larry shook his head when he remembered how the guy had behaved and spoken. He was an odd one, didn't seem quite all there. Casper had said the delivery was on Larry's way home, the bastard. The guy lived somewhere near The Kelvin Hall, completely in the opposite direction for Larry.

As he pushed the café door open, he spotted Tina at the counter. She was full of the joys, singing along to a song on the radio. She waved when she saw him come through the door.

'What can I get you, pet?' She'd used this line before, obviously thinking it was funny because of where Larry worked. Despite his worries, he didn't want to disappoint her so he smiled to acknowledge the joke. He gave his order and chatted to her for a couple of minutes while she got his tea and roll. She was full of questions and speculation about Tony's murder and Larry started to feel on edge. He said as little as possible and when another customer came in he went over to the window and took a seat from where he could watch Black's car.

As he drank his tea he wondered what Black was saying to Casper. And what was that 'other business' that Black had mentioned? Larry wasn't sure if he really wanted to know. He shivered as he remembered Black's words and that cold look he'd given him.

The main thing was that, for the moment, Casper, and more importantly, Black, had no idea what Larry had seen on Friday and what he'd told the cops. There was nothing more he could do for the moment except keep his fingers crossed. He tried to relax and enjoy his tea. A few minutes later he saw Black and his two gorillas come out of the pet shop, saunter across to the car and drive off. He jumped when he heard Tina's voice right behind him.

'They're an evil-looking bunch. Do you know who they are? I've seen them before, talking to Casper. Come to think of it, I'm sure I've seen them talking to Tony.' She paused and looked at Larry. 'You don't suppose…'

Larry stood up and looked her straight in the eye. He liked Tina but he had to put her straight. 'Listen, I don't know who they are, or anything about them. With guys like that it's better not to speculate and definitely not to gossip. Understand?' As he said this, the image of him sitting in the police station identifying the three of them came back to haunt him. He finished his tea. 'I better get back. You take care. Okay.' He put a finger to his lips, gave her a wink and left.

When he got back Casper was slumped against the counter, staring into space. As Larry turned the handle, the bell rang and Casper reacted to the noise, jumping up and looking round. When he saw it was Larry he leaned back against the counter.

'Is that them away then?' Larry asked. He wasn't going to pry, he knew Casper was secretive about any dealings he might have with Black. In any case Larry didn't really want to learn too much about the gangster and his business. The less he knew, the less there was for him to tell the police.

Casper shook his head and continued to stare into space. He had the look of a man with serious problems. Larry assumed it was to do with what had gone on between him and Black, but Casper wasn't going to share it with his brother-in-law.

'That man is pure evil,' he said still not looking at Larry. 'Pure fucking evil.'

Despite his shaky relationship with Casper, Larry felt sorry for him. 'Do you want a cup of tea?'

At first Casper appeared not to have heard. After a minute he looked at Larry, seeming to take an age to answer the simple question. 'No. Thanks anyway. I might just head out for half an hour, grab a quick pint round the corner.'

Larry nodded, waiting for him to move but before he could do so, the doorbell sounded. Casper jumped and when Larry saw the look on Casper's face he didn't turn round but braced himself to hear that rasping, menacing tone. But it was another, equally unwelcome, voice that spoke.

'Mr White? I'm Detective Sergeant McNally. This is my colleague Detective Constable Wallace. We'd like a word.'

The two detectives brushed past Larry, giving him a nod. As Casper led them into his office McNally turned and gave Larry a wink and a knowing smile.

Larry spent the next twenty minutes in a cold sweat. He wandered to the front of the shop and stared aimlessly at the passers-by. He tried to busy himself with routine tasks, checking the animals' food and water were sorted. He was sure the cops would tell Casper all about what Larry had seen last Friday and what he'd later told them in his meetings with them. Casper was bound to go nuts at the thought of Larry involving him and his business in the murder enquiry and especially in inviting the wrath of Black. And once Casper knew, it wouldn't be long before Sharon did too.

He moved about the place pretending to be busy but all the time trying to hear what was being discussed in the back office. He wondered if he could go into the office on the pretence of offering them a cup of tea or asking Casper some question about the stock. No, that was crazy, it would just make the cops mad and make Casper suspicious.

He was leaning into the door, trying to hear what was being said, when it was flung open and he nearly fell into the office. Fortunately whoever had opened it, stood there for a minute longer finishing the conversation, giving Larry enough time to hurry over and pretend to be busy feeding the fish.

The two detectives emerged, followed by an unhappy-looking Casper. Larry tried to imagine what had been said and braced himself for the reaction.

'Don't forget, Mr White,' McNally said. 'If we find out you've been holding information back from us we won't be happy.' He glanced at Larry. 'I've already told Mr McAllister the same, haven't I, sir?' He turned and left without waiting for a reply and the door slammed behind them.

Larry held his breath, waiting for the onslaught, but, amazingly, it didn't come. When Casper looked at him, it was with an air of understanding, not of anger and menace. Larry wondered whether he should speak, venture a question to try and find out where he stood, but Casper saved him the trouble.

'Shower of bastards. I told them I knew nothing about Tony's murder, that I'd no idea who might have wanted to kill him. They asked me if I'd seen anybody suspicious hanging around but I just said no. No way was I going to mention Eddie Black's name.'

Larry nodded, trying to show understanding but hardly daring to breathe. Was it possible the police hadn't mentioned anything to Casper about what Larry had seen and what he'd told them? He thought about it. Maybe they had to be careful about who they shared information with. It might come out later, but it seemed he was off the hook for now. Or was Casper playing with him? Had the cops in fact told him everything? He looked at Casper for a sign that he was hiding something but he couldn't read anything there. He'd just have to keep his fingers crossed. Eventually he broke his silence and changed the subject.

'I could load up the van with the hutch and the rest of the stuff for that guy's rabbit.'

At first Casper didn't seem to hear him. 'The van's knackered. Failed its MOT. I meant to tell you.'

'Right, well that's okay, I brought my car in today, because I was late. If I fold down the back seats there'll be enough room. I could nip round and bring it into the lane.'

Casper nodded. 'Aye, that would be an idea. I'll have the details written down for you when you get back.'

Chapter 21

Larry was always glad to have some excuse to get out of the shop. Any reason to get away from the smell of the animals was welcome. There was also the added bonus of not being under Casper's scrutiny.

It was a cold day, but sunny, the sort of day where he loved taking the kids for a long walk in the park, kicking through the leaves. Thinking of that immediately made him feel better despite everything that had happened in the last few days. He strolled round to get his car, taking his time, nodding to a few people on the way.

As he approached the lights, a heavy vehicle rumbled past. It was one of the large flatbed lorries that were used to lift illegally parked cars. He'd been caught that way a couple of years ago. Not only was there a fine, but it meant a trek to a depot on the outskirts of Glasgow where he had to pay a hefty sum before they would release his car. He could still remember Sharon's reaction. Apart from the money being an issue, the whole thing had made him late for a family outing and she had seethed for the rest of the evening.

He watched the lorry turn the corner and suddenly had a horrifying thought. He broke into a run and dodged across the road, not waiting for the lights to change, ignoring the curses and blaring horns. The lorry was turning into the street where Larry had parked earlier that morning. He increased his pace, managing to narrowly avoid a woman pushing a toddler in a buggy and sprinted round the corner with her curses ringing in his ears. He ran down the street, straining to see where the lorry was heading. He didn't have to look far, it was stopped beside his car, and there was a traffic warden standing there smiling as he spoke to the driver. A brand new parking restriction notice had been attached to the lamp post beside his car. The other cars that had been parked beside his that morning were gone.

Larry swore and increased his pace. As he reached his car, he saw the ticket tucked in behind the windscreen wipers. He grabbed it and got into the car, started the engine and drove off as fast as he could. In the rear view mirror he could see the warden and the lorry driver not looking too happy. If the lorry had started to lift his car he would have had to pay the full fee of £200 and had the hassle of going to the depot to collect his car. He had avoided a disaster but he still had a problem, a £60 fine to pay or £30 if he paid it quickly. If Sharon found out, she'd have yet another reason to nag him.

As he drove the short distance he tried to calm down. A thirty pound fine. It could have been a lot worse. If that guy, Arthur, hadn't come in for his rabbit then Larry wouldn't have gone for his car. He tried to look on the bright side, the guy had brought him a bit of luck. Rabbits were meant to be lucky, weren't they? He navigated his car up the lane behind the shop and parked as near as he could to the back door.

When he stepped out of the car, he saw the crime scene tape at the back door of the bookies. He nodded to an officer who seemed to be standing guard and rang the bell. While he waited for Casper to let him in, he thought about the events of last Friday. Black and his men were ruthless, there was no doubt about that. He hadn't known Tony all that well, but he was a decent guy just trying to make a living.

Tony's wife, Maggie, would have been told the news when she was away at her hen weekend in Spain and would presumably have flown straight home. He wondered if she'd been asked to identify the body. A thought forced its way into his brain. He remembered a programme on TV where the wife had killed her husband, or at least had paid someone to kill him, while she was away for the weekend with her pals. Could Tony's wife have been responsible? Maybe, like Tina said, he'd been playing away and she had found out. If so, who would have done the actual murder? He gave himself a shake. It was a waste of time and nothing to do with him anyway. But it reminded him that he didn't actually know how Tony had been killed or exactly when it had happened. Maybe Tina would know.

As Casper opened the door for him, Larry decided not to mention the parking ticket. The man always told his sister anything that Larry had done wrong and he didn't need any more grief. He'd find some way of paying it on the quiet.

128

He loaded the hutch and the various accessories into his car and left it parked in the lane. With all the police activity outside Tony's back door there was no through traffic down the lane. He wouldn't be heading off with the delivery for a while yet so, rather than leave the rabbit in his car for a few hours, he placed its cage near the back door to be ready for a quick getaway. Eventually, at five o'clock, Casper gave him the nod and he made his escape.

Chapter 22

Casper had said it would be no problem for Larry to deliver the rabbit, that it wasn't even a detour. But that was just his salesman's patter, nothing was too much trouble for a customer and so on. The reality was that the shop was in the centre of town, Larry lived on the south side and the delivery address was out to the west. He wouldn't have minded except for the fact that Casper didn't really let him away early. He hadn't remembered to let Sharon know he'd be home late so he'd need to remember to do that when he got to the guy's address.

Despite his grumbles, Larry grudgingly acknowledged that it was only a few extra miles in each direction. He was lucky not to hit too much traffic. So just before six that evening he pulled up in front of a tenement close in Argyle Street. He checked the address on the sheet of paper lying on the passenger seat. This was the place and the flat was ground floor, right. He turned off the engine. As he stepped out of the car he was struck by the enormous tree in the front garden. Though, in truth, it was an overstatement to call it a garden. It was just a patch of earth where the tree was the only thing growing. He glanced up and saw that the tree rose all the way up to, and slightly beyond, the roof of the building. He wasn't a natural when it came to recognizing trees but he'd picked up some tips from walks in the park with Kelly and Joe. They had both done some sort of school project about trees. So he recognised this as an ash tree, and it was definitely old. Ok, he thought, let's get this done and I'll get home for my tea.

Like most tenement closes, there was a door at the entrance to control access. When Larry was growing up the closes were a free for all, something that had its good side and its bad. As the times changed, people wanted a bit more privacy and security. He scanned the list of names and flat numbers, confirmed he was at the right address and pressed the button for the ground floor right, occupant, A Simpson.

A minute later the tinny voice spoke to him and he stated his business. The door buzzed open and he stepped into the close to be greeted by the guy from that morning, Arthur Simpson, according to the piece of paper Casper had given him. When the man saw Larry he smiled and clapped his hands together. Larry got the impression of a wee boy at Christmas.

'The rabbit man,' he said.

'Aye, that's me,' Larry replied. 'And you're Arthur. Right, do you want to give me a hand to get this stuff in? We'll start with the hutch. We always transport the rabbits in a cardboard box so they don't get bashed about in the hutch. So we'll get the hutch in first then you can put him straight in there.'

Larry turned and headed back to the car. He unlocked the hatchback door and turned to look for Arthur only to find him about two inches from his face.

'Christ, you gave me a fright there,' Larry said. 'Stand back a bit and give me a bit of room.' He lifted the boot door up and reached in to pull the hutch nearer.

They piled the boxes of rabbit food on top of the hutch and carried the hutch between them, Larry walking backwards and Arthur directing him as best he could. As they neared the close Larry saw they had an audience and heard a voice call out with a slightly mocking tone.

'What's all this, then, Arthur? Going to start breeding rabbits?' Another voice joined in. 'Let us know if you need any help.'

As Larry moved back he saw the faces that went with the voices. A couple of fly guys, by the look of them. He nodded non-committally as he went past them.

'Who's your pal, Arthur?' The question followed them down the close as they reached the door. Once inside Arthur directed Larry to the living-room where he would be keeping the rabbit initially. They placed the hutch in a corner and went back for the rabbit and the rest of the stuff.

Arthur insisted on carrying the rabbit and Larry brought in the rest of the bits and pieces. As he came back into the house he had more time to have a look around. His own place wasn't exactly all mod cons but this was place was a museum in comparison. There was an ancient wireless set sitting on a sideboard. Larry went closer to examine it. It was brown and made of some sort of plastic but not plastic. He searched his memory for the term, Bakelite. It had a whole series of stations marked on it including Athlone, Hilversum, Paris. He'd seen radios like this in second-hand shops years ago. He remembered his dad saying they used to have one like that. The old man had always insisted on calling it a wireless instead of a radio.

'Does this thing still work?' he asked Arthur.

'Don't touch that,' Arthur said, hurrying over, 'or we'll lose the station.' It sounded like he was repeating a message that had been drummed into him.

'Ok, ok, I didn't mean any harm.' Larry let his gaze travel round the room. It wasn't just the radio, or wireless, there were lots of old things here. He spotted a lamp, about five feet tall, carved in the shape of a dragon and two elephants standing guard on either side of the fireplace. Always on the lookout for some quick cash, Larry wondered if any of them might be worth something.

Arthur had moved away from the radio and was kneeling down, fussing over the rabbit. Larry started to think about the possibilities, his mind working on options. This guy, Arthur, seemed none too sharp, he had produced a wad of cash earlier at the shop, and here he was living in a house with what could be a load of valuable antiques. Maybe Larry could turn this to his advantage.

'Do you just live here yourself?' he asked. He looked upwards and saw a shelf running round the wall, with what appeared to be a full dinner service displayed on it. The plates were blue and white with intricate illustrations of what looked like Japanese scenes. Larry reached up to lift a plate off the shelf.

Arthur came scurrying over. 'You don't touch that, it'll break. They're mum's special plates.'

Larry backed away, hands up in surrender. 'Okay, okay, no problem. I was just looking.' He glanced up at the plates again. 'So you live here with your mum then?'

'Mum died a month ago,' Arthur replied, 'just me now.'

'What about your dad?'

Arthur closed his eyes and shook his head, he seemed to be remembering something. 'Just me,' he repeated.

'Listen,' Larry said, scrutinising the various objects that were on display on shelves and in cabinets, 'I'll help you get things set up here for the rabbit. They can take a bit of getting used to. Have you ever had one before?'

'Only in my book,' Arthur replied.

Larry nodded slowly. 'Right. Well, if you like, I could pop in from time to time to see how you're getting on. Make sure everything's going okay. As I say, rabbits can take a bit of getting used to.'

Arthur clapped his hands again in that same child-like gesture. 'Thanks, mister, that would be great.'

'No problem, Arthur, and call me Larry.' He put his hand out to shake the man's but Arthur was already down on his knees again, playing with the rabbit.

'Right, well, I'll see myself out, but I'll pop in again in a couple of days.'

Chapter 23

Larry whistled to himself as he drove home. He had his window down and he tapped his hand on the outside of the door as he made his way back to Battlefield. This would need some careful thinking, he told himself, but there were definitely possibilities here. He didn't think of himself as a dishonest person, he'd only ever done minor stuff and only to people who could afford it. This guy Arthur seemed to have more money than sense. He was definitely a bit short in the brains department.

Was that a problem then? Was Larry taking unfair advantage of someone who, in some ways, seemed more like a child than an adult? On the other hand, the guy was living by himself, getting out and about and there was probably more to him than met the eye. Plus, Larry didn't see any point in things sitting in a room gathering dust when they could be put to good use. It's not as if he'd actually be hurting Arthur. It looked like most of his energies would be focused on his rabbit from now on.

But how exactly would he go about liberating a couple of choice items? Was Arthur likely to notice if something went missing? Larry decided he would test the water in the next day or so. He'd come back on some pretext and might be able to pocket something that would pay his parking ticket. He'd need to be careful, make sure Sharon didn't catch on.

Ten minutes later he pulled up outside his close in Battlefield Road. As he locked the car, he looked up at the living room window. What sort of mood will she be in tonight?

He trudged up the three flights of stairs, searching through all his pockets for his key as he went. By the time he reached the front door he realised he must have forgotten it when he left the house in a hurry that morning so he had to ring the bell. He had pressed it for the third time when he remembered that Sharon had asked him to fix the bell two weeks ago. He would have bet that she knew he was at the door but was deliberately not answering it to make a point.

He crouched down and peered through the letterbox. He could see lights on in the kitchen and the living room and he could hear Sharon's laughter and the sound of the telly. He stayed there for a minute, just listening. She always seemed to enjoy herself fine when he wasn't there. When he was there, she just had a go at him most of the time. Why? He wasn't sure, but he knew that he was partly at fault, losing jobs, not getting things done around the house. But you couldn't do everything and Sharon had to take her share of the blame.

'What are you up to?' He hadn't heard Sharon opening the door; he straightened up and followed her into the kitchen where the kids were finishing their tea.

'What kept you?' Sharon said, not bothering to hide her irritation. 'I tried calling you but your phone went to voicemail.'

'Sorry, it was out of charge again.'

She shook her head. 'Typical. I managed to get hold of Casper and he told me you left the shop ages ago.'

'So he must have told you I had to make a delivery for a customer. It was away at the far end of Argyle Street. Then I got caught up in rush hour traffic.'

'Your dinner's in the oven,' Sharon said. 'We couldn't wait any longer.'

'Sorry Dad,' Joe said. 'I had been at the swimming earlier and I was starving.'

'Don't worry about it,' Larry said. 'How did you get on tonight?'

'A personal best in the breaststroke.'

'Well done, wee man.' Larry reached over and ruffled his son's hair. 'I could never get the hang of that breaststroke. Couldn't get my legs to move at the right time.'

He did a swimming motion with his hands and made a face like he was drowning to show how confusing he found the whole thing. The kids laughed while his wife just shook her head at him.

Sharon produced a plate of food from the oven, shoved it into the microwave, set it to reheat for two minutes and headed for the living room to watch the telly. When the microwave pinged Kelly got up and took the plate out and placed it in front of her dad. The kids sat with him while he ate his dinner, telling him about how they had got on at school that day. Both of them seemed to be doing well in class and thankfully they had no bother making friends. He remembered his own school days, made to feel stupid by the teachers and teased, if not exactly bullied, by the pupils. Still, that was life and at least his two didn't have those problems. He finished his dinner, cleared the table and they went in to join Sharon. She was watching a recording of 'Tipping Point' and the four of them spent the next half hour shouting advice and answers at the screen.

DCI Helen Flint surveyed her team as they settled down in the incident room. 'First piece of business, the post mortem. I was there earlier today. We'll get more details over the next few days but we now know that Tony Hamilton was killed by a single violent blow to the back of the head. Your proverbial blunt instrument. From the description of the wound, the thinking is that a baseball bat would be a good fit.'

'Baseball bat, the low-tech weapon of choice for your modern-day criminal who likes keeping things simple,' McNally said.

Flint paused to read from the report in front of her. 'The blow was delivered with considerable force and death would probably have been instantaneous.' She looked up again. 'That's what the PM says. Hamilton was a heavy-made guy and about six feet tall. From the angle of impact, indications are that his attacker would have been a few inches shorter.'

McNally spoke up. 'One of Black's thugs. Vinny Stuart, is about five feet eight and Black himself is roughly the same size.'

'Good point, Tom.' Flint nodded and checked her notes. 'Time of death is estimated at between six and midnight on Sunday night.'

'Can't they narrow it down a bit more, boss?' McNally said.

'Maybe later, Tom, but that's as good as they can do at the moment.'

'So that means that the alibi that Black gave us for himself and his men doesn't really take them out of the equation,' McNally said.

DC Wallace cleared his throat. 'Isn't that a bit odd, boss?'

'What's that, Willie?'

'Well, if Black killed Hamilton, he obviously knows when he did it. So why would he say he was back in Glasgow about nine or ten on Sunday evening. That means he's offering an alibi that doesn't do him much good?'

Flint looked round the room for any comments but nobody spoke for a moment. 'I see what you mean, Willie. Black might be working some angle that we're not seeing yet. Let's not lose sight of that. In any case as soon as we get a more precise time of death we'll review it again.'

'I still can't think what Hamilton would be doing in the shop at that time on a Sunday.' McNally said, looking round the room.

Wallace hesitantly raised his hand, glancing at McNally as he did so. 'Maybe he was meeting somebody and wanted to make sure nobody else saw them together.'

McNally gave a chuckle. 'You think he was having a wee bit of the extra-maritals? Surely not in that bookies shop.' He paused for effect. 'What would be the odds of that?'

Flint's icy glare quickly silenced the laughter that went round the room. 'Highly amusing, Tom, I'm sure.' Her tone left no doubt that she did not appreciate her sergeant's attempt at humour when it ran the risk of undermining one of the team. 'Go on, Willie.'

'I didn't mean that he was, you know, doing that.' Wallace's face was slightly red. 'But it could have been something illegal, something he didn't want us to know about. Or maybe something he didn't want Eddie Black to know about.'

Flint looked thoughtful. 'And maybe Black found out about it, whatever it was, and decided to teach him a lesson.' She pointed to various members of the team. 'We need to chase up the CCTV. I want a full report covering the immediate area around the shop by first thing tomorrow. Now that we have a better idea of the time of death we need to check out the alibis of Black and his two heavies.'

McNally spoke up again. 'What about this guy McAllister, boss? He's lied to us more than once. Even now, we might not be getting the full picture from him.'

'Good point, Tom. Do we have any more background on him?'

It was Wallace who answered. 'He's been in trouble with the law on a few occasions. Nothing major, resetting stolen goods, petty theft and the like.' Wallace glanced at his notes. 'He was sacked from his last job, at a whisky bonded warehouse, after some stock went missing.'

'From what you say, Tom, he was certainly trying to tell us as little as possible at first. Could he be involved in the murder somehow? Could he even have done it?'

McNally rubbed his chin. 'I hate to give any of these scumbags the benefit of the doubt but I somehow don't see it. I just don't think he would have the bottle for it.'

Flint didn't seem convinced. 'People can do desperate things when their back's against the wall.'

'Maybe he's up to his old tricks again.' It was Wallace this time. 'Resetting stolen goods and Tony Hamilton found out and was blackmailing him.'

'Let's keep an open mind on this guy,' Flint said. 'He's certainly no angel. We can put some pressure on him and see where it takes us. Tom, you and Willie go and knock on his door after we finish here. Tell him we want to see him in here tomorrow morning, nine sharp. Don't give him any explanations. Just leave him to sweat about it overnight.'

The kids had gone to bed and Larry and Sharon were settling down to watch the latest episode of 'Unforgotten'. It was just getting to a bit where they might find out the identity of the killer when there was a loud knock at the door.

They looked at each other. 'Who in God's name is that at this time of night?' Sharon said, pausing the television. Larry shrugged, but experience told him it was unlikely to be good news.

Sure enough, when he opened the door the two cops that had been in the shop yesterday were standing there, smug smiles on their faces.

'Evening, Mr McAllister,' McNally said. 'I hope we're not disturbing you.' He stepped forward to come in.

Larry didn't move out of the way and pulled the door over behind him. He felt the anger rise but tried to remain calm. 'As a matter of fact you are disturbing me. The kids are in bed and me and the wife are trying to get a bit of peace and quiet. What do you want?'

'We need you to come into the station tomorrow, nine o'clock sharp.'

'What the hell do you want now? I've told you everything I know.'

McNally didn't say anything for a moment, just fixed Larry with his aggressive stare. 'Well, that's good, sir, because if you start telling us lies again you'll be in trouble. There's just a few things we need to clarify.'

Despite himself, Larry asked the question. 'What do you mean clarity? What things?'

'McNally glanced at Wallace then gave Larry a smirk. 'It'll be better if we talk about it at the station.' They turned to go. 'Remember, nine o'clock sharp.'

Larry stood there for a minute, wanting to throw something at them as they went down the stairs.

They'd obviously come here late at night to make sure he'd be wondering all night about what they would be asking him, the bastards. Surely he'd told them everything, not willingly, that was true, but they now knew what he knew. So there should be nothing to worry about, but as he closed the door and prepared an explanation for Sharon, he knew he wasn't convincing himself.

'Who was it?' Sharon asked, as he came back into the living room.

He tried to keep his voice relaxed. 'The cops. They want me to pop into the station tomorrow in case I've remembered anything that might be of help to them.' He could feel the reaction from Sharon and he decided to ignore it, he couldn't face another row tonight. He pointed at the handset. 'Right, let's watch this. I want to find out who the killer is.'

Sharon gave him a sideways look. 'You better not be up to something dodgy. I mean it. If you ruin this job with Casper you know what'll happen.'

She restarted the programme and they settled down to watch it. His mind was going over everything that had happened and he wondered what trap they might be setting for him. Surely they didn't suspect him of having anything to do with Tony's murder. He was a witness, not a suspect.

The bastards had probably dug around and found that he'd been in trouble a few times over the years. All Micky Mouse stuff but he knew what the cops were like. They liked to twist the facts to put pressure on people. He thought back over the weekend, trying to remember where he'd been, who had been with him and when. Then again, he didn't know exactly when Tony had been killed or how. He'd need to have his wits about him and, he'd need to explain to Casper why he was going to be late tomorrow.

Chapter 24

By the time Flint met with her team the next morning she had received an update from the pathologist and was bringing them up to speed.

'The time of death is now confirmed at between eight and eleven on Sunday night so that gives us a slightly narrower window than we had before. Where have we got to with the alibis for Black and his men?'

McNally glanced at the sheet of paper on the desk. 'Staff at the hotel have confirmed that all three were there over the weekend. From about half past seven on Friday evening to about seven on Sunday evening. But there was something a wee bit odd. They were originally scheduled to stay until the Monday morning but decided to leave early.'

Flint raised an eyebrow. 'That's interesting. And of course Black didn't mention that to us. Did the staff know why they left early?'

McNally shook his head. 'No, just asked for their bill to be ready after dinner and they were off.'

'Could they have left earlier than seven on the Sunday?'

'They said it's theoretically possible but highly unlikely. The waiter was sure they were all in the restaurant for dinner until about then. They remember that one of them wasn't drinking, said he was the designated driver.'

'They're criminals, I wouldn't have thought drinking and driving was likely to worry them too much,' Wallace said.

Flint read McNally's reaction in his face and she stepped in to answer before he could do so. 'I take your point, Willie, but think about it. It's not so much about obeying the law as being careful. If they were heading off to commit a murder they wouldn't want to risk being caught on a drink driving charge, have their journey on record and so on.'

Wallace reddened when he realised his mistake. When he turned to acknowledge his error to McNally, the DS wagged an admonishing finger at him but gave him a wink and a smile to soften the blow.

'What about the pub in Broxburn, The Fiddler's Rest?' Flint asked, 'a very appropriate place for someone like Black to stop off at.'

'The barman was a bit reluctant to give out information about any of his customers,' Wallace said. 'But after a bit of persuasion he agreed he recognised the photos of Black and his cronies and said they were there for about an hour around eight o'clock. Apparently they were in deep conversation with another bloke. The barman said he looked pretty dodgy, to quote his words, but he'd no idea who it was.'

Wallace spoke up. 'Maybe that's why they left early, Boss. To meet this guy.'

Flint didn't look convinced. 'Maybe, Willie, but surely he could have come to their hotel. Or they could have met him and gone back to the hotel. It was only about a half hour's drive away.'

The DCI was about to move on to the next point when DS Louise Spencer knocked on the door to her office. Flint had asked her to come in again so they could all compare notes on Eddie Black.

Spencer handed Flint a folder. 'This is a summary of the email I sent you earlier today, boss.'

'Thanks, Louise, I know you can't share everything but can you highlight the main points for us.'

'Eddie Black, like many criminals these days, likes to diversify; doesn't keep all his illegal eggs in the same black market basket,' Spencer said. 'We suspect he's into people trafficking but we've not got the evidence yet. He's certainly involved in prostitution, we've heard from several sources that he's got a string of flats in and around Glasgow that he rents out to girls and no doubt he also takes a share of their income as well.'

'Are you planning to do anything about the prostitution? See if he's got any trafficked girls in those flats?' The question came from McNally and it contained the hint of a challenge.

Spencer tucked a long strand of her blond hair behind her ear. 'As you can imagine, Tom, we don't want to go off half-cocked. We do have plans to disrupt his activities, yes, but the main thing is to make sure we gather the evidence to make a case stick.'

Flint watched the exchange. She had always been impressed with Spencer; the DS had a much more privileged background than her own; private school, riding lessons, skiing in the Alps. Flint had grown up on a rough estate in Newcastle, eldest of four, her dad had been a drunk and a loser and had taken off when Flint was just eight. But despite their different backgrounds, Flint and Spencer had hit it off right from the start.

Spencer's father was one of the most successful lawyers in Glasgow. Apparently the man almost had a stroke when his daughter told him she was joining the police and not his law firm. She had the tall blonde looks of a model and she carried herself like one. But in the DCI's opinion she was as tough as the rest of them, and twice as smart. McNally was a bruiser, came up the hard way too. Flint had seen the little germ of resentment when he watched Spencer progress faster than him. He liked to wind Spencer up, but Flint knew, deep down, that he respected her.

The DCI didn't think Spencer needed her help but this was her team and she decided to get the discussion back on track. 'We know how hard it is to get the evidence against people like Black. Louise is giving us good insights from her team's investigation. What we're most interested in right now is if there's anything that might tie Black, or one of his cronies, into the murder of Tony Hamilton.'

Spencer looked at her colleagues. 'I know from what the boss has told me that one of the angles you're looking at is that Hamilton was paying protection to Black, that he decided it was a bit on the high side, he protested and that led to his death.'

It was McNally who responded. 'So what do you think?'

'We know he's definitely running a protection racket among certain shops in the centre of Glasgow. Tony Hamilton's was one of them.'

'What about White's pet shop?' Wallace asked and immediately blushed as all eyes turned towards him.

'Yes, White too, the whole row of shops in that street as far as we can tell, and beyond, no doubt. But we think there's more than just protection going on there.'

'Like what?' Flint asked.

'We're not sure, maybe something to do with property development, but that's just a theory.'

'So, what do you think about the theory that Black killed Hamilton in an argument about money?' McNally said, wanting to nail the point down.

Spencer shook her head before answering. 'You can never rule out mindless violence with someone like Black. But, honestly, I'd have to say in my opinion it's unlikely. The boss has told me the alibi doesn't really take him out of the picture. Despite that, I don't see why he would kill him. If Black wanted to ensure Hamilton continued to pay up he would beat him up, or more likely, threaten his wife. Killing him would be counter-productive.' Spencer shrugged an apology as she said it.

McNally threw his pen down in disgust. 'Brilliant. So do you have any better suggestions for us?'

Flint glared at him. 'There's no point in Louise simply telling us what we want to hear. In any case, all she's saying is that it wouldn't make sense for Black to kill Hamilton, and we said more or less the same thing ourselves.' The DCI looked at her team. 'But we don't rule him out. Okay?'

Flint noticed Wallace fidgeting in his seat. 'Something to say, Willie?'

Wallace chewed his lip. 'Just something else that might make it less likely that Black was responsible for the murder.' He heard the mutterings from McNally but carried on. 'Well, we've already said it was unusual for Hamilton to be in his shop at that time on a Sunday evening. Did somebody know he was going to be there? Was he meeting someone? Or was it maybe a break-in gone wrong? A burglar might think there could be money in the place and that the shop would be empty on a Sunday night.

'So how does that impact on Black?' McNally said.

'Well one of the possibilities we're considering is that Black or one of his men killed him by accident. Why would Black want to meet Hamilton in his shop on a Sunday evening? Why would he make a journey all the way from Edinburgh and go straight to the bookies to do it? We know that Black had visited the bookies on several occasions, during the day. So why arrange to go there at night, on a Sunday?'

'Fair point, Willie,' Flint said. She looked round the rest of the team to see if anyone had an answer to that but was met with blank looks. She nodded to Spencer. 'Have you any more for us, Louise?'

'As well as his day-to-day protection racket, it's likely that Eddie Black is into black market cigarettes and drugs,' Spencer said. 'We've got plenty of intelligence on that but not a strong enough case yet to charge him. He has an interest in the casino, though nothing on paper, and of course that offers him all sorts of possibilities for laundering illicit cash.'

'Apart from the protection money, the casino is the one element of Black's business that would have had the closest link to Tony Hamilton's bookies business,' McNally said.

'Are you thinking some sort of gambling scam, Tom?' Flint asked.

McNally spread his hands wide and shrugged his shoulders. 'No idea, boss. Just wondering about possible connections. We've speculated that Tony Hamilton had been paying him protection and had started to complain about it but we're not convinced by that theory.'

Wallace nodded. 'Then again, maybe it's not that daft. If someone else takes over the bookies, somebody more compliant, they would have to continue with any payments, so it makes life easier for Black.'

Flint frowned. 'We've covered that already, haven't we? Black wouldn't have any problems getting the money out of Hamilton. His racket has apparently been going on for ages.' She looked at the ceiling as if for inspiration. 'Maybe Black wanted to take over the bookies himself and he just wanted Hamilton out of the way and he refused to play ball.'

McNally nodded his head in agreement. 'You know, you might be on to something there, boss. Louise has confirmed that Black owns the casino, or as good as. So the bookies could be another way for him to pull in the punters' money.'

Flint stood up to signal that the briefing was drawing to a close. 'I'm still waiting for that CCTV footage. We don't forget about other lines of inquiry, the people in the other shops, his wife. Okay, we've got lots of possibilities but nothing concrete yet. Black remains a prime suspect despite the problems with motive and opportunity and we've got several angles to pursue on him.' She checked her watch. 'In the meantime, Tom, I believe you and Willie are due to see Larry McAllister.'

Chapter 25

Larry was feeling rough. He'd had a restless night, full of dreams where he was being chased by the cops and by Eddie Black. It was one of those dreams where he was trying to run but his legs wouldn't work and the people that were chasing him just got closer and closer. He'd obviously been shouting in his sleep because Sharon had punched him in the ribs a couple of times and told him to shut up. He rubbed his bruised ribs at the memory.

He'd called Casper first thing and explained that he had to go into the police station before work. Casper went mental, as expected. Wanted to know why the cops needed to see him again and demanded to know when he'd get into the shop.

Larry had done a lot of lying over the last few days but this time he could truthfully answer that he'd no idea why they wanted to speak to him again or how long it would take. He told Casper about the cops turning up at the door late last night and how they'd refused to give him any clue about what they were after. As for when he'd get into the shop, Casper's guess was as good as Larry's. He'd ended the call with Casper's curses ringing in his ears. Well, he'd soon find out what it was all about, he told himself as he pushed open the door of the police station.

'Thanks for coming in, sir,' McNally said as he ushered Larry to a chair in the sparsely-furnished interview room.

Larry rolled his eyes as he sat down. 'You didn't really give me any choice, did you? I mean, why did you have to turn up at my house like that, late at night? You could just have phoned, couldn't you?'

The two officers shrugged their shoulders, clearly not prepared to respond to the point.

'Anyway, we just want to tidy up a few loose ends,' McNally said. 'Can you tell us again about your movements over last weekend? Say from Friday evening through to Sunday morning.'

So his guess had been right, Larry thought. They were going to see if they could somehow tie him into Tony's murder. 'I've already told you that.'

'You might have remembered some more details, sir.'

Larry had lain awake going over what he'd done over the weekend and he recounted the details to McNally and Wallace, the launderette, the quick pint, making the tea for the family. Then on Saturday in the shop all day, playing cards with the kids on Saturday evening, out with them at the park on Sunday and then dinner at Casper's on Sunday night. As far as he could remember, it was the same story he'd already given them.

'McNally raised an eyebrow in mock surprise. 'Very good, Mr McAllister.'

Larry saw no reason to pretend. 'Well it was only a few days ago. Anyway, after you left last night I was thinking about it. I assumed you'd want to go over that stuff again so I went over it in my head while I was lying in bed.'

He wasn't quite as confident as he was letting on. Because he had gone out again on Friday night, after the argument with Sharon and got plastered. He decided the cops didn't need to know about his late-night drinking session and the hangover on Saturday. He'd no clear recollection of when he'd got home but Sharon had laid into him the next day about the state he'd been in. So he knew it had been late but he didn't remember the details.

According to what Tina had told him, and Casper, Tony was still alive and well on Saturday. Why should Larry bother the cops with the fact that he was out late on Friday night? He knew he hadn't killed Tony Hamilton, so what was the harm?

'Of course we'll be checking all of this, make sure you haven't made any mistakes,' Wallace said.

Larry gave him a cold look. 'Check away.' He started to get to his feet. 'So is that me finished?'

McNally waved him back into his seat. 'Not quite, sir. We just want to discuss any other activities you might have been involved in recently, you know, outside of your work in the pet shop.'

Larry's heart sank. So this was what they were really after. They obviously knew his record. He'd kept a low profile for the last few years, but there was no way he could stay completely clean. He needed the money, even if Sharon liked to pretend otherwise. He had a few wee deals going on to bring in some extra cash. But he'd kept them all low key and he didn't think the cops knew anything about them. Anyway, surely they weren't interested in that. They had a murder to solve. Larry didn't have to wait very long before he found out what they were up to.

McNally flicked through the file of papers in front of him. 'We've been having a look at your background.' He glanced up at Larry. 'Makes for interesting reading. You've been a naughty boy over the years, haven't you?'

Larry shrugged and put on his best innocent face. 'It was never anything serious. Just stuff that nobody really wanted. I was like a market trader, you know, getting people things they wanted, things they needed. Not everyone can afford to pay the full prices they charge in the shops. Some of it's daylight bloody robbery. So I was just helping the economy.'

McNally laughed and looked at his colleague. 'Helping people, helping the economy, he says. You're a real Robin hood, aren't you?'

Wallace took up the line. 'The only one you were helping was yourself, to other people's property.' He shook his head as if saddened by Larry's criminal activities.

Larry put his hands out as if he could appeal to their better natures. 'Come on, for God's sake. It was Micky Mouse stuff, and it's all water under the bridge now anyway. I don't get involved in anything dodgy these days.'

'So it's all in the past, is it?' McNally turned over a page in the file. 'So you wouldn't know anything about a few crates of knocked-off whisky getting sold to a couple of our finest city establishments or to a couple of pubs up the east end?'

'Whisky?' Larry stammered, stalling for time. The fact was he'd kept in touch with one or two of his old contacts, a guy who still worked in the whisky warehouse and a few bar owners in the city. He'd no idea how the cops had found out about it, how they knew he was involved. They must be bluffing, but what if they weren't? Even if they weren't sure yet, it wouldn't take them much digging to show that Larry was the one organising these sales of black market whisky. 'I mean, I don't even drink whisky,' he said finally.

'No, but you sell it. Or you used to.' McNally leaned forward across the desk. 'The stuff you were nicked for three years ago has been doing the rounds again. I thought, with your previous connections to the trade, you might know something about it.'

Larry shook his head, not trusting himself to speak.

Wallace took up the questioning. 'Maybe you thought now that the dust had settled you could start up with your old tricks again.'

'The thing is, we don't really want to spend our time chasing after all that stuff.' McNally pushed the file to one side as if it offended him. 'We're trying to solve a murder, not petty pilfering. You know how these things work. We're getting pressure from above. It's a numbers game.'

McNally waited for Larry to nod before continuing. 'And of course, it's a distraction when we're trying to solve a murder.' He looked at Wallace. 'I've just had a thought. If we were able to give the high heid yins a result on this murder they probably wouldn't bother chasing us up on this whisky caper.'

Wallace nodded slowly as if considering the idea for the first time. 'You mean…?'

'If Mr McAllister here could keep his eyes and ears open for anything that might assist us in sorting out this murder case then we'd have no need to go raking about into any whisky-related activities he might be involved in.'

'Eyes and ears?' Larry stammered. He felt the sweat breaking out on his back. 'What would I see or hear that would help you?'

McNally fixed him with that hard look. 'Well, look how much you've already helped us. There's probably stuff you'll hear and see that we would never know about. Stuff that people who might be of interest to us, are involved in. Stuff that might give us a lead into Tony Hamilton's killer. For example what was going on between Eddie Black and Tony Hamilton? Was Black trying to take over the bookies?'

'What about your own boss, Mr White? What dealings might he have with Eddie Black?' Wallace added.

Larry tried not to react. Christ, he was already asking himself that same question. 'What dealings? As far as I know he doesn't have any dealings with Black.'

McNally glared at him then started up the pressure again. 'A word of warning, don't think you can take your time with this and string us along.'

'What do you mean?' Larry didn't like the way this was going. 'I've no idea if I'm going to find anything I can tell you. Or how I would find it in the first place. So I've no idea when I might have any information for you.'

McNally looked at Wallace and then at Larry with a reaction that almost seemed to be genuine regret. 'That's too bad, Mr McAllister.'

Was the man genuinely sorry for him, Larry wondered?

'Our boss, DCI Flint, doesn't have much patience. She likes to get results quickly. That's maybe because she gets the pressure from the ones at the top. Wherever it comes from, it means that pressure makes its way down to us guys at the front line.' He paused and looked at Larry to see if he was following. 'So that means we all need results right away.'

'But that's bloody ridiculous,' Larry said.

McNally held up his hands in a gesture of helplessness. 'I know, I know. That's how we feel a lot of the time. I'm not the bad guy here. It comes from up there.' He pointed at the ceiling. 'So we're giving you one week to come up with something useful for us. Something that will help us nail Eddie Black.'

Wallace chipped in again. 'Otherwise, we'll get a couple of our colleagues to poke around into your wee sideline activities.'

Larry felt sick. He was getting drawn in deeper and deeper. He didn't know who to be more scared of right now, the cops or Eddie Black. Then there were the consequences if Casper found out. Not quite in the same league as Black but it would screw things up with his job and with Sharon. His only saving grace was that Black still had no idea that Larry had seen him that day and knew nothing about what Larry had told the cops. He'd also managed to keep that from Casper and Sharon.

He looked from McNally to Wallace and back again. There was no help there. He struggled desperately to see a way out of this but there was none. He couldn't give up his wee whisky deals, he needed the money to give the kids their wee treats, take them on holiday. God knows they got little enough. Somehow or other he'd have to give the police one or two wee titbits of information, hope that they were happy with that, and pray to hell Black never found out about it. He continued to stare at McNally, he could see the guy's lips moving but he couldn't hear a word because there was a roaring in his ears as if he was ten feet underwater.

About an hour later, Larry left the station in a blind panic. Despite his best efforts to lead them astray, the police had somehow got him to tell them that Eddie Black had been a frequent visitor to the pet shop and that he was involved in some sort of business with Casper. He thought back over the conversation and shook his head in frustration. It had been like watching a magician hypnotising someone or a pickpocket exercising his craft. Larry had known what McNally and Wallace were trying to do but, despite trying to mislead them, he'd ended up telling them everything they wanted to know. Now here he was, sitting in the back of their car as they drove to the pet shop. They were very keen, to use McNally's words, to have another conversation with Casper. As he sat in the back of the car, Larry tried to piece together a credible story that he could tell Casper and Sharon.

Chapter 26

When the car pulled up outside of the pet shop, Larry's head was still all over the place. McNally and Wallace got out of the car and beckoned Larry to go ahead of them. He walked into the shop feeling like a condemned man walking onto the scaffold. As soon as Casper heard the bell on the door he got ready to interrogate Larry about what had transpired at the police station, but he did a double take as the police officers walked into the shop.

Larry tried to avoid Casper's threatening glare and the question in his look. He was saved from thinking of something to say by McNally.

'Good morning, Mr White. I think we need to have a chat. Follow up on a couple of points.'

Casper tried to put on a show. 'Points? What points?' He indicated the shop. 'I'm a busy man, I've got a shop to run.'

McNally nodded as if he was agreeing with him. 'I'm sure Mr McAllister will take care of the shop.' He smiled at Larry who was caught between appearing more than happy to look after the shop and not seeming eager to have Casper carted off by the police. In the end he nodded and said nothing.

Wallace followed Casper into the back shop as he went to fetch his jacket. When Casper came out his face was white with rage. 'I'll speak to you when I get back,' he hissed, as he passed Larry.

Larry watched Casper being led away by McNally and Wallace. He tried not to think about what Casper would say when he got back. A couple of customers were over by the bird cages trying to decide which one to buy when the doorbell sounded. Larry put on his best customer-friendly smile and started for the door. But his guts turned over when he saw Eddie Black and his two thugs strut into the shop. The images and names from the police computer cane back to him, Shug Dunbar and Vinny Stuart.

Black strolled straight up to Larry, stopping a few inches from him, and gave him an ice-cold smile. Meanwhile Dunbar went over and spoke to the two customers while Stuart stood guard at the door. A moment later the two customers scurried out. As soon as they had left, Stuart closed it firmly behind them and turned the sign to read 'Closed'.

'How're you doing?' Black asked, almost gently. 'Everything ok?'

Larry nodded and managed to squeeze out a 'yes'.

'Good. That's good. I see you've been getting cosy with the cops.' Black made it sound almost like a question and Larry started to shake his head, putting on a puzzled expression.

Black put a finger on Larry's lips. 'Don't bother lying to me, you wee tosser,' he said in a whisper. He shook his head slowly as if saddened by what Larry had done. The tone changed suddenly. 'We were watching you from across the street. We saw you arriving with the Chuckle Brothers, then two minutes later they cart Casper off to the station.' Black looked at Larry, eyebrows raised in question, waiting to see if he could offer any explanation for this sad state of affairs.

Larry felt his insides churning and his left leg started twitching. His skin felt chilled and clammy at the same time.

'I was wondering how come the police were asking me about Tony Hamilton,' Black went on. 'Now it all makes sense. Somebody's obviously been talking out of school.' His hand flashed out and Larry's head was rocked to the right. 'And that somebody is you,' Black continued, as if the slap hadn't taken place.

Larry raised his hands, pleading for understanding, but what was he going to say? There was no point denying he'd been talking to the cops. Black had seen him. So this was about damage limitation. The most important thing was that Black didn't find out that Larry had seen him assaulting Tony.

'They were just following up on a couple of points. You know, tying up loose ends.'

Black's expression was unreadable. He must have given a signal because all of a sudden Vinny Stuart strode over and punched Larry on the side of the head. He staggered back against the counter, dizzy from the blow and trying not to throw up. His eyes darted left and right, looking for some way out.

At a slight nod from Black, Shug Dunbar walked over to the rabbit cages. He picked up one of them and placed it on the floor, a couple of feet from Larry. It was the white rabbit with the black foot, the one that had escaped on Friday and started this whole thing off. The rabbit twitched its nose in what might have been curiosity or fear. Dunbar produced a baseball bat from beneath his jacket. Larry looked at the weapon, then at the rabbit, then back at the heavy implement.

Black spoke. 'How's your wee family getting on? What is it, a boy and a girl? Is that right? You're married to Casper's sister, of course. Nice.' A nod to Dunbar and the weapon came crashing down on the rabbit cage. With a deafening sound, the cage shattered apart. The door flew open and the rabbit hopped out through the gap, looking terrified but apparently unharmed. As it sat there quivering, several of the parrots in the shop screeched at the outrage. A moment later Larry heard a piercing scream that turned his blood to water.

Black looked at his men and laughed. 'God almighty, I never knew rabbits could fucking scream.'

Larry looked at the rabbit. Sure enough the rabbit was emitting a high-pitched squeal. It was like something from a horror film.

'Does your wee girl like rabbits?' Black whispered. His mouth was so close to Larry's left ear that drops of spittle sprayed on to it. 'I bet she does. Your wee fella too, I'm sure. Kids are great, but you always need to keep your eye on them. They can so easily get hurt, just like rabbits.'

The rabbit continued its banshee wail. Another nod and the baseball bat came down in a blur. Larry felt the wind as it passed in front of his face. He squeezed his eyes shut just in time. There was a squelching thud and Larry realised the screaming had stopped.

'Open your fucking eyes,' Black growled. 'Open them, now.'

Larry opened his eyes, one at a time and, inch by inch, turned his head to where the rabbit should have been. But the rabbit had gone. In its place was a mess of blood and fur smeared across the floor. He lurched against the counter and threw up.

The voice grated in his ear. 'Remember, kids are every bit as fragile as rabbits.' So, just what exactly did you tell the cops?

Larry turned to look at Black. The man's face sent out a message that was clear, don't mess with me. Larry nodded in apparent resignation and related his various encounters with the police. As he picked his way through his narrative he concentrated furiously and somehow managed to keep back the most dangerous piece of information.

Black hadn't built up his criminal empire by taking things at face value and he quizzed Larry, trying to trip him up to see if there was anything that Larry was keeping from him. Eventually he appeared to be satisfied and he nodded to his two men. After giving Larry a final warning about talking to the cops, Black sauntered towards the front of the shop, Dunbar and Stuart following in his wake. Larry heard the bell ring as the door was wrenched open, he glanced towards the men and Stuart gave him a cold-eyed stare and drew his hand across his throat in silent warning.

Chapter 27

As the door slammed behind Black and his team, Larry slumped onto a chair, averting his eyes from the horror on the floor. He sat there for some time, waiting for his heartbeat to return to something approaching normal and trying to assess how bad things were.

When the panic started to subside, he gradually realised that his face and the side of his head were throbbing with pain. He hauled himself up and went into the toilet. There was a small mirror on the wall. He could see a hand-shaped red mark on his cheek and a swollen lump on his right temple. He touched it with the tip of his finger and then wished he hadn't. Would there be any internal damage? He laughed grimly as he imagined Sharon's reaction to that question. It could only be an improvement, she'd say. He ran a towel under the cold tap and carefully dabbed at his injuries. He'd live.

He stood there, leaning on the wash hand basin trying to gauge the impact of what he'd told Black. The good thing was that he'd managed not to tell him about last Friday. But Black now knew that the cops were interested in him and that it was partly because Larry had told them he was a regular visitor to the pet shop. That being the case, the cops had assumed Black was also a regular at Tony's. At least, that was what Larry had told Black and the man had seemed to accept that. In any event, surely Black couldn't be surprised that he would attract the attention of the cops when there was a murder and when he'd been spotted in the neighbourhood on several occasions.

Larry lifted his head and stared at his face in the mirror. It was a mess of bruises and cuts. A pint, that's what he desperately needed. He checked the time. Maybe he'd just close the shop early and catch up with Casper later. What would Casper be saying to the police? More importantly, what would they tell him, if anything, about what Larry had said? That thought made the decision for him and he headed for the door.

For a moment he couldn't understand what the shapeless mess on the floor was, he'd somehow blocked it from his mind. Christ, the fucking rabbit. It made him sick to even think of it but he knew there was no way he could go home and leave that for Casper to find, he would already be raging after his interview at the station and was going to go mental when he heard about Black's visit. Having to deal with this mess would send him over the edge, and Larry would be the one who would suffer.

As he swayed against the counter he saw in his mind's eye the rabbit quivering in its cage and he remembered how it had almost seemed to wink at him on the day it had escaped and hopped down the lane. In a remote corner of his mind a tiny thought was forming and, even though he tried to blank it out, he couldn't. You brought this on yourself, he was thinking. If you hadn't escaped from your cage and run down the lane none of this would have happened.

He dragged his eyes away from the rabbit, went to one of the bins and filled a bucket with sawdust. Slowly he tiptoed towards the obscene mess and poured the sawdust over it. After a couple of further trips and bucket loads, things were looking slightly better. Eventually he could no longer make out any of the detail. The sawdust would also absorb some of the liquid he told himself. He went back to his chair to think about his next step.

After a few minutes he got up again, rummaged around in the stores and unearthed two heavy-duty plastic bags. Last winter Casper had invested in a snow shovel, to keep the pavement clear for customers in the winter. Larry had seen it in the back shop. He supposed his previous assistant had done the actual shovelling. Casper didn't like breaking sweat if he could help it. The shovel was still where he'd last seen it, wedged behind a pallet of bird seed. With the shovel in one hand and the bags in the other, he slowly approached the rabbit.

It was completely obscured, hidden under its sawdust covering. He put the bags to one side and placed the shovel on the floor, a few inches from the rabbit. As he slid the shovel forward it scraped against the floor and made a screeching noise that reminded him of the unearthly squealing the rabbit had made as it waited to be pummelled into oblivion. He tried to slide the shovel under the sawdust-covered mess but it just sort of squelched into the middle. Brilliant, he thought. Come on, I'm trying to help you, you wee bastard. You could at least cooperate, for Christ's sake.

This is what it's come to, he told himself, swearing at a dead fucking rabbit. He still couldn't really believe they could scream like that. He paused and looked at the other rabbits in their cages. A chill ran down his back. None of them were making a sound but every one of them was silently watching Larry as he did his best to dispose of their dead companion. Did they blame him? What if…? Suddenly, he had a vision of the other rabbits ganging up on him, taking revenge. It wasn't me, it was Eddie fucking Black and his team. He gave himself a shake. I'm going bloody crazy here. This isn't some Steven King film. Rabbits don't gang up and attack you. Anyway they're all locked up in their cages. He had to stop himself from checking that the cages were indeed locked.

Right, come on, get a fucking grip. You can do this. He needed some sort of brush to push the rabbit onto the shovel. He looked around for inspiration. He saw a stout cardboard box on one of the shelves. That might do. He lifted it off the shelf and glanced inside. There were about a dozen rubber bones for keeping dogs' teeth sharp. He emptied them on to the counter and set to with the box, pushing and tearing at one corner. It finally gave way with a satisfying ripping noise. He continued with a combination of breaking and

172

tearing and managed to get one side of the box separated. He tested it for strength and was satisfied. After taking a deep breath, he once more approached the rabbit mess.

The worst of it was over after a few minutes. It was relatively easy to get it onto the shovel and he then had to scrape it off the shovel and into the bag. Again the box came into its own. He got into a pattern of shovel, scrape, drop. He tried to block out the noise each time a bit dropped into the bag. He was surprised at his progress and soon all that remained was a dark red smear on the floor. That would need a different approach.

He found an old mop and pail out the back, filled the pail with warm water and bleach, gritted his teeth and set to. The mop slapped onto the floor with a heavy thud, sending small pieces of matter flying up and splattering onto his trousers. He was convinced some of it had landed on his face and he threw down the mop, ran over to the sink and scrubbed at his face, ignoring the pain.

Right, it's only one fucking rabbit, he told himself as he went back to his task. He placed the mop more gently this time and swirled it back and forth, round and round. He wrung the mop into the bucket and stared mesmerised as the water quickly became scarlet. With each swishing pass the mess on the floor gradually became less red and less sticky. He straightened up and examined his efforts. Not too bad.

He emptied the pail, rinsed the mop, repeated that process and after one final effort he was satisfied. As a final touch he sprinkled bleach over the area and wiped it over. He took a step back to survey his efforts. As he did so, he stepped on something. He turned and looked. It was white, with a black patch but covered in red. It was the rabbit's foot. It must, somehow, have been flung clear with the impact. He just had time to remember that a rabbit's foot was meant to be lucky before he threw up all over the area he had just cleaned.

Chapter 28

He downed the first pint of heavy in one go and ordered a second and a Bell's to go with it.

'You look like you've been in the wars,' the barman said.

Larry shook his head slowly. 'You've no idea, Willie. What a fucking day I've had.'

'Difficult customers?'

Larry knocked his whisky back and looked at the man. 'Aye, you could say that.'

Willie shook his head. 'Christ, you wouldn't expect that in a pet shop.'

Larry held his whisky glass out for a refill. 'As my old man used to say, it's a funny old world.'

He had another couple of pints before he felt able to face the world. His phone had rung a few times but he'd ignored it. He checked it now as he headed for the bus, missed calls from Casper and Sharon. Business as normal. Sitting upstairs on the bus, he looked out at the people in the streets. Just going about their lives quite happily, most of them. Not giving a minute's thought to the likes of Eddie Black and his two sidekicks. Ruthless bastards who would crush you if you got in their way. He fingered the side of his face. Not quite as sore as before but it would be a while before it was back to normal. As for the mental scars, the rabbit, the mess on the floor, the fucking screaming. That would stay with him forever.

As soon as he got through the door, Sharon was on at him. Where had he been, what happened to his face, how much had he had to drink, had he spoken to Casper?

He tried to stay calm. The image of the baseball bat swinging down was running through his mind. He shook his head as if he could rid himself of the memory.

'Don't shake your head at me,' Sharon said, misunderstanding the gesture.

He put his hands up as if he could stop the torrent of accusations. 'Look, just..,' he hesitated and looked at her, '…just give me five minutes, ok.'

Maybe she saw something different in his face, or maybe she was just fed up getting on at him. Whatever it was, she nodded and took herself off to the kitchen and Larry slumped wearily into an armchair. He sat staring into space while various images and sounds whirled around in his head, Black, the rabbit, the baseball bat, the parrots screeching, the rabbit squealing, its foot lying there on the floor, those two cops, Casper's face as they led him away, the rabbit again, Sharon and finally his kids, Kelly and Joe.

He was stirred from this waking nightmare by his phone ringing. He glanced at the display. Casper. He hit the green button and braced himself for the onslaught. He held the phone away from his ear for a couple of minutes until Casper had got the initial anger off his chest. Larry took some comfort from the fact that he wasn't having to deal with the man face to face. He could hear the occasional word through the phone and it was obvious that Casper's interview at the police station had not gone well. He waited until Casper paused for breath then spoke.

'So did they tell you what exactly they think happened?' Larry was trying to find out how much Casper knew, if anything, about what Larry had seen last Friday.

There was a sigh of exasperation from the phone. 'They're hardly going to confide in me, are they? They were very fucking interested in the fact that Eddie Black was a regular visitor to my shop and they wanted to know what that was all about.' Larry waited for the barb and it wasn't long in coming. 'And we all know who told them about that, don't we?'

'But why do they care about that?' Larry asked. Then, before he could stop himself, he added. 'Anyway, why does he keep wanting to see you?'

There was a torrent of swearing. 'I've told you before. Don't ask. The less you know the better. The reason they want to know about Black visiting me is in case he'd also been visiting Tony.' Casper paused and Larry could hear him taking a drink before continuing. 'So did anything else exciting happen today?'

Larry hesitated. Exciting? That depended on your point of view. Anyway, did Casper already know what had happened? Had he been back to the shop? Or had Black had a quiet word with him? Let him know what's what? In any case, he was bound to find out about Black's visit sooner or later and there was no real reason to keep it from him.

'He came into the shop again,' Larry finally answered, deliberately not speaking the name of the bad guy, just like in his daughter's Harry Potter books. He heard Casper choking on his drink.

'Black? What did that bastard want this time?'

'He'd been on his way to see you but he spotted me arriving with the cops and then saw them taking you away so he hung back. A few minutes later he came in with his two gorillas and started giving me grief.' As soon as the words left his mouth Larry replayed them in his head. Giving him grief? Did that really cover it? He touched the bruise on his head and saw Black's brutal face again.

'What did you tell him?'

'More or less the same as I've told you.' Larry paused while he did a mental cross-check. Was he managing to keep his story straight between Black and Casper? He'd better fucking hope so. 'I had to tell him. He battered me and he was threatening the kids.'

'The kids? Jesus Christ.' There was silence on the other end of the phone and Larry knew Casper could easily imagine the scenario. He'd be filling in the blanks for himself. 'Did he cause much damage?' Casper asked after a moment.

Larry wasn't sure if he was asking about damage to him or to the shop. The image forced its way into his mind's eye, the rabbit quivering and squealing as the baseball bat came smashing down. The sawdust and the mop and the bucket and the bits of rabbit sticking to him. He didn't want to go there right now. He'd deal with that tomorrow. 'Gave me a slap and one of his men punched me on the side of the head. Could have been worse I suppose.'

Casper grunted in reply. More silence. Then: 'He's a vicious bastard.'

Larry realised that was the closest he was going to get to sympathy from Casper. He decided to play a bluff, pretend to change the subject. 'So, had Black been visiting Tony?' he asked, picking up on something Casper had said earlier and trying to keep his voice neutral.

For a minute he thought Casper had ended the call. Then he broke the silence. 'Don't stick your nose in where it doesn't belong, right?' Casper snarled. The hint of sympathy was gone, and this time he did end the call.

Larry looked at the phone for a minute, as if he could read Casper's thoughts by staring at the screen. He thought about the conversation he'd just had. Okay the guy was mad at him, but that was to be expected. In a way, following Casper's logic anyway, it was justified. After all, Larry had told the police about Black coming to see Casper and that had obviously opened up a whole can of squiggly things. The fact that the police had given Larry no choice was of no interest to Casper.

But right now, Larry wasn't all that bothered about that. The important thing was that the police had obviously decided not to tell Casper about Larry seeing Black threatening Tony that day. If they'd told him, then his answer would have been different when Larry asked if Black had been visiting Tony. Casper would have said something like: 'Well you should know, you daft bastard, cause you told them about it.' But Casper hadn't said that, so that meant he didn't know.

Larry hadn't often had reason to be grateful to the police but on this occasion he was glad they were keeping his little secret to themselves. But that could only last so long. There was no doubt that, when it suited them to tell Casper and, even worse, Black, they would do so. Then Larry would really be in the shite.

Chapter 29

Larry made a point of getting up early the next day. He wanted to get to the shop before Casper. He wasn't sure where this spark of dedication to the job had come from. Maybe some sort of bonding with Casper since they were both up against Eddie Black as well as the cops, but maybe there was also an element of self-preservation in it. Had he done a good enough job of cleaning up the rabbit? Or would it be obvious to Casper what had happened? No, Casper might spot a stain on the floor but there was no way he would guess the reason for it. Nobody would imagine that. You had to have been there to see what those sick bastards had done.

Whether Casper noticed any mess on the floor, Larry would, in any case, have to explain why they were one rabbit cage short and the only white rabbit in the shop was gone and no money in the till to account for them. Casper didn't miss things like that, not when it meant that he'd lost money. Larry knew it wasn't his fault that the rabbit had been bludgeoned into a pulp, but he knew that somehow he'd get into trouble for it.

Surely Casper would sympathise this time. Larry had detected that note of solidarity on the phone last night. It hadn't lasted long but still, maybe it was a positive sign. Then, Black had threatened Kelly and Joe, and Casper was their uncle and fond of them. Family matters, he'd heard Casper saying that more than once. In fact he'd said it to let Larry know that was the only reason he was giving him the job in the pet shop.

All these thoughts ran through his head as he quickly got showered and shaved. Before he left, he took tea and toast into Sharon who was still in bed. She gave him a look of pure astonishment, sniffed suspiciously at the tea and examined the toast before favouring him with a smile.

'This is a nice surprise. What's the occasion?'

He shrugged his shoulders. 'Do I need an excuse to treat my wife?' He opened the blinds to let in a peep of daylight. 'I want to get in early today. There's stuff to sort out from yesterday.' He'd given Sharon an edited version of yesterday's events after the kids had gone to bed. It was always tricky deciding how much to tell her because in the first place she would go mental that he was getting into trouble again. In the second place she would tell Casper and Larry wanted to be the one to tell him. 'See you tonight,' he said, pulling the door closed behind him.

He popped in to see the kids, made sure they were ok. They had noticed something was wrong last night but thank Christ they had no idea what it was about. He'd given them some story about the bruise on his face, said he'd bumped into a shelf in the shop. Both of them had seen that he was a bit drunk but that wasn't exactly front-page news. Anyway, they both seemed fine and looking forward to school. When he thought back to how Black had threatened them Larry realised he was clenching his fists and grinding his teeth. He gave them both a quick hug and made his escape.

When he got to the shop, Casper was already there, standing staring at the spot where the rabbit had been clubbed to death.

'What the hell happened here?' He glanced at Larry then went back to staring at the floor.

Larry joined him and looked at the floor. He was pleasantly surprised to see that he made a good job of cleaning up. It was a pity Sharon couldn't see it. She was always going on about how he never cleaned up properly after himself. But it was so clean, he wondered how Casper could tell that something had happened. He decided to play for time. 'How do you mean?'

Casper was in no mood for games. 'Look, I've got enough going on, what with the cops and that scary bastard Eddie Black. So don't fuck me about. We keep the place reasonably clean, for a pet shop.' He swept his arm in a half-hearted gesture in case Larry was unaware that this was, indeed, a pet shop. 'But this bit of floor here has obviously been scrubbed to within an inch of its life. You could eat your dinner off it.' He looked at Larry and waited.

Larry couldn't believe it. How was that for luck? He'd been worried that he hadn't cleaned up properly and that Casper would know something had happened. Instead of which, he'd gone over the top, he'd made too good a job of it and Sherlock here had worked it out. Christ, he couldn't win.

He spread his arms wide in a gesture of defeat. 'Well, you know how I told you Black was here and that he threatened the family?'

'What the fuck happened,' Casper growled, making 'get-on-with-it' gestures with his hands.

Larry swallowed hard. He'd just have to dive straight in. 'One of his thugs smashed a rabbit cage with a baseball bat.'

Casper flinched. 'A baseball bat?'

Larry nodded, trying not to retch as he relived the incident. 'Then he battered the rabbit into a pulp. That white one with the black foot. It was screaming. I never knew rabbits could scream.' He looked at Casper to see if it was news to him as well, but Casper just stared at him, so Larry went on.

'There was blood and bits of fucking rabbit everywhere. Then he told me that the same thing would happen to the kids if I kept speaking to the cops.'

Casper was now looking at the floor again as if trying to visualise the horror that had taken place here. He remained silent for so long that Larry wondered if he had heard him.

'I spent ages cleaning up the mess,' Larry finally said. Still no reaction. 'I didn't want to tell you about it over the phone.'

Finally Casper turned and looked at him. His face was haggard and bloodless. Larry wondered what else was going on in Casper's world. To Larry's amazement his boss simply nodded and clapped him on the shoulder.

'Ok thanks. Don't worry. You've done a great job of cleaning it up. These bastards are pure fucking mental.' With that, Casper made his way to his office at the back of the shop leaving Larry standing there relieved and a bit bewildered.

The shop wouldn't open for another half hour and it was always quiet for the first hour at least, so Larry put the kettle on and nipped into the café and got a couple of doughnuts. The café was busy so Tina had to content herself with a quick 'How're you doing?' but she gave him a wide-eyed expression and mouthed that she'd speak to him later. Maybe she'd heard the racket yesterday or just seen all the comings and goings or maybe she'd spotted the cuts and bruises on his face.

He got back to the shop, made a pot of tea and took a cup in to the office with a doughnut. Casper was on the phone but gave him a thumbs-up. Christ, Larry thought, were they actually starting to get on with each other?

The rest of the day passed uneventfully. There was no visit from Black and there was no word from the cops either. As soon as he thought about the cops Larry remembered that he was supposed to be acting as their eyes and ears, their inside man. He'd forgotten all about it when Black and his men started battering him and killing rabbits.

The familiar chilling sensation ran up his spine. How in God's name could he even think about trying to dig up dirt on Black? The guy would destroy him. Larry deliberately blanked out the guy's threats against his family. He'd need to tell the police that it wasn't on. They could do their worst. At least they wouldn't smash his kids' heads in with a baseball bat.

He stared out the window and took a drink of his tea. A dialogue with himself ran frantically through his mind. How are the cops going to know I'm not trying to get any information about Black? I'll just tell them that all I hear is chitchat, nothing of any interest. That whenever he comes into the shop he goes into the office to talk to Casper. No, Christ, don't tell them that. That'll stick Casper right in it and he'll know who told the cops. I'll just say I never hear anything. Anyway, it's not up to me to do their job for them. They must be looking at CCTV, talking to other people, checking forensics. That's what I'll say to them next time. All those evenings watching 'CSI' and 'Unforgotten' would come in handy after all.

Casper stayed in his office for most of the morning and Larry could hear him on the phone from time to time. Things were starting to get back to normal and Larry was kept occupied as a few customers came in with their various requests.

Although Casper had treated him reasonably well about the rabbit incident, Larry was aware of a feeling of depression creeping up on him. Maybe the fact that he hadn't seen or heard from Black or the police wasn't necessarily a good sign. Were they both, in their own way, planning their next move? A move that would see Larry caught in the middle?

On the odd occasion when Casper emerged from his office he would spend a few minutes chatting to a customer or have a look at the till to see how they were doing on takings. As far as Larry could tell, takings were never all that impressive. In fact it had occurred to him more than once that it was a bit of a mystery how Casper could afford the lifestyle that he had.

His house was worth a fortune. His wife, Christine, didn't work. Well not really. She used to work in a beautician's and that was how Casper had met her, when he went for a manicure. Larry looked down at his own hands. For him the thought of a guy getting a manicure was ridiculous, but Casper liked to make an impression. He'd obviously made an impression on Christine. So now she spent her time shopping or eating in fancy restaurants with her pals. According to what Casper had told Sharon, Christine still did the occasional stint at the beautician's but it was all a bit vague and Larry couldn't quite see her in the role.

Anyway, Casper, with all his fancy ways and his fancy wife didn't seem to fit the role of someone who ran a pet shop. Larry didn't know what a pet shop owner should look like but it wasn't Casper. The guy sometimes came into work dressed like he was going for a day in some office, not dealing with animals. Having said that, it was Larry who did all the real work. Casper was not one to get his hands dirty.

There had been another assistant before Larry started here, a woman, foreign apparently. She'd stormed out one day, having had enough; and who could blame her, Larry thought. As luck would have it, Larry had lost his job in the whisky warehouse just about the same time and Sharon persuaded her brother to give Larry the job.

He was pulled out of this daydreaming when he heard Casper shouting on him. He looked up and saw Casper standing at the door.

'I'm just nipping out for half an hour or so. If anybody asks, you don't know where I am.'

Larry laughed to himself as the door slammed behind his boss. I don't know where you are, whether anybody asks or not. He rolled his eyes, even though there was nobody to see him. So that was Casper away out again. The more Larry thought about it, the more he was sure Casper had some other way of earning his money. Was that why he was always nipping out, with nobody knowing where he was or who he was seeing? Larry dealt with most of the customers, and most of the deliveries. He nodded to himself. Yes, Casper was up to something. Well so what? So was Larry, in his own small way. So were most folk, given half a chance.

He wondered if Sharon knew what Casper was up to, since she was his sister. Probably not, given how she went on at Larry when she found out he was doing something a wee bit dodgy. So the question was, what was Casper up to?

Then it hit Larry. It was so bloody obvious. He must be doing something for Eddie Black. All those times Black came in to see Casper and they went in to the back shop to talk. What was it Black had said a few days ago? He wanted to know if Casper had an answer for him about that 'other business'. Jesus Christ, no wonder Casper was on edge. If Casper was working with Black on one of his schemes and the cops were able to get Black for murdering Tony, who knows what that might mean for Casper.

But what could he be doing? Black was probably into protection, re-setting stolen property, drugs. Larry had heard the rumours about prostitution and that the man owned a luxury villa somewhere in the South of France. Larry smiled to himself. Maybe he could give the police these stories to keep them happy. Everybody seemed to have heard them so he wouldn't actually be doing Black any damage and he wouldn't be taking any risks. If he called them, rather than speak to them face to face, then who would know? They'd probably tell him that sort of stuff was useless but at least he would be giving them something. Yes, he thought, this could work.

He wasn't used to thinking things through like this and was feeling a bit tired. No wonder, when he stepped back and thought about it; he had been battered mentally and physically from all sides. The shock of Tony's death, then the pressure from the cops and the threats from Black. Not to mention the usual grief from Casper and Sharon. He could murder a pint but there was no way he could leave the shop. He'd need to make do with another cup of tea. Just at that moment the bell on the front door sounded.

Chapter 30

He stopped and looked round, bracing himself in case it was the cops, or Black. But, in fact, it was Arthur Simpson, standing at the door, holding it half open, as if he wasn't sure he'd come to the right place. He looked to left and right before continuing into the shop. Larry guessed what was going through the guy's head. The last time Arthur had been here, Eddie Black and his cronies had been in and Black had given the guy a mouthful of abuse. He was lucky it hadn't gone further but that was obviously what was worrying him.

Larry strolled towards him. 'Come on in. Don't stand there like a frightened rabbit.' As soon as the words left his mouth, the all-too-familiar image leaped to the forefront of his mind. 'I mean, come on in. What can I do you for?'

Still Arthur hesitated, clinging to the door handle as if for safety.

'It's fine. He's not here,' Larry said. 'That guy you met last time. The big, scary guy. He's not here today. It's safe. You can come in.'

Arthur still hesitated and looked all around him again before venturing further. Finally he made his way over to where Larry stood.

'So what are you after?' Larry asked.

Arthur just looked at him.

'Is there something else you need for your rabbit?'

Silence.

How are you getting on with him anyway?'

Arthur continued to stare at him before finally replying in a rush of words. 'He's nice and friendly. He lets me pat him, but sometimes he won't take his food.'

Larry nodded. 'You need to remember to make sure he's got enough water in his dish.'

Arthur laughed. 'I've been doing that. I remember you told me.'

'Good man. So what do you need today?'

Arthur looked confused and Larry could see the panic rising in his face. He tried to control his frustration. What does this guy want? Does he have any idea of how to take care of a rabbit? Christ, maybe it's already dead.

He decided to try another tack. 'Do you want to have a look round, see if there's anything else you fancy?' While he wandered round the shop, Larry might be able to get his tea. Arthur nodded but didn't move. 'Right, I'll come out and see you in five minutes, see how you're getting on,' Larry said.

He made his way to the back shop but when he looked round to see what Arthur was doing, the man was two inches behind him. He'd done the same thing when they were carrying all the rabbit stuff into his house.

'Christ almighty, you gave me a fright.' He glanced down at Arthur's feet. 'How do you manage to walk so quietly?'

There was no reply. Larry could feel his frustration getting the better of him but he reminded himself that maybe the guy wasn't quite all there. So he would tread carefully, but it was like pulling teeth. What did he want? Why was he here? But then Larry remembered something he'd forgotten over the last couple of days with all the aggro from Black and the hassle from the cops. He remembered what he'd seen the night he'd taken the rabbit to Arthur's house. All those antiques and valuables that had been sitting around Arthur's house.

It was odds on this guy had no idea of how valuable some of those items might be. In truth, Larry had no real idea either if any of them had any great value. But they must be worth something, some of them anyway, and, if he was lucky, he might turn up something really valuable. There could be money in this for him if he played his cards right.

Sharon was always on at him about how they could be doing with more money. God knows how she thought he could get more. He didn't get that much from Casper, the guy was notorious for being tight with his cash, seemed to think he was doing Larry a favour even employing him in the first place. Sharon's job in Asda wasn't that well paid but she wasn't shy of letting him know that she was bringing more into the house than he was.

Okay, he had his sideline of black market whisky and a few other odds and ends that brought in some extra cash but he kept that quiet because he knew Sharon would kill him. In any case, now the police were taking an interest in his whisky activities so that might dry up. If Larry could help himself to some of Arthur's valuables nobody, including the police, would be any the wiser and the extra cash would put him in Sharon's good books. He would find some way to explain it to her.

He gave the man his best smile. 'Listen, Arthur.' Arthur looked pleased that Larry had remembered his name. 'When I was at your house the other night, I told you I'd come over and help you with your rabbit from time to time.'

There was a faint nod and smile from Arthur. Larry wondered if this was why Arthur had come to the shop today.

'Well, there's been a lot happening here over the last couple of days and I sort of forgot about it, you know. But it I'm still happy to do it if you want. Give you advice about feeding and all that.'

Another smile and nod.

'I mean, rabbits can be a wee bit tricky especially at the start. Well, I've got a bit of spare time on my hands. So what do you say?'

Arthur just stared at him. 'What do I say when?'

Larry realised he'd have to take it even slower. 'So what I'm saying is, would you like me to come over to your house from time to time and make sure everything is ok with your rabbit?'

Arthur smiled and clapped his hands together just like he'd done in the house. Larry thought he actually might have given a little jump of excitement but maybe he imagined it.

'Okay then, great. I'll pop over to your place at some time between this evening and Sunday evening. It just depends on what's happening at home. Is that ok?'

For a minute Larry thought Arthur was going to hug him, but he contented himself with a 'yes, please.'

Larry had one of his light-bulb moments. 'It might be an idea to get a few boxes of rabbit food supplement.'

Arthur gave him the same blank-eyed look that Larry was starting to recognise.

'It helps the rabbit get the most from its food. It makes the food more interesting for the animal.' The truth was Larry had no idea if this was true. Stuff like that was one of the wee money-spinners that Casper had in the shop. Not a lot of money from each item, but it all built up. The boxes usually sold for a couple of pounds each but Larry took twenty quid off Arthur and he didn't blink so that was a nice wee bonus for Larry.

Casper made a point of never ringing that sort of item through the till. There was a tin box where the money from those sales was kept, the idea presumably being so the taxman would know nothing about them. Larry shrugged. No skin off his nose and on this occasion it meant he had a nice bonus.

He put a few quid into the box and quickly pocketed the rest while Arthur was loading the boxes into his bag. It wasn't much but it would go towards his parking fine and hopefully it would be just a small taste of what was to come. Larry smiled to himself; it was a sign that his luck was finally changing.

'Remember, I'll pop in to see you in the next few days, Arthur. See how you're doing.'

'Thanks, that would be great,' Arthur said.

Just then the door bell sounded and they both jumped. With the events of the past few days, Larry was on edge and no doubt Arthur still had the menacing image of Eddie Black in his mind. Larry held his breath as he waited to see if it was the cops or Black, but he felt the tension leave him as the cheery face of Tina peered round the door.

'How're you doing?' she said as she approached. 'I never got a chance to talk to you earlier when you were in the café.' She stopped as she noticed Arthur. 'Sorry, I didn't realise you had a customer.'

Larry followed her gaze and saw that Arthur's face had turned bright red and he seemed to be trying to hide behind the counter.

'This is Arthur, a new customer. He bought himself a rabbit the other day and he's just nipped back in to get a few wee bits and pieces. Isn't that right, Arthur?'

Arthur's face got even redder. He mumbled a few words, squeezed past Larry and Tina and shot out the door.

'I'll see you soon, Arthur,' Larry shouted to his back.

As soon as the door closed, Tina burst out laughing. 'What's his problem?'

Larry shrugged. 'He's a bit shy, in fact I don't think he's quite all there. Then you come in, full of the joys and, you know, maybe scared him off. I

195

don't think he's too confident with most people, let alone somebody like yourself.'

Tina raised a well-groomed eyebrow and laughed. 'What does that mean? What's wrong with me?'

Larry looked at her balanced precariously on her high heels, blonde hair combed up in an elaborate style and the face with its dramatic make-up. 'Absolutely nothing wrong with you, Tina, but he's obviously not used to being up close to that much personality.'

Tina thought about this for a moment but Larry could tell she was pleased by the roundabout compliment.

'Aye, well, maybe I'm a bit of an acquired taste,' she said as she flicked her hair. 'Anyway, I wanted to see how you were. I saw they guys coming into the shop yesterday and they didn't look too happy with life.'

She paused and peered at Larry's face. 'In the name of the wee man. What's happened to you? You're all cuts and bruises.' She reached out to touch Larry's face but he jerked back.

'It's still a bit tender,' he said. 'It was Eddie Black and his heavies. Came in here throwing their weight about. Wanting to know what I'd said to the cops and gave me a couple of whacks when they didn't like what they were hearing.'

Tina shook her head. 'Bastards, but why take it out on you?'

Larry shrugged to give himself time to think. He got on well with Tina and she was trying to be sympathetic but he had to be careful about how much he could tell her. 'Who knows?' he said. 'These guys don't need much of a reason to start handing out a doing.'

Tina nodded. 'That's how I wanted to come in and see you. I'd heard through the jungle drums that he's really bad news. So when I saw him getting out of his car yesterday with his team I wondered what was going on. Just before that, I'd seen the cops dropping you off and then taking Casper away.'

She waited for Larry's answer. He had to laugh at how Tina came out with this stuff. Casper had said she was a gossip and it was true. She loved to know all the comings and goings of the street. The way the road and the building curved meant that, from the window of the café, Tina a front row view of everything that happened in the short street, and she made the most of it.

'The cops had asked me to come in to follow up on a couple of things. That made me late for work, so they offered to drop me off. I wasn't too happy about it, in case somebody saw me getting out of their car.'

'Which is exactly what happened,' Tina said. 'I saw you and I said to Rosa, there's Larry getting dropped off by the cops.'

So the whole street probably knew about it by now, Larry thought. 'Anyway, what did she say?'

'Told me to keep my mind on my customers, but I knew she was desperate to know more as well.' She looked to her right as if she might see Rosa through the wall of the shop. 'Anyway, how come they took Casper away?'

197

'Wanted to speak to him, just like the rest of us, I suppose.'

'Aye, but they never took me or Rosa away. They just spoke to us in the café. So what was different about Casper? You as well, come to think of it.'

Larry knew she was fishing and that whatever he told her would be all round the street before the end of the day. 'They were passing my place on their way into the station so they just thought they'd save everybody time. I don't know about Casper. He was quite friendly with Tony, so maybe they thought he'd know more.'

He could see her considering his answer to see if it made sense. 'I suppose so,' she finally said. 'I was going to tell you what I'd heard about that guy Black and his mob. Seems they're into all sorts of dodgy stuff.'

Larry gave a non-committal grunt. 'Where did you hear that?'

She gave a shrug. 'You know, the usual. Here and there. Do you think I should tell the cops?'

Larry thought his heart was going to stop. 'No. No way. Definitely not.' He looked at her. 'I mean it. You've just said it yourself. They're into all sorts. Look what they did to me, for no reason at all.' He knew that was a bit of a lie but the truth was too complicated and, in any case, not to be shared with Tina.

'Apart from anything else, the cops are bound to know about Black and what he gets up to. So even if you told them what you'd heard, it wouldn't be anything new and it wouldn't be any sort of evidence that they'd killed Tony.'

A mixture of disappointment and relief crossed over Tina's face.

'I suppose you're right,' she said. 'These guys always seem to get away with it. I mean, Tony never did any harm to anybody, not really. His poor wife must be in pieces.' She was silent for a minute. 'Anyway, I better get back, or else Rosa will be docking my wages. Right, look after yourself. I'll see you tomorrow.'

Once she'd left, Larry thought back over the conversation. Did Tina know something? Did she somehow know that he'd seen Black and his men beating Tony up last Friday? No, it couldn't be that. There was nobody else in the lane that morning. And if she had seen something there was no way she could keep it to herself. No, she was just doing her usual. Trying to find out what was going on in the street. He realised he hadn't managed to get his cup of tea and he headed for the back shop.

Casper reappeared about half an hour later. He looked thoughtful, maybe still troubled by Larry's revelations earlier in the day.

'Anything new?' he asked.

'Nothing much,' Larry said. 'We got an order for a couple of parrots from an elderly couple who live in Springburn. Then that guy who bought the rabbit the other day, you remember the one who doesn't appear to be too smart, he was in and bought a couple of boxes of food supplement. I dropped the money into the box in the back shop.'

Casper nodded, apparently, for once, finding nothing to criticise in Larry's actions. 'Right, why don't you take yourself off home early for once? I'll finish things off here.'

Larry looked at him, surprised at this generosity but he didn't want to jinx it by saying anything. Casper wasn't in the habit of giving him time off. Maybe the recent events were causing him to have a rethink. He'd certainly been sympathetic when he heard what Black had done to Larry. Still, Larry wasn't a hundred per cent convinced. Was Casper up to something and wanted Larry out of the way for some reason? But that didn't make sense. If he wanted to speak to someone in private he did it in his office or just went out to see them.

So Larry didn't question it. 'Right, that's great. If you're sure it's ok. Thanks a lot. I'll see you tomorrow.' He picked up his jacket and headed for the door, thinking he might even treat himself to a couple of pints with his wee cash bonus, the parking fine could wait.

He had crossed the road and was about to turn into The Saltmarket when he saw Eddie Black's now all-too-familiar Range Rover turning into the street. Larry stepped into the shadow of a shop doorway and watched as the car drew up in front of the pet shop and Black got out, followed by Shug Dunbar and Vinny Stuart, and none of them looked happy.

Chapter 31

'Right, Tom, bring me up to speed,' Flint said as she perched on a corner of her desk.

McNally glanced at his notes. 'We've got the time of death confirmed for the Sunday evening, between nine and eleven. Cause of death a single blow with a blunt instrument to the back of the head. Judging by the shape of the wound, the best guess is a baseball bat. Small fragments of wood were found embedded in the scalp. We're getting them analysed to see if that will nail down exactly what weapon was used.'

'Well, we know that gangsters like Black will often use a baseball bat or a pickaxe handle so that would fit,' Flint said.

'Some people also keep them behind the counter for protection so we're checking to see if Hamilton kept one in the bookies,' McNally said. 'The blood spatter pattern tells us the murder happened where the body was found, namely in the back shop of Tony Hamilton's bookies. The scene of crime guys have gone over it as you would expect and come up with several sets of prints and some other trace evidence and we'll be working on identifying who they belong to.' McNally nodded to Wallace to take over.

Flint nodded. 'But no sign of the murder weapon?'

'No, we've checked all bins in the vicinity and within a one-mile radius in case the killer chucked it away.'

'Obviously The River Clyde isn't that far from the shop. Downside for the killer would be that a wooden implement wouldn't sink but on the plus side for them, it could float downriver. If that happened, could it possibly float all the way to the sea, or would it get caught up on a weir or something?'

McNally raised his eyebrows and looked at Wallace. 'Good question, boss. I don't know but we'll get straight on to that.'

Wallace cleared his throat. 'We know from speaking to the people in the other shops in the street that White, the pet shop owner, was a fairly frequent visitor to the bookies.'

Flint nodded as she considered the information. 'Who told you about that?'

The waitress in the café, Tina Callaghan, she seems to be the eyes and ears of the street and she likes to gossip. She said she's seen White going in and out of there a lot.'

'As a customer or a friend?' Flint asked.

'According to Tina Callaghan, a bit of both. We plan on speaking to White today to follow up on that. Interestingly, he failed to mention these frequent visits when we spoke to him yesterday.'

Flint looked thoughtful. 'When was the last time that we know he was there?'

Wallace checked his notes. 'Callaghan says Saturday, late morning. The day before Hamilton was killed.'

'Hamilton was still alive and well when he closed his shop on Saturday evening.'

McNally shrugged. 'Exactly, boss. So I'm not sure if that tells us anything. It wouldn't be unusual for these guys to pop in and out of each other's shops.'

'So, why was Hamilton in his shop on Sunday evening and who was with him?' Flint asked. She looked at her team but no-one could provide that particular answer.

'So far we've drawn a blank with CCTV,' McNally said. 'Too many gaps or not clear enough to be of any use. So we're hoping the forensics from the back shop of the bookies will help narrow things down.'

'We might need to consider widening the CCTV radius. What about the alibis of Black and his men?'

'So far, they're solid, boss.' McNally said. 'We'll check out another couple of angles but, as we've said before, Black's own alibi doesn't actually take him out of the picture and, in any case, he could easily have paid somebody to do the business while he was safely having a drink fifty miles away.'

'We've been putting some pressure on Larry McAllister, the guy that works in the pet shop,' Wallace said.

'This is the one who saw Eddie Black and his team assaulting Hamilton on the Friday morning?'

'That's right, boss,' McNally said. 'We already know from McAllister, that Black and his thugs were in that back shop on the Friday morning, so we're expecting to find evidence to support that.

'So what's this pressure that Willie mentioned?' Flint said.

'McAllister has a history of petty crime, some proven, some not. We've got information that he's currently running a wee scam along with one or two of his former colleagues at a whisky warehouse, selling black market booze. We've suggested to him that if he can keep his eyes and ears open and let us know what he sees and hears then we might not feel the need to pursue any enquiries into his freelancing deals.'

Flint raised an eyebrow, apparently not convinced that this was an appropriate way of doing things. 'You're not worried about putting him in danger, Tom?'

'It will just be intelligence and all he needs to do is call us. We don't expect him to come up with evidence that would entail him standing up in court.' He paused. 'But you never know.'

Flint pursed her lips. 'Just make sure it's done properly. If it goes wrong, for example if Black found out, then McAllister could be in danger.'

McNally glanced at Wallace and both men nodded.

Wallace cleared his throat, his trademark way of letting DCI Flint know that he had something to say.

'Spit it out, Willie.'

'I was just thinking, as well as visiting Hamilton as a friend or customer, White also had something in common with Hamilton.'

McNally was about to ask the question but Flint was ahead of him.

'You mean the fact that, according to Louise, they were both paying protection money to Eddie Black?'

Wallace nodded. 'Maybe they felt the need to talk about it from time to time.'

'Interesting thought, Willie,' Flint said.

McNally nodded approvingly. 'Nice one, wee man. We'll make a proper cop out of you yet.'

Chapter 32

Larry stayed in the doorway until Black and his men were well inside the shop. He had no intention of getting involved with them today. He slipped out of the shadows and headed for Sloan's. The place was a Glasgow legend and laid claim to be one of the oldest establishments in the city. There were three entrances to the place. One was from the plush Argyll Arcade, a covered arcade of expensive jewellers, the second from a narrow lane off Buchanan Street, the third from a more dodgy-looking lane off Argyle Street. Larry always went in from Argyle Street.

He ordered a pint of Tennents and downed half of it in one swallow. Seeing Black arriving at the shop had unnerved him, but it also set his mind thinking. It looked like Casper had wanted Larry out of the way after all. Black had dropped into the shop plenty of times. With all the extra police activity in the area, he must realise there was a good chance of the cops spotting them meeting up. Maybe Black didn't care. From what he could gather, the man seemed to be able to do what he liked and the cops, so far, had not been able to stop him. This time it was murder but maybe Black had killed before. Larry wondered if Casper really knew what he was getting himself into.

He suddenly realised he could do himself a favour. The cops were putting the pressure on him to dig up some information about Black. Maybe he could buy a bit of time with no great risk to himself. All he had to do was call McNally and tell him Black was in the shop with Casper. Nobody would suspect that he'd told them. After all, the cops had been in and out of the street in the last few days so there was a good chance that they would spot him anyway. Larry could give them info that was probably going to be public knowledge soon anyway.

Before he could talk himself out of it, he keyed the number into his phone. He was about to press 'call' but he looked around him. Even at this time of the day there were too many eyes and ears about. He stepped out into the lane and found a quiet corner.

The familiar gruff voice answered with just the one word. 'McNally.'

Larry looked around him and kept his voice low. 'It's me, Larry McAllister.'

'To what do I owe the honour? Have you got something for me?'

'I thought you might want to know. Black and his men have just paid a visit to the pet shop to see Casper.'

'What about?'

Larry was taken aback. 'I don't know. I was on my way out as they arrived. I just thought you'd be interested.'

There was silence for a moment then a curt 'thanks'. Larry imagined McNally nodding at the other end of the line. A minute later, the call was ended. On balance McNally seemed pleased that Larry had given him something and said they'd 'look into it'.

Larry congratulated himself. That gave him something in credit with the cops. Not a bad move. Then, a moment later he started to doubt himself and he felt a wave of panic. Christ, now he was a grass. What would people say if they found out? More importantly, what would Black do to him? He stepped back into the bar to finish his pint and order a second.

Maybe this was the day that things changed. He ran through the list of points in his mind. He had a possible new sideline with Arthur. Things had gone well in his last conversation with Casper. He'd managed to navigate his way through Tina's questions. Even Sharon had been more sympathetic than normal last night. He'd kept the cops happy with a simple phone call. Most important of all, nobody, apart from the cops, knew that he'd seen Eddie Black laying into Tony last Friday.

Was his luck finally beginning to turn? Okay, he still had absolutely no idea how he was going to dig up any serious information about Black for the cops in under a week. But maybe he'd come up with something and at least he'd given them a wee snippet today. In the meantime he should do something for himself, strike while the iron was hot. He could go over to Arthur Simpson's house right now. He might not be able to take anything from the house today but he could make an initial survey of the place. There was no shortage of problems in his life, the cops, Eddie Black, Casper always giving him hassle and Sharon with her threats about divorce and custody. This was maybe something where he could take control and make some extra cash into the bargain. He nodded to himself, his mind made up.

Sloan's was at the eastern end of Argyle Street and Arthur lived two miles away at the opposite end, near Kelvingrove Art Gallery. Although he thought nothing of walking a few miles when he was with the kids in the park at the weekend, he wasn't in the mood for a long hike, given everything that had happened to him over the last week. St Enoch's Square subway station was just across the street and that's where he headed.

The Glasgow underground, the 'Clockwork Orange', as it was known locally, wasn't in the same league as London's but Larry liked it. When he was a young boy, his dad used to take him and his sister on it to see the Christmas lights in Buchanan Street and George Square. Happier times, he thought. When had life started to get so difficult? He gave himself a shake and started to plan how he would approach things with Arthur.

He exited the subway at Partick and, as he passed the Kelvin Hall, he remembered the Christmas 'shows' that he used to go to with his sister and their dad: waltzers, merry-go-rounds, big wheel and candy floss. Now it was reincarnated into a world-class sports venue as

Glasgow reinvented itself and he'd never had the chance to take his own kids.

Across the road was the Glasgow Museum and Art Gallery, another favourite of his dad's. He loved telling Larry and his sister about Glasgow's historic buildings. The three of them spent many an afternoon wandering the city streets, his dad pointing out features that most people never noticed. He had taught himself about the city's history and its architecture, and loved the fact that the city's list of protected buildings covered a wide range, from museums like the Art Gallery to pubs like Sloan's.

The Art Gallery was still a favourite for Larry and his kids on rainy Sunday afternoons. He shivered at the threats that Sharon uttered about denying him access to his children because of his brushes with the law. He didn't really think she meant it but you never knew. It was another reason why he had to tread carefully with Arthur. If he could get money out of him, it meant he could treat Sharon and the kids. He'd find a way of disguising where it came from. But if he got caught doing something dodgy then it could spell disaster.

As he approached Arthur's tenement he again noticed the huge tree in front of the building. He had mentioned it to Sharon after his first visit and she had called it 'the only tree in Argyle Street'. Apparently it was famous and had been written about in books and newspaper articles. He had no idea if it was still the only tree in the two-mile long street but it was certainly impressive.

He checked the number, pressed the button for ground floor right and waited for the buzzer to sound. Arthur didn't even ask who was there, he just let him into the close. While he waited for Arthur to open the house door, he tried to assess the man. Arthur had happily paid the inflated price that Larry had asked for the rabbit food supplement and he'd spread a wad of money on the counter during his first visit to the shop. He put Arthur's age at about forty, not much different from his own but as far as Larry was concerned that was the only similarity between them.

He wondered how the guy got on with normal day-to-day living. From what he'd said last time, it seemed he'd lived with his mum until she had recently passed away. His dad had apparently died, or left, some time ago. Was there someone who came in from time to time to help him cope?

He heard a noise from inside the house and a shape moved towards the glass-panelled door. There was money to be had through Arthur. He didn't know how or how much, but his gut told him it was the case. He would take it one step at a time, build the relationship, win Arthur's trust.

When Arthur opened the door he was holding the rabbit. 'Look Larry, it's the other Larry, your uncle Larry come to visit. Are you going to say hello to him?'

Larry winced at the play acting. He had no desire to be a rabbit's uncle. He was also momentarily confused, then horrified. Had Arthur called the rabbit 'Larry'? He pointed uncertainly at the animal. 'What did you call him?'

Arthur beamed and nodded. 'Larry. I named him after you.'

Larry tried to smile. Christ almighty, that's all I need. Godfather to a fucking rabbit. Then he remembered the other rabbit, the one that had been smeared across the floor of the shop. 'Thanks, that's nice.'

Chapter 33

He followed Arthur into the wide hall, expecting to go into the big living-room like last time. But, instead, Arthur led him to the opposite corner of the hall and into an old-fashioned kitchen. Larry stopped in surprise at what he saw on the far side of the room.

As he moved closer to examine it, his face brushed against a shirt sleeve. He glanced up and saw that Arthur still had the traditional clothes pulley suspended from the ceiling and that it was fully-laden with damp laundry. He brushed the shirt aside to peer at the fireplace. 'Good God,' he said, 'you've still got the original, cast-iron range? That's incredible.'

Arthur turned to look at the coal-black range but he didn't seem to understand why Larry thought it so unusual. 'It's just the fireplace. Keeps the room warm,' he said simply.

Surely he didn't actually do his cooking on there as well, Larry thought. He looked around him and saw an ancient electric cooker in the corner near the window. Okay. Well at least that's sort of normal, he thought.

Arthur didn't say anything to Larry. He didn't seem surprised to see him. He just plonked himself down in an armchair with the rabbit on his lap. 'Countdown,' he said, pointing to the telly.

Larry turned to see where he was pointing. The television was completely out of keeping with the rest of the room. It was a huge plasma screen, squeezed into an alcove that had obviously been built long before enormous televisions, or maybe even any televisions, had been thought of.

Larry had watched the programme a few times but he usually wasn't home in time to see it these days. The kids enjoyed it and so did Sharon but Larry wasn't a fan. He wasn't much good at the letters games and he was hopeless at the numbers. He heard muttering from behind him and turned to see Arthur staring at the screen where the competitors were unsuccessfully trying to solve the number puzzle. Arthur seemed to be talking to himself. Both of the competitors on the programme had failed to solve the number puzzle. The host was asking the resident mathematical genius if it could be done and she said it was a tricky one and she'd get back to him later.

Arthur laughed and gave a dismissive snort. 'Easy,' he said, 'then muttered a series of numbers.'

Larry tried to follow his thinking but he spoke too quickly and too quietly. A few moments later, as the programme was about to break for adverts a word puzzle appeared, there were eight or nine letters and the host offered a clue that seemed complete nonsense to Larry, something about swallowing a joke. Even before the man had stopped speaking Arthur shouted the word 'ingested'. Then he hit the mute button and helped himself to a chocolate digestive from a packet sitting on a stool beside him.

Larry looked at the guy. This was a new side to the man. He'd thought Arthur was a bit simple and, in a way, he was, but maybe not really or not for everything. Could be he was just shy or awkward around people. From the way he'd mentioned his mother it sounded like she'd given him a sheltered life. So maybe he'd never had the chance to do things for himself.

He wasn't sure how to react. 'You like that programme, then, Arthur?'

Arthur crammed another chocolate digestive into his mouth. 'It's okay,' he said, spraying crumbs over his lap and the rabbit. He glanced down at the rabbit and made a half-hearted attempt to brush the crumbs off it on to the carpet.

Larry had visions of the rabbit being covered in all sorts of food after a few weeks living here. 'But you're good at the puzzles. You always get the answers,' he went on, trying to draw the guy out.

The man shrugged his beefy shoulders. 'They're easy.'

'Do you want to talk about the rabbit?' Larry thought he better get on to the point of his visit.

'After Countdown.' Arthur nodded at the screen to indicate the programme was starting and hit the mute button again to bring the sound up.

The answer to the word puzzle was revealed and sure enough it was 'ingested'. Arthur gave a little grunt of satisfaction and turned his attention to the next puzzle.

Larry sat in a chair off to the side and watched Arthur for the rest of the programme. The man solved all the puzzles more or less instantaneously. Not that Larry could follow everything he was saying, but he could tell from the self-satisfied smiles that he was correct every time. He'd heard about people like this, they didn't seem all that bright but they were brilliant at certain things, solving puzzles, remembering things. There had been a film about it but he couldn't remember the name. As he watched Arthur muttering the answers, munching chocolate digestives, spraying crumbs and stroking the rabbit, he wondered if the man was as good at remembering things as he was at solving puzzles.

Eventually the programme finished and Arthur switched the telly off. Larry was eager to talk about the rabbit and then get on to the real purpose of his visit, getting another look at all the stuff in the room next door. But Arthur wanted another cup of tea first. While they waited for the kettle to boil, Larry talked him through the basics of looking after a rabbit. He laughed to himself at the irony, he had no time for pets and the little he knew about them had been drummed into him by Casper. He'd brought a few leaflets that would reinforce the message, though he was far from confident that Arthur would read them. Arthur nodded and looked interested as Larry went through the points, so maybe some of it was going in after all.

Of course, Larry now knew that Arthur wasn't actually stupid. He searched for the right word and decided 'special' would do for the moment. He was also wondering if there was some way he could use Arthur's skills to his advantage. One of the things he remembered from the film was that the guy's brother had used him to help them win money in a casino.

Larry started to imagine all sorts of possibilities. He could see himself and the family staying in top-class hotels, lounging by the pool and having waiters bring them as many drinks as they wanted. A new car. Of course, he'd chuck in his job in the pet shop, tell Casper where he could stick his tropical fish.

He'd only been to a casino once before, it was after a works night out from the whisky warehouse. A lot of the guys had loved it but Larry had found the whole thing a bit confusing. He enjoyed playing cards in the house, always had done. His dad had taught him lots of card games over the years and he liked passing them on to his two. In the casino it just wasn't the same. There were too many people, everything happened too quickly and people were spending scary amounts of money.

If he could somehow manage to persuade Arthur to go with him, things might be different. If the man had a great memory to go with his apparent phenomenal skill with numbers, who knows what might happen? Could the guy cope with that sort of atmosphere? Larry had found it hard enough himself. He realised this would need some thought. With his one solitary experience of casinos it would be like the blind leading the blind.

So he might have to pick somebody's brains for advice on how to make it work. But who? There was no way he could ask Sharon. She would kill him. Casper was also out of the question. Maybe some of his pals could help.

He remembered Tina talking about how she liked to go to the casino with her pals. He got the impression she was a regular and knew her way around. Could he trust her to keep things quiet? And how would Arthur react? He'd seemed scared stiff when Tina spoke to him in the shop earlier. He'd need to be careful how he asked her.

Larry realised he was getting way ahead of himself. Sharon would have put it less kindly, said his head was full of wee motors and to screw the nut. So one thing at a time, this could be risky and he didn't want to rush it. Anyway, before that, he wanted another look at the antiques.

'Listen, I just remembered something,' Larry said. 'I'm sure my mum used to have fancy plates like the ones you've got next door.'

There was no response from Arthur and Larry realised he had to be more specific. 'Do you think I could see them again?'

After a moment's pause, Arthur nodded and led Larry into the living room. Larry made a show of examining the one plate that Arthur fetched down from the shelf. It was unusual, and pretty, no doubt about that, but Larry had no idea if it was of any value. After getting permission from Arthur, he got his phone out and took a picture of the plate and said he'd check it against the one his mother used to have. As he said the words he realised how ridiculous they were. Most people would have challenged him on it. Where's your mother's plate now? Have you not got a picture of it? And so on. Arthur simply gave his trusting smile and nodded.

As they spoke, Larry's eyes drifted round the room picking out the various objects he'd spotted the last time. He knew absolutely nothing about antiques, the square root of bugger all, as his dad used to say. The closest he'd come to an antique was that his mum and dad used to have an alarm clock that only worked when it was lying face down.

But he knew someone, Dixie Finnegan, who, although not exactly an antiques expert, had a stall down the Barras. The man was more of an acquaintance than a friend but they'd got chatting one day and Dixie told him you could make a fair bit of money by picking up old family heirlooms. Larry hadn't worked out how he was going to do it but he somehow had to let Dixie see a couple of these items and get his opinion on them.

On the sideboard there was a little green statue of a Buddha and the word 'jade' popped into Larry's mind. Dixie had spoken of green jade and how it could be valuable. Next to it there was a soldier on a horse. It was brass or bronze and was about twice the size of the Buddha. It reminded Larry of a picture he'd seen in the Art Gallery once when he'd taken Kelly and Joe one wet Sunday afternoon.

Larry walked closer to the Buddha. He was about to pick it up when he remembered how Arthur had reacted the last time he'd touched something without permission. So he put his hands behind his back and leaned forward to inspect it. 'Where did you get this wee thing? It's really unusual.'

'Mum got it from a friend,' Arthur replied, 'one of her special friends.'.

No point in asking what 'special friend' meant, Larry decided. 'Must have been a generous friend. It looks expensive.' Larry thought he might as well try and impress him. 'Is it jade?'

Arthur nodded. 'Jade, yes, mum always called it her wee jade man.'

Larry tried to hide his excitement. If this was the real thing then it could be worth a lot. He somehow had to get a picture of this and let Dixie see it. Arthur had put the rabbit in its cage in the kitchen when they had come in here. Larry suddenly stood up straight and seemed to be listening to something. He put on a worried face and looked at Arthur.

'I think that's the rabbit trying to get out of its cage. You better check on it.'

As soon as Arthur scurried out of the room, Larry whipped his phone out and snapped off some photos of the Buddha from a few different angles. At the last minute he remembered something Dixie had mentioned and he picked the statue up. Although it was small, it was heavy. Quickly he turned it over and took a couple of photos of the base. He placed the statue back on its stand just as Arthur came back in to the room.

'Was the rabbit okay?'

Arthur gave a single nod. He looked a bit annoyed and Larry wondered if he was suspicious. He pointed to the little Buddha.

'Yep, really beautiful that is,' he said, as calmly as he could. He moved over to the statue of the soldier. 'This one reminds me of something I saw once in the Art Gallery, years ago.'

Arthur nodded enthusiastically. 'Yes, mum said it was from the Art Gallery.'

Larry looked at him. 'No, I mean, it looks like one that's in the Art Gallery. It can't be the same one. I don't think they sell them off.'

Arthur's face went red, whether from anger or embarrassment, Larry couldn't tell. Arthur walked over to the door and put his hand on the light switch. 'You have to go now. I have to get my tea.'

Larry put his hands up in a gesture of apology and moved to the door. 'Okay, no problem. I'm sure you're right, no offence.'

As soon as he stepped out of the room, Arthur switched the light off and closed the door firmly behind them. When Larry came out of the close he saw a pub right across the street, 'The Park Bar'. He'd never been in but he'd heard it served a good pint. He decided to treat himself to a wee celebration drink. A minute later he was standing at the bar, pint in hand, his mind spinning with all sorts of wild dreams.

Chapter 34

When Larry got home Sharon wasn't happy.

'Where the hell have you been?' she said. 'You know I always go out with my pals on the last Thursday of the month, it's the pub quiz.'

So much for the improvement he'd seen in her mood the night before. Every time he thought he was getting somewhere, things were soon as bad as ever. One step forward, two steps back. She was right, he did know about the last Thursday of the month. But, with everything that had happened over the last week, it had gone right out of his head. Simple as that. It was his fault, but surely, it was understandable.

'Sorry. I just forgot.' He fumbled in his pocket and pulled out a tenner. 'Here, get a taxi at the corner so you're not too late.'

Sharon looked at the money suspiciously. Was she going to ask why he was being so generous? But she was in a hurry and sometimes even Sharon knew when to take the money and run.

'Have a nice night,' he shouted after her as she clattered down the stairs.

The kids were doing their homework so he had a quick chat with them, reheated his dinner, cheesy pasta and ham, and sat down to watch the latest episode of 'The Wire'. Sharon would be out for a few hours. Quite often, after the pub quiz, they would go on to 'The Horseshoe', for the karaoke. So hopefully he could have a quiet night. He pulled out his phone to look at the photos of the green jade Buddha. He'd done a good job. On Saturday or Sunday he'd show them to Dixie and see what he made of them.

He was jolted out of admiring his handiwork when the phone rang and the name 'Casper' come up on the screen. He had to admit he'd a real talent for compartmentalising things. If something wasn't right in front of him, he could completely forget about it. Because he'd been so caught up with what he'd found at Arthur's house, he had, unbelievably, wiped from his memory the fact that he'd called the police earlier to tell them that Black was in the shop with Casper. He considered ignoring it but Casper would keep calling and if he didn't answer then there would be hell to pay tomorrow.

He pressed the pause button on the telly, put his plate on the side table and tried to think himself into a nonchalant mood. 'Hi, Casper, how's it going?'

He held the phone away from his ear as Casper roared a string of expletives at him. 'What the hell's going on?' Larry asked, once the shouting tailed off.

Casper let rip with another torrent of abuse but this time not quite so loud or so long. 'Guess who showed up at the shop not long after you left?'

Was this a trick question? Had Casper spotted that Larry was still near the shop when Eddie Black turned up? Even if he had, there was no

223

way he could know that Larry had seen Black. He definitely hadn't seen the cops arriving so he was safe on that score. He better go in with somebody relatively neutral.

'I don't know. Tina from the café?'

'Tina from the café?' There was another bout of swearing. 'Do you think I'd be going off my nut just because Tina the mouth pops in for a gossip?'

Larry shrugged his shoulders. He speared some cheesy pasta on his fork and crammed it into his mouth. 'Who was it then?' he mumbled through the food.

'They two fucking cops, McNally and Wallace, plus their boss, that Geordie bitch.'

Larry was about to offer the name. 'DCI Flint', but he held back. He couldn't remember exactly how much detail he'd given Casper about his meetings with the cops. 'I don't think I remember her,' he said vaguely.

'Flint, that's her name and she's as hard as flint as well. You could probably sharpen a knife on her fucking arse.'

Still no mention of Eddie Black, Larry noticed. Maybe he left before the police got there. 'What did they want?

'The usual, how well did I know Tony? What was my relationship with him? Had anyone threatened him recently? Had anyone threatened me recently? What did I talk about when I went into his shop? Where exactly in the bookies had I been?'

Larry swallowed another mouthful of food. 'I thought they'd asked you all that already.'

Casper sighed. 'They had, more or less, but there was a bit more detail on a couple of points. It was like they had something new.'

'Where was all this happening? Were there customers in the shop?' Larry thought he should play up his concern about the shop.

'Thank Christ there were no customers. They only stayed about ten minutes. They checked out the back shop and the lane. Then that was it. They left.'

Larry didn't know whether to be relieved or disappointed. He'd told the cops Black was there and when they arrived he had gone. Would they think he'd been winding them up? No. That would be stupid. What could he gain from that? He picked his words carefully. 'That sounds a bit weird. To turn up mob-handed like that and then only stay for a few minutes.'

There was silence for a minute then Casper said: 'Aye, definitely weird. Anyway, I'll see you tomorrow.'

As Larry hit the button to restart the programme, the screen was showing a police informant being tortured, then killed, by the gangster he had informed on. The man was held down by his hands and feet and one of the heavies hammered his arms and legs with a baseball bat before finally crushing his skull with a huge blow. Larry had been about to take another mouthful of food but suddenly he'd lost his appetite. He switched the telly off and went to check on Kelly and Joe.

Chapter 35

Next morning over breakfast Sharon told Larry and the kids about the quiz night and the karaoke. 'Our team came in second after a tie-break.'

'Did you sing anything at the karaoke, Mum?' Kelly asked.

Sharon laughed. 'I might have given them a wee rendition of 'Crazy''.

Larry was relieved to see she was in a good mood. When she asked him what had happened yesterday, he adopted his usual practice of some truth mixed in with some lies. He told her that Arthur, the weird guy with the rabbit, had come in looking for help, that he'd gone to his house to help him and the guy had given him a few quid as a tip. He told Sharon he wasn't telling Casper about it because it had happened outside of work. She seemed to think about it for a moment, then nodded.

'Seems fair enough,' she finally said, and went to get ready for work.

As Larry approached the shop he kept his eyes peeled for the cops ambushing him. They'd promised not to compromise him but he didn't trust them to stick to that. He gave them the tip-off yesterday but it seemed it had come to nothing so they might turn up looking for more. It wasn't his fault if they weren't quick enough off the mark.

They'd given him a week to come up with what they called 'inside information' about Eddie Black but how the hell was he supposed to do that?

He was also wary of Black turning up like he'd done the day before. Casper hadn't cracked a light about what the man had wanted or in fact even that he'd been at the shop at all. What did that mean? Was Black putting the pressure on Casper the way he'd done with Tony? Did that mean Casper might be the next to be beaten up? Or even killed? Maybe Black had given him a doing yesterday; that would explain why Casper was so angry on the phone last night. But surely Casper would have mentioned it when he called Larry.

Anyway, he'd soon find out, he could see his boss through the window of the shop. As he got to the door, he saw Tina, standing in her favourite spot at the window of the café, keeping an eye on the comings and goings of the street. He remembered he wanted to speak to her about casinos. She waved to him and gave him a thumbs-up, then turned away to serve a customer.

Casper looked worried and tired, which wasn't unusual these days, but there was no sign that he'd been on the receiving end of a beating. Before Larry could say anything, Casper jerked his head towards the back of the shop. 'There's somebody waiting for you back there,' he said, and gave Larry a cold smile.

Larry's blood froze. Who was it? It wouldn't be good news anyway, that was for sure. It had to be either Black or the cops. For a crazy moment he imagined it would be both of them, somehow teamed up against him. That made no sense at all but that was the state his brain was in these days.

He edged his way to the back of the shop trying to prepare himself for the worst. When he saw who it was, he released the breath he'd been holding in. There, peering into the rabbit cages, was Arthur.

Casper's voice came from behind him. 'I couldn't resist winding you up,' he said. 'I knew you'd think it was probably the cops in to hassle you again.' He nodded at Arthur. 'He was waiting outside when I came to open up. Wanted to speak to you, I wasn't good enough for him. I'll leave you to it,' he said as he headed to his office.

After the initial relief, Larry started to worry again. Had Arthur said anything to Casper about the price of the food? Or was he here to complain about something? Only one way to find out.

'All right, Arthur? What can I do for you?'

'I think Larry's lonely.'

Larry was confused. 'I'm not lonely.'

Arthur burst out laughing. 'No, my Larry.' He clapped his hands together. 'He needs a friend.'

Christ, he was talking about his fucking rabbit. Larry managed to force a smile. 'Okay, we can definitely sort that for you.'

Larry glanced towards Casper's office. He didn't think it was a good idea for Arthur to take on a second rabbit until he was more used to the first one. But Casper wouldn't be impressed if he caught him talking a potential customer out of a sale.

'I'll tell you what. You have a wee look round and see if there's anything in particular you fancy.' Larry thought for a minute. This might be another opportunity for him to make some more cash out of Arthur. 'You don't need to decide now. I can come to your house and talk to you about it.

Arthur spent a half hour looking at the rabbits then called Larry over and pointed out the rabbit he was interested in. It looked identical to the rabbit he'd already bought. 'I want this one, please.' His face was flushed with childlike pleasure and excitement.

'Right, not a problem. I'll come over to your place later and we'll finalise the details. Okay?' Larry glanced round to make sure Casper wasn't within earshot. He'd probably wonder why Larry wasn't closing the sale right away.

Once he'd safely ushered Arthur out the door Larry spoke to Casper.

'The guy's not really sure if he wants to buy another rabbit. I think he gets nervous when he's away from his house. So I told him I'd pop over and talk him through things slowly.'

'What's so special about this bloke that he gets home visits?'

'He's a wee bit odd, you must have noticed. I think if he's comfortable in his own house, I'll be able to sell him all sort of extras.'

At the mention of extra cash, Casper was happy to agree. 'Right, fair enough. Just don't make a habit of disappearing out of the shop.' He headed for the door. 'I'm nipping out for a coffee and a roll and then I've got some business to take care of.'

As soon as Casper left, Larry went to the back door to have a smoke. As he stood there, leaning against the doorframe, he realised it was exactly a week ago that the rabbit had escaped and that he'd seen Eddie Black dragging a knife down Tony's face. He glanced up the lane towards the back door of the bookies. The police seemed to have moved on but there were a few straggling bits of police tape blowing in the wind. He stubbed his cigarette out against the wall and dropped the butt. As he stepped back into the main part of the shop he heard the ding of the bell as the front door opened.

Chapter 36

For the second time that morning he braced himself for an unwelcome visitor, but was relieved to see Tina, no doubt coming in to give him all her news.

'Hi, how you doing?' she said, wearing her trademark smile and waving the usual bag of goodies. 'It's a bit quieter in there just now so I thought I'd grab the chance to nip in and have a catch-up. I've brought you a wee treat.'

Larry made the tea and they talked over the events of the last week. Tina was clearly dying to see what Larry could tell her about yesterday's visitors.

'So I saw that gangster was here yesterday,' she said. 'What was he after?'

Larry shrugged. He was surprised that if Tina had seen Black arrive, she hadn't seen Larry leave. He decided to play dumb. 'I don't know, I left the shop early, he must have come after I'd gone. Did you see him from the café window?'

'No, I was coming back from a wee message. How come you were away early?'

'Casper told me to take an early finish. I wasn't going to argue. Was Black with his two pals?'

She took a drink of tea and a bite of her snowball. 'Aye, the three amigos. A right bad lot. But guess what?'

Larry shrugged his shoulders again, and munched his cake. 'What?' he said, though he had a good idea what was coming.

'Well, once I got into the café I tried to keep an eye on what was going on. Just in case, you know. And guess what?'

He managed to keep calm and pretend to look interested. He was intrigued to see if Tina knew whether Black and the cops saw each other. 'Haven't got a clue,' he said.

'While that guy Black and his men were in the shop, the cops arrived. The two that spoke to me and you the other day. You know, the mean-looking one with the scar and the quieter one. Plus a woman was with them, and she seemed to be giving out the orders.'

Larry tried to look impressed. 'You're kidding.'

Tina was now satisfied with the way this was going. She liked nothing better than to have an audience hanging on her every word. She slowly shook her head. 'Nope, they waltzed right in there.'

'So what happened? Did they arrest them or what?'

She seemed to realise she'd overplayed her hand. 'I don't think so,' she said, clearly aware of the anti-climax. 'The cops were only in there for about ten minutes and then they came out on their own.'

'That's funny,' Larry said, and he meant it.

'I know. I mean I was expecting a big fight or something. So I grabbed a couple of cakes and nipped along to the shop. Went in expecting to see you and Casper and the bad guys. But it was just Casper, on his tod. So what do you make of that?'

Larry shook his head. 'They must have seen the cops arriving and nipped out the back door and along the lane.'

'Exactly. When I got back here, the three of them were sitting at a table waiting to get served.' She was back on track with her story now and enjoyed the look of surprise on Larry's face.

'How did they get in?'

'Quite often Rosa wedges the back door open cause the place can get really hot. She didn't say much to me about it but I got the impression they'd come in that way and just sat themselves down at a table.'

Larry was trying to picture the scene. He'd seen them arriving, they'd parked their car out front as usual. If they went back to the car the cops would see them. So they'd decided to have a nice wee cup of tea. Why wouldn't they just brazen it out with the cops? Black would surely enjoy facing them down. For some reason he wanted to avoid the cops catching him in the shop with Casper.

'When I saw the cops, I thought maybe you'd phoned them,' Tina said.

Larry froze. Did she know what he'd done? 'What would I do that for?'

'You know, in case they were going to give you or Casper a doing.'

He heaved a sigh of relief. 'Right, I see what you mean. No, well I wasn't there anyway, so I

233

couldn't have called the cops. They must have just turned up by luck.'

He thought back to what Tina had said earlier. 'How did they behave when they were in the café? Did they give you or Rosa any hassle?'

Tina finished her tea and shook her head. 'No, I mean they've been in once or twice before but I never knew who they were then. When they finally left I said to Rosa that they were bad news but she said she didn't need me to tell her.' The eyebrows were raised again.

'What did she mean by that?' Larry asked.

Tina looked all around her before answering even though there was no-one else in the shop. She beckoned Larry in closer. 'After a while she told me that Eddie Black as good as owns the café.' She paused for effect and nodded when she saw Larry's reaction.

'You're kidding. I thought all these shops were owned by the people that ran the businesses.'

'I know. It seems Rosa used to own hers as well. But a while back he made her one of those offers you can't refuse. Know what I mean?'

Larry stopped with the last bite of snowball halfway to his mouth. 'What did he do? Threaten her?' Rosa was a small, gentle woman from The Hebrides and he couldn't imagine Black beating her up like he had Tony. But you never knew with an animal like that.

Tina shrugged her shoulders. 'She wouldn't go into details. Just said that he'd more or less bought her out and would be letting her renew the lease on a three-monthly basis.'

234

'So the café could close and you could be out of a job within three months?'

Tina stood to leave. 'Yep.' She gave a shrug. 'Anyway I better get back in case there's people waiting. You take care.'

He remembered his plan about taking Arthur to a casino. He wanted to approach it carefully. How could he persuade Tina to help him without giving away too much of his plan? He hadn't even thought how he might get Arthur to come to a casino anyway.

'Before you go, Tina,' he said. 'You remember that guy Arthur?'

'The one that you said I had frightened? Aye, I remember. What about him?'

'I think he'd be interested in going to a casino and I remember you said you've been a few times.'

Tina gave him a look. Did she suspect something? 'A casino? He doesn't really seem the type. He could hardly look me in the eye.'

Larry shrugged. 'It takes all sorts.'

'Well, we've got a few casinos in Glasgow. I usually go to the one near Glasgow Green, The Green Rooms. When is he thinking of going?'

'I'm not sure. Probably quite soon. I wondered if you fancy coming with us. I think he might appreciate somebody who knows the ropes being there.'

This time she definitely looked suspicious and her eyes bored right through him. 'So you're going with him? When did you two become best mates?'

Before he could answer she went on. 'Is this some sort of dodgy thing?'

Despite how she looked, Tina didn't miss a trick. Larry couldn't believe how close she was to the truth. 'Dodgy? No. He's never been and I said I'd go with him. But we'd want somebody who knows what they're doing.'

She said nothing for a moment then slowly nodded her head. 'Maybe. I'll let you know. Right, I need to go.'

When Tina left, Larry sat at the counter trying to assess how he'd done. The casino thing had gone quite well. At least he'd started the ball rolling and she was going to think about it. He'd need to have a word with Arthur and see how he could sell the idea to him. He was getting quite good at this lying game.

He tried to make sense of what Tina had said about Eddie Black buying the café. There were eight shops in the short street, with tenement flats above them. He knew from what Casper had told him some time ago that the shops were owned by the people that ran them. Or at least they had been. Now Rosa had apparently sold the café. Who else had sold to Black? Was this why Black had killed Tony? Because he refused to sell his premises to him? If so, what would happen now? Presumably the bookies would pass to Tony's widow, Maggie, and she would be the next one to feel the pressure.

He remembered how Black had mentioned wanting an answer from Casper about 'that wee bit of business' when he came in to the pet shop.

Casper was obviously holding out, no doubt trying to get a better price. How long could he do that before he ended up dead in his shop? He had to try and find out from Casper what stage things had reached.

Larry was no brain of Britain but he knew that property prices in Glasgow had jumped in recent years. The city had 'reinvented' itself as a tourist destination, the Clyde had been cleaned up and new pedestrian walkways had been built. The Saltmarket was right in the centre of all of this and that meant there was money to be made.

Black was obviously up to something and whatever it was, he was willing to commit murder to get it. Maybe Larry had something else he could pass on to the cops. Since other people already knew about it, there might not be too much risk to himself. He got his phone out and keyed in McNally's number. It took a minute before he heard the now familiar growl. Larry took a deep breath and quickly told him what Tina had said about Black buying the café. McNally actually sounded interested for once.

'That's great, Mr McAllister, really useful. Keep the information coming.'

Larry could hardly believe his ears. 'What do you mean? Keep the information coming? Surely to Christ I've kept my side of the bargain.'

McNally was unmoved. 'It definitely helps, no question, but we need more than that. You keep your eyes and ears open and let me know as soon as you have anything else.'

Larry was about to protest but he realised McNally had ended the call. He was staring at his phone and calling the DS all the names he could think of when the bell on the shop door sounded. He looked up to see Eddie Black and Shug Dunbar striding towards him while Vinny Stuart stood guard at the door.

Chapter 37

Flint looked up from her desk when McNally knocked on her door. Wallace was with him. 'Come in Tom, what have you got for me?'

'I've just had Larry McAllister on the phone, the guy from the pet shop. You remember we'd asked him to keep his eyes and ears open. He's told us that Eddie Black has bought the café next door to the pet shop.'

Flint stood up, her interest clearly sparked. 'Where did he get this?'

'He wasn't willing to say, boss, but Willie did a quick check before coming to see you. It seems to be accurate. Or at least, that's how it's looking,' McNally added. 'The café was bought up a few weeks ago by a company called 'Pangloss Investments', though the deal might not be absolutely final yet.'

'There's nothing on paper,' Wallace added, 'but the intel unit says that Pangloss is a cover for Black. They've been looking at it for a while now and trying to find proof that it's one of Black's.'

'So maybe this could be the proof they need,' Flint said. 'Though we all know how hard it will be to prove the link.' She thought for a moment. 'Any other property deals in that block?'

Wallace nodded. 'We've just been checking the registers. Pangloss has bought another three of the shops in that street in the last few months.'

'So it looks like Black's trying to buy up all the shops in that street,' McNally said. 'He's maybe planning some sort of development.'

Flint's expression showed what she thought about that. 'Christ, that's just what Glasgow needs. A thug like Black getting his hooks into one more part of its economy. How are these people allowed to get away with it? You wouldn't think the council would be too happy about it.'

'Presumably it's all legal, boss and the council might not care as long as it brings money into the city. Either that, or else they can't do anything about it.'

The DCI looked at him. 'I know, you're right, Tom, but it sickens me. I saw the same thing in Newcastle.'

'We don't know for definite that's what Black's up to, boss. But if it is,' McNally said, 'then it could give us the motive for him to kill Tony Hamilton. Black wants to buy the bookies, Hamilton refuses to sell, or holds out for more money and Black loses his temper.'

Flint heard a grunt from Wallace. 'What is it, Willie?'

Wallace hesitated. 'Well, Black is obviously up to something. He sees the possibility of profit in those properties.'

'So what's your problem?' McNally said.

'It comes back to the same point we talked about before. Black's a pro. He's a villain and a thug. But when it comes to violence, he knows what he's doing. If he kills Tony Hamilton it doesn't actually get him the property. It will presumably go to Hamilton's widow, Maggie.'

Flint wasn't convinced. 'I think you might be over-complicating things, Willie. Black's well known for having a violent temper. He could easily lose it and clobber Hamilton. So that doesn't help his property plans, but he might not have been thinking logically.'

'That's probably why he's been such a regular visitor to White,' McNally said, 'he clearly wants the pet shop as well.'

Flint nodded. 'That's something Mr White neglected to tell us. I think we need another word with White. We'll see what we can get from him before we tackle Black. We should also have another word with Louise and our colleagues at 'Organised Crime.'

Suddenly Flint gave a bitter laugh.

'What is it, boss?' McNally asked.

'I've just realised, we're after Mr White and Mr Black. It's like a bloody monochrome version of 'Reservoir Dogs.'

Chapter 38

Larry felt as if he was trying to shrink and disappear as the two men walked towards him. The look on their faces was like something out of a horror film he'd seen. A guy was strapped into a chair in the basement of a hotel and a pair of deranged psychos were using all sorts of tools to wreak havoc. In most normal faces you could spot a little bit of humanity, even if you didn't like the person. But these two were like stone, completely indifferent to what other people thought of them, and giving nothing away.

'Where is he?'

Larry cringed back as Black leaned into his face. He could smell stale beer and whisky from the man.

Larry stuttered. 'Who, Casper?' As soon as he said the words he knew it was a mistake.

Black leaned his forehead against Larry's so that their eyes were inches apart. 'What the fuck did you say?'

Larry felt the breath on his face before he heard the words. He was confused. 'I just asked if it was Casper you wanted.'

The gangster leaned back slightly and turned to look at Dunbar. 'Can you believe this wee prick?' He turned back and dropped his forehead on to Larry's with full force. 'Who the fuck else would I be looking for?' Black paused. 'Unless you think

242

I'm here wanting to buy a rabbit.' He grinned coldly and his men laughed on cue.

Larry was having trouble swallowing. 'He's not here, he's away out.'

Black nodded slowly. 'Don't tell me, he's out somewhere on business.'

'Aye, that's right.'

The forehead was withdrawn and came crashing down on Larry's nose. 'I told you not to tell me that.'

Again the grin and the echoing laughs.

Larry was sure his nose was broken. He was finding it hard to breathe, his eyes were watering and he could feel his heart racing. All this because he had tried to be helpful. The man was a nutter.

Black stood up, distancing himself from the blood running down Larry's face. 'I came to see him yesterday, but we got interrupted when the boys in blue turned up.' He whirled back and leaned into Larry's face again. 'You wouldn't know anything about that, would you?'

Larry shook his head and immediately wished he hadn't. His nose felt like it was moving in the opposite direction from the rest of his face. 'No,' he groaned.

Black patted him gently on the cheek. 'Good, that's good. Just keep it like that. There's nothing I hate more than somebody that grasses me up to the cops.'

'I would never do that,' Larry mumbled. He was acutely aware that his phone was sitting on the counter and that the last number dialled was DS McNally's. If Black decided to be nosy, all he had to do was pick up the phone, hit redial and that would be that. Images of dead rabbits and dead bookies ran through his mind.

But Black was ready to leave. 'Tell that wee bastard that if he's not here the next time I come looking for him, I'll pay a visit to his house. He won't like that and his wife will like it even less.'

What the hell have I got myself into, Larry thought, as he watched the three men leave, the door clattering shut behind them? His attention was caught by one of the hamsters in its cage running endlessly in its wheel and getting nowhere.

'You and me both, pal,' he muttered.

When Casper got back to the shop and saw Larry's bruised and bloodied face he shook his head in anger. 'Not that bastard, Eddie Black, again?'

Larry remembered not to move his head this time. 'He came in looking for you. You weren't here and he went mental. In fact, no, he didn't go mental. He was calm as you like, icy cold. I think he just likes hurting people.'

'You're right there,' Casper said. 'When did it happen?'

'Ten minutes ago. You just missed hlm.' Larry carefully touched his nose with the tip of his fingers. 'I think I better get to the hospital, get this checked out.'

'Definitely. Did he leave a message for me? Apart from that,' he nodded towards Larry's face.

'He said you better be here when he comes back. If not he'll go to your house.'

Casper's face paled. 'My house? Did he threaten Christine?'

'Not in so many words, but, aye. He said that when he was here yesterday you were interrupted by the cops arriving.'

Casper looked surprised that Black had told Larry about that. 'He'd been here about ten minutes and the next thing we saw the cops pull up outside. Black and his two heavies nipped out the back door just as the cops came in the front.'

Larry was keen to get to the hospital to get his nose checked. But, since Casper had opened up a little, he thought he might as well strike while the iron was hot. 'Tina was in earlier. She said Black and the other two turned up in the café, they must have gone along the lane and gone in through the back door.'

Casper looked uneasy. 'Did she say anything else?'

Larry hesitated, but he was sure Casper would already know about the café and Tina hadn't said that what she'd told him was a secret. 'She said that Rosa had more or less sold the café to Black. Apparently he made her an offer she couldn't refuse.'

The look on Casper's face was indeed not one of surprise but of resignation. 'Aye, he's good at that. He's trying to buy up the whole block. A few people, like Rosa, have already caved in.'

'Is that how he keeps coming here, wanting to know if you're going to accept his offer?'

Casper nodded. 'In the end, I won't have any choice, if I want my face to stay the way it is.'

Larry kept quiet. Under different circumstances he might have made a crack about how Casper could do with getting his face rearranged. 'What about Tony?'

'What about him?'

'I suppose Black was after his place as well. Do you know where it had got to? I assume Tony said no and that's how come Black, or one of his men, killed him.'

Casper nodded slowly. 'I'm not sure, but that's what I'm thinking as well. Tony told me Black was really piling on the pressure. A couple of days later he turns up dead.' He looked thoughtful for a moment. 'And I could be next.'

Larry picked his next words carefully. 'Maybe the cops will find out that Black was pressuring Tony. That would give him a motive, wouldn't it?'

'Aye, but who's going to tell them? Not me, and I doubt if you're daft enough to grass on Eddie Black.'

'Me? No way.' Larry wondered if he'd said too much. Would Casper find out that Larry had just done that very thing? 'But they'll be looking at all the angles. Searching for a motive, trying to find out who might have had any problems with Tony. That's what they do. You see it on the telly. So they'll probably find out that Black's been buying premises in this block and they'll put two and two together.'

'I hope you're right.'

'So, are you going to call Black? Cause you've no idea when he might come back here and if he turns up here again and you're not here, then he'll be coming round to your place.'

'I need to think about it. Anyway, you better get yourself along to The Royal, get that nose looked at.'

Chapter 39

The nurse who did the initial assessment quizzed Larry about the incident, what had happened, where, when, did he know the person responsible and so on. He gave her a watered-down version of events; said he'd been coming out of the pub, had accidentally bumped into a guy and the guy had gone nuts.

'Next thing I knew, there I was, lying on the ground, with blood streaming down my face.' Larry could actually picture the scene, he could almost believe that was had happened.

The nurse gave him a look that let him know she knew he wasn't telling her the full story. 'You should report it to the police,' she said, knowing that he probably wouldn't. 'When they check our register they might come and speak to you. They sometimes do follow-up calls for assaults.'

Larry thought she was probably winding him up but he just said that would be fine. The nurse wrote something in her notes then said the doctor would see him shortly.

In fact it was another half hour before the doctor appeared. He gave Larry a thorough examination and an x-ray. The nose wasn't broken but he put a dressing on it and told Larry to avoid any knocks to it over the next few days. Try telling that to Eddie Black, Larry thought.

While he waited for the bus, he thought about the story he would tell Sharon. Should he just be completely straight with her for a change? Was there any down side to that? All that had happened was that Black had been looking for Casper, didn't find him and took his anger out on Larry. Sharon couldn't find fault with him for that, surely. Then he thought about it from Casper's point of view. Maybe he hadn't told his wife, Christine, about all this hassle. If that was the case, he probably wouldn't want Sharon to know. The two wives weren't exactly close, but you never know. These things had a way of getting out there. He decided he should probably keep the full story from Sharon. He sent Casper a quick message to that effect and Casper messaged back 'Agreed'.

So while he travelled home, Larry came up with a slightly different version of the story he'd told the nurse. He didn't want to tell Sharon that he was coming out of the pub in the middle of the day but after a few minutes thought he was satisfied with his new story and he messaged Casper with the new version.

He'd lost track of the fact that it was Friday so when he got home he couldn't understand where Sharon and the kids were. Then he remembered it was Friday evening. Swimming was something they'd started up with Kelly and Joe from an early age and the kids loved it, so they kept it up. They were both great swimmers and put Larry and Sharon to shame. Sometimes they both went with them but Sharon liked to do the Friday evening sessions.

He looked in the fridge. There was all the stuff he needed for a fry-up. Brilliant, he'd have that ready for them coming in from the swimming. He remembered Friday nights when he was a boy. His mum almost always gave them either a fry-up or fish and chips. The fish dipped in an egg and coated with breadcrumbs and the chips done in oil in the big pot. His dad would come in from work, stand at the door, sniffing the air, pretending to be surprised that they were having fish and chips. He'd pick up Larry and his sister, Mary, and swing them round through the air, then he'd grab Larry's mum and dance her round the kitchen, telling her what a great wife she was.

He still got angry when he thought about how his mum and dad had both died much earlier than they should have done, in their fifties, in a car crash. Larry and his sister had been in their early twenties and suddenly their family was over. His sister had moved to Newcastle shortly afterwards and things had started to go downhill for Larry.

He realised he was standing staring into the fridge. He gave himself a shake and went into the bathroom to check his face in the mirror. As well as the nose being swollen and covered with a plaster, the area round his eyes was a lovely shade of black and blue; a nice wee present from Eddie Black.

He found the frying-pan in the sink, sitting there in all its glory. Bits of food were sitting in a bed of semi-liquid, brown-speckled gunge. He picked it up to scrape the mess into the bin and remembered too late that the handle was loose. The pan spun on its handle and dumped its contents all over his trousers. Sharon's cat, Sammy, had wandered in to observe the proceedings. It was licking its left paw but he would have sworn it was doing it to hide a smile.

'You knew that was going to happen didn't you, you smug wee bastard.'

He grabbed a towel and roughly mopped his trousers. He surveyed the damage. There was a greasy smear down his left leg but it would do for now. He scrubbed the pan and finally got it clean enough to use. He sat it on the hob, poured in some oil and turned the gas on. He laid everything out on the worktop. Ham, eggs, tottie scones, square slice, and a fresh Mother's Pride loaf with a nice hard crust. He'd give the outsider to wee Joe. He loved the thick crust, just like his dad.

Larry looked at the clock. They should be back in about fifteen minutes. Perfect timing. He'd always enjoyed cooking. Sometimes, at the weekends, he tried something a bit different, chicken jalfrezi or goulash, but he hadn't done it for a while. The kids appreciated it, and even Sharon would give a little nod of approval. It took his mind off other stuff, like his job, what had happened to Tony, and evil people like Eddie Black.

Anyway, he'd try not to think about any of that tonight. Try and make this a special evening for the family. He worked away, between the grill and the hob, whistling some half-forgotten tune as he did so. Every so often he saw the cat, Sammy, regarding him solemnly with an air of disapproval. He realised he should probably have fed the animal. Well, it could wait until after the family had eaten.

Twenty minutes later he had everything ready, but they still hadn't arrived so he was keeping it warm in the pan and under the grill. Another fifteen minutes and they still hadn't shown up. He'd tried calling but Sharon wasn't answering her phone. Finally, he decided to have his own meal. He served up a plate, making sure to leave enough for Sharon and the kids and sat down to enjoy his meal. He was just wiping up the last bit of egg yolk with a piece of bread when he heard the front door opening and the children's excited chatter.

So much for his idea of them all sitting down together for a nice Friday night tea. But he was determined to keep his cool.

Wee Joe was first through the door but stopped dead when he saw the damage.

'What happened to your face, Dad?'

Kelly and Sharon heard the question and came over to see what was going on. Kelly gasped and gave Larry a hug. Sharon looked concerned but thoughtful at the same time and he could see the questions forming in her mind.

'Don't tell me you've been fighting, at your age.' She had one of those looks that said 'I know you're going to come out with a story so at least make it a good one'.

He gave them the story he'd agreed with Casper. It was a complete accident. A customer had been peering into one of the fish tanks, Larry had come up behind him to see if the man wanted help and, as the man turned round, his head had caught Larry right in the nose. He tried to make it into a bit of a joke, mainly for the benefit of the kids, but for Sharon as well, though she didn't seem convinced.

After a few more questions he changed the subject. I've got a nice big fry-up ready for you.' he said, getting to his feet. 'You'll be hungry after all that exercise. I'll just dish it up for you.'

'Fry-up?' Sharon said. 'We've all been for a MacDonalds. You know we usually go for one after the swimming. That's more money down the drain.'

The kids looked at him as if to say sorry, but Sharon had that look on her face that made him feel like an idiot. She always seemed to find fault with whatever he did. He did know that they usually went for a MacDonalds but it had gone right out of his head when he thought of doing the fry-up. He looked at Sharon, but she just shrugged her shoulders. He looked at the kids, they were standing waiting to see what would happen next.

Larry's shoulders drooped, he said nothing, stepped over to the cooker and picked up the pan with the intention of dumping the lot in the bin.

'Can we not have a piece and sausage and potato scone?' Mum, Kelly said, her brother nodding in agreement.

Sharon didn't look too happy about it but she gave a curt nod then went out of the kitchen. The kids sat up at the table and made their pieces while Larry had another cup of tea and they told him all about the swimming.

A minute later Sharon came back into the kitchen. 'Don't bother saving any of that for me, I'm going out to the bingo with the girls.'

At least that means she won't be here to interrogate me, Larry thought. He picked up the pan, he set some of the food aside for putting in the fridge later, scraped the rest into the bin and clattered the pan into the sink.

The cat strolled over to Sharon and rubbed against her leg. She bent down to stroke it and it purred. It looked at Larry and then at Sharon as if to say 'I told him you wouldn't want a fry-up, and he never fed me either.'

Sharon picked up on the cue. 'I don't suppose you gave wee Sammy his dinner.'

Larry glared at the animal. 'Hang on, I'll just get it something.' He reached down and pulled a bit of square slice out of the bin. It was dried up and rock hard. He skited it at the cat and caught it right on the nose. The creature fixed his eyes on Larry and hissed from its refuge under the table, plotting its revenge.

Chapter 40

Larry's face was still aching but Saturday was their busiest day in the pet shop so he knew he had to go in. He went through the events of the last week as the bus made its way into the centre of town. His nose was still painful and served as a vivid reminder of his most pressing problem, Eddie Black. So far he'd escaped relatively unscathed. Okay he'd been beaten up, threatened and traumatised but Black still didn't know that Larry had seen him in the lane the previous week. That was a big plus.

On the down side, Casper and Sharon were still giving him grief and Sharon's threats about divorce were a constant worry. There was no way he could live without seeing his kids every day. The occasional softening of tone from his wife and his boss never lasted.

He was also worried about the pressure from the cops even though he'd managed to slip them a few useful snippets about Black without putting himself at risk. But Larry knew they wouldn't let up until they'd arrested the man.

On the plus side, his relationship with Kelly and Joe was in great shape. They were brilliant kids, they sensed the friction in the house but they looked out for him without taking sides between their parents.

Then there was Arthur, a potential source of cash. Despite his worries about Black and the cops, he was determined to see what he could conjure up with Arthur. He thought through the things he wanted to do in the next couple of days. He'd go to the Barras tomorrow and show the photos of the green Buddha to Dixie Finnegan. He'd tell Dixie that a mate of his had inherited it from his granny and was wondering if it was worth anything. It was almost true.

Then he wanted to speak to Arthur about a visit to the casino. He still had no idea how he was going to make that happen, let alone any idea what he would do if he ever got Arthur into the place.

He'd checked Google on Friday night. Rainman, that was the name of the film. In the story it had seemed fairly simple. Tom Cruise was a regular at casinos so he knew exactly how things worked. Larry would be depending on Tina. He thought he might have a game of cards with Arthur beforehand and try to assess how he could use his skills. Another possibility was roulette as Arthur might be able to remember all the winning numbers. Larry had never played roulette though he'd seen it in James Bond films and the like. No, cards seemed the more natural route. He'd speak to Tina later today and sound her out. What exactly would he ask her? He gave a mental shrug, he'd think of something.

Would there be any word from the cops today? The information he'd given them was useful, he knew that. McNally had played it down but that was just so he could keep Larry under his thumb, the bastard. They were bound to come in and ask Casper if Black had been pressuring him to sell his premises. Casper might suspect the information had come from Larry but he'd deny it. He could suggest the cops had simply come across it through their routine searching of any records relating to Eddie Black and Tony. In fact, for all Casper knew, Tony's widow, Maggie, could have told them.

Talking of unwelcome visitors, would they be getting another wee social call from Black and his two cronies? Casper had definitely got the message yesterday when he'd seen what Black had done to Larry's face. So surely he'd have already called the man and given him an answer one way or another. Larry would try and find out from Casper as soon as he got to the shop.

He didn't have to wait long. Casper was waiting for him as he went through the door.

'Did you tell the cops about Eddie Black trying to buy up the properties in the street?'

Larry had been rehearsing this in his mind. 'Me? No, are you mad? I wouldn't tell that lot a thing.'

'Well they called me last night, wouldn't tell me what they were after, but said they'd be round at the house first thing. And they were. The bastards obviously wanted me to sweat, wondering all night what the hell they were going to ask me about.'

'Aye, they did that with me as well. So what were they after?'

257

'Like I said. They wanted to know about Black trying to buy up the properties around here.'

'They came to your house, first thing in the morning? What did Christine say?'

'That was one good thing. She's away to a spa with her pal for a couple of days, so she's none the wiser.'

'So do they think there's something dodgy about Black going after these properties?'

Casper shrugged. 'I mean, they didn't tell me that. In fact they never really told me anything. It's all one way with them. They want information and they only give you a wee snippet if it helps them.'

'Aye, that's how they've been with me when they interrogated me,' Larry said, remembering his various run-ins with McNally and Wallace. He realised that Casper was continuing to be a bit more open with him than he'd been before. Previously, when Larry had asked him anything he would say, 'Don't ask', or 'You don't want to know'. Larry didn't understand what had brought about this change in Casper but the man now seemed more ready, even keen, to talk.

Larry realised he'd have to be careful in this new spirit of chattiness not to get drawn in and blurt out something that he didn't want Casper to know. With everything that had happened in the last week, he was losing track of the many variations on the truth that he'd told Casper.

Casper gave Larry a few more details about what Black had been up to and Larry filed them away in his brain under the heading of things he might tell the cops. He was surprised at how easily he'd fallen into the way of conspiring with McNally and his colleagues. His parents had always told him to respect the forces of law and order but ever since they'd died and he'd gone off the rails he'd got used to seeing the cops as the enemy.

There were quite a few customers over the course of the morning so it wasn't until late afternoon, when things quietened down, that Casper announced that he was nipping out on some business. Again, Larry wondered what business the man got up to. Whatever it was, it obviously helped Casper to fund his lifestyle.

Could it be drugs? There was no shortage of people involved in it these days. If so, was he doing it on his own, or was he somehow involved with Black? He recalled Black's reaction when Larry had told him that Casper was out on business. He had been angry, yes, but also puzzled. No, if Black knew that Casper had another source of income then he would surely already be muscling in on it. Larry remembered how Casper had reacted when he found out that Larry had told Black he was out on business. So, whatever it was, it was something Casper was desperate to keep secret from Black.

The rest of the day passed easily enough. No visit from Black or the cops. Tina popped in for her usual chat and with her usual bag of cakes. He told her that he'd try and speak to Arthur about the casino tonight. Tina said, with a wry smile, that she'd just broken up with her latest romance so she was available at short notice if the need arose.

She produced an Empire Biscuit from the pocket of her apron and took a bite. 'When are we talking about?' she said through a mouthful of crumbs.

'Sometime this week. What's a good day and time to go?'

'It's open seven days a week, from the afternoon right through to early morning. So it depends on when suits you.'

Larry thought about it, he hadn't really worked out how he was going to explain all of this to Sharon. He imagined the conversation. 'I'm going to the casino with Tina from the café and that daft guy that bought the rabbit.' Sharon would give him one of her looks. 'Oh aye, do you think so? And where would you get the money for that?'

'How much would it cost?' he asked Tina, trying to sound casual about it.

She laughed. 'You can actually spend a night there for nothing. Membership's free and you don't really have to gamble. If you do want to have a wee flutter, sometimes they offer deals for new people. I'll have a look online. The drinks can be quite expensive, right enough. Right,' she said, getting to her feet, 'I better get back before Rosa sends out a search party.'

Okay so you don't have to gamble, Larry thought, when Tina had gone. But if he didn't gamble, how could he make any money? He remembered the wad of money that Arthur had produced when he bought the rabbit. Arthur seemed to be a genius with numbers but he didn't really appear to understand money. Larry smiled, maybe he could work something out, after all.

When Casper got back Larry asked him if he could get away early.

'I was thinking. The shop's quiet now. I could pop over to that guy's house and chat him on about getting that second rabbit.'

Casper thought about it for a minute, then nodded. 'Fair enough. Make sure he buys the hutch and all the rest of the stuff.'

'No bother. In fact maybe I should take a few packets of that food supplement with me. I'll give you the money on Monday.'

Chapter 41

Just before four that afternoon, Larry left the underground station and made his way towards 'the only tree in Argyle Street', whistling as he went. Casper had told him to take four packets of the supplement so that would be another nice wee bonus for Larry after he added his own profit margin.

For once he remembered to call Sharon and let her know he'd be a bit late. She was mollified when he told her that the guy was a big tipper and in any case they had nothing planned for this evening.

Arthur seemed delighted to see Larry again but disappointed that he hadn't brought a new rabbit with him. As Larry walked down the hall he remembered that he still hadn't worked out how he might convince Arthur that a visit to a casino would be a good idea.

'I'm going to talk to you about a new rabbit, don't worry,' he said. He gave Arthur some more leaflets he'd picked up from the shop and this appeared to pacify him for the time being. After the mandatory 'hello' to his namesake, they spent some time talking about the pros and cons of Arthur getting a second rabbit.

Larry was torn about the idea. Casper expected him to make the sale and Arthur himself wanted the rabbit. Considering how much trouble the man had coping with one rabbit, Larry was convinced it would be too much for him. They eventually decided on a couple of options and agreed that Arthur would come into the shop next week to make a final decision.

With that out of the way, Larry gradually brought the conversation round to Arthur's prowess at 'Countdown'. He went on about how impressed he'd been and said that he was sure if Arthur ever decided to go on the programme as a competitor he'd easily win. Arthur seemed genuinely pleased at this, giving a shy smile.

'They don't get any money for winning on that programme, do they?' Larry asked innocently. He knew the answer but wanted to see how Arthur would react.

Arthur shook his head vigorously. 'No money, no. Mum said it would be a waste of time.'

This was unexpected. 'So you spoke to your mum about you going on 'Countdown'?

A nod of the head this time. 'She said it wouldn't be worth it and it would give the game away.'

Larry was intrigued. 'Game, what game?'

Arthur seemed to fold in upon himself. 'I'm not supposed to tell. It was a secret.'

What the hell was this about? 'So your mum had an idea for a game that would maybe make you money?' No response. 'You said it was a secret. So maybe it's not a secret any longer, now that….'

He stopped himself, not wanting to remind Arthur that his mum was dead, but he might have to. He studied him, it was like trying to coax a child. Arthur seemed to be wrestling with his own thoughts. 'Did you ever play the game?' Larry finally asked.

The head shook from side to side, the cheeks went red, the eyes started to fill up with tears. 'Mum died.'

Larry nodded. 'So you wanted to play it, but you never got the chance?'

For a moment Arthur said nothing, appearing to stare inwardly, maybe seeing memories of his mum. Larry had a thought.

'Have you got a picture of your mum?'

Arthur looked up, nodded.

'Can I see it?'

He chewed his lip, obviously a big decision for him. Finally, another nod and he went over to an old sideboard, opened one of the drawers, returned with the picture and thrust it under Larry's nose.

Larry wasn't sure how to react. It wasn't what he'd been expecting. From the little he knew of Arthur, he was a timid, naïve soul. Somehow he'd assumed the mother would be more or less the same. You couldn't always judge people by their photographs but the face staring out at him was the opposite of timid and naïve. It seemed full of craftiness and deceit, sharp nose, prominent chin. A hard face, cruel even, it reminded him of the witches you saw in the old children's fairytale books.

He remembered seeing a face like that one year when he went to the shows with his dad and sister. The woman was operating a stall with a card game in a dark corner at the back of the fairground. She had tried to draw Larry's dad in to chance his luck but he took one look and shook his head, his instincts obviously warning him to avoid it. As they walked away Larry had glanced back and the woman was glaring at them, muttering under her breath. Larry imagined she was putting a curse on them and he had nightmares about her for weeks afterwards. Arthur's mother was not quite in the same league, but nonetheless she had the look of a woman that you wouldn't want to mess with.

'She looks lovely,' Larry managed to say. 'What did she do?'

Arthur looked blank. 'Do when?'

'Did she have a job?'

Arthur's face took on the cagey look again. 'She helped people.'

Larry nodded. It was like drawing teeth. 'What people? How did she help them?'

Before he answered, Arthur looked all around as if someone might be listening even though there were only the two of them unless you counted the rabbit nibbling away at some lettuce leaves. He leaned forward so that their faces were almost touching. 'She helped people sell things.' His voice was almost a whisper. His face had such a secretive air that Larry wouldn't have been surprised if he had tapped the side of his nose and winked.

'Helped people sell things?' Larry imagined her as a telesales assistant or something like that. 'What people?' Larry repeated.

'Friends, special friends.'

'Okay, and what sort of things?'

Arthur got up and took the jade Buddha from the shelf. 'Things like this,' he said. 'For special friends.'

A picture was starting to form in Larry's mind. He glanced again at the picture of Arthur's late mother. Probably not a telesales operator. He looked at Arthur. 'Things that they couldn't sell in the normal shops?'

Arthur nodded, pleased that Larry seemed to understand.

Larry sat there trying to work out what this meant for his plans. It looked like Arthur, the shy, naïve Arthur, had a mother who had acted as a fence for stolen goods. Suddenly Larry felt a new sense of kinship with the man.

By treading carefully, Larry managed to piece the story together. As far as he could understand, Arthur's father had been part of the criminal fraternity and in his later years had become a fence.

When he had died, his wife, Arthur's mother, had kept the business going. Arthur seemed to have no real idea about the illegal nature of the activities but he did know he wasn't meant to talk about it to outsiders. Larry took it as a good sign that he'd felt comfortable in confiding in him.

It was only by luck, he wasn't sure yet if it was good luck or bad luck, that he'd got Arthur to talk about his mother's illegal activities. Larry was amazed at what he'd just found out and he had more questions about the mother's dealings. But, even though his curiosity was killing him, he didn't want to rush things, he'd come back to it later. Right now he was going to concentrate on his immediate plan. Larry watched while Arthur dipped an Abernethy biscuit into his tea.

'So, your mum wanted you to do something else, something more profitable, rather than go on the telly.'

A nod, a munch of the biscuit and a gulp of tea. 'She said if I went on the telly it would spoil the game.'

Larry dunked his own biscuit into his cup. 'What game? What did she want you to do?'

He watched Arthur struggle with the decision, to tell or not to tell. Finally he blurted it out. 'She wanted to take me to the casino, to play cards and to play the wheel game.'

Larry sat there open-mouthed. Could this be happening? The wheel game was obviously roulette. Arthur's mum had wanted her son to play roulette and some card games. With her criminal background she'd clearly realised the money-spinning potential of her son's unusual talents. But before she could put it to the test, she had died and now Larry could take on the role.

He'd been worried about how he could persuade Arthur to go to the casino. Larry had assumed the man would hate the idea of being put under pressure to gamble and win money. Maybe he would, but Arthur didn't see it like that.

He saw it as a game, a game that he and his mother had wanted to play but that he never got the chance to try out. Well, Larry was the man who could take care of that. He realised his biscuit was still dipped in his tea. He attempted to raise it to his mouth but it collapsed into the cup in a soggy mess.

With a few encouraging nods and prompts from Larry, Arthur told him about his mum's plan for the casino.

'She thought we could make money because I'm good at numbers.'

Larry couldn't believe his luck but did his best not to look too interested. 'She was right. You definitely have a talent.' He took a sip of his tea. 'But casinos are big noisy places. You might feel a bit out of place there.'

Arthur looked anxious, obviously struggling with himself. Eventually, he blurted out the words Larry was waiting for.

'Do you think you could take me to the casino?'

While laughing inside, Larry made a big show of appearing reluctant, said he didn't really have any spare time what with his work and his family. But when Arthur got upset Larry reluctantly agreed, on one condition. There were enthusiastic nods and hand-clapping from Arthur.

An hour later Larry sat in a daze as he made his way home on the underground. He touched his hand to his jacket, opened it slightly and peered down into the large, inside pocket. There, peeping out at him, was the green jade Buddha. Larry's luck was finally changing.

Chapter 42

It was early Sunday morning as Larry made his way along the Gallowgate with the Buddha safely stowed in his jacket. He'd persuaded Sharon to look after the kids for the morning. In fact he had to persuade the kids as well. The truth was that he loved spending Sundays with Kelly and Joe but he wanted to be on his own for what he was doing today. He'd told Sharon he had to get something for a customer and that was partly true. The Barras was Glasgow's traditional open-air market and it operated every weekend. It was scattered over a small group of streets about a mile east of the city centre, bounded on the south by London Road and on the north by the Gallowgate. In centuries gone by the Glasgow crowds would throng along the Gallowgate to watch their favourite entertainment, public executions. Today, the street still attracted the crowds, but they were there to see what bargains could be had.

The place was, famous, or infamous depending on your point of view, for offering Glaswegians the chance to acquire goods at knock-down prices. There was a huge range of products available, from second-hand sci-fi novels, to decrepit record players, crockery, duvets, watches, jewellery and devices, hacked TV-top boxes that let you watch any television channel you wanted for free.

Some people said the cheap prices were only to be had if you were prepared to compromise on quality, or turn a blind eye to the fact that much of the stuff probably figured on police 'wanted property' lists. In Larry's opinion that was an unfair judgement. Sure, there was knocked-off stuff to be had there, in fact he'd supplied some of it over the years, including his black market bottles of malt. But there were also some genuine bargains to be had if you knew where to look.

As well as the stalls and market halls themselves there were plenty of permanent shops and more than a few pubs. The bars wouldn't be open for another half hour and Larry noticed small groups of men and women waiting outside some of them, counting the minutes until the doors were flung open.

His dad occasionally brought him and his sister here, sometimes on a Saturday but more often a Sunday. His mother didn't often come with them but, when she did, she was after something specific, like bed sheets or dinner plates. Larry could still remember the patter of the stall-holders as they drew their customers in. Incredible bargains for the first person to put their hand up. Then a flurry of hands went up, not always sure what they were going to get for their money. The phrase 'a pig in a poke' came to mind.

When it was just his dad, then it was more of a browsing expedition. With no particular purpose in mind, they would pick through the second-hand books and CD's, the toys and the foreign coins. At some point during the day his dad would nip in to one of the many pubs for a pint of Guinness while Larry and his sister sat on the wall outside munching away at a bag of doughnuts.

Maybe it was just the different ways that a child and an adult looked at the world, but Larry felt the place had gone seriously downhill when he compared it to his childhood visits. It had always been a bit of a magnet for fly men and chancers but now, as Larry looked around him, there seemed to be dozens of people who were completely out of it on drugs or with that desperate look of the addict waiting for their next fix. A man and a woman were standing in the middle of the road, screaming at each other, enraged faces no more than inches apart, ignoring the looks from passersby.

Across the street, three men and a woman marched towards the city centre, one behind the other, stiff-legged and with vacant eyes, leaning forward as if that would get them to their destination more quickly. The leader had a plastic carrier bag clutched tightly in one hand and with the other he gestured angrily for people to clear out of his way.

From time to time Larry had to navigate round a person with outstretched hands and pleading eyes muttering 'help the homeless'. Others sat on pieces of cardboard with hand-written signs on the pavement in front of them and a tin with a few coins within safe reach. He ignored all of them as he weaved his way towards his destination.

Many of the stalls were outdoors and customers had to brave the notoriously changeable Glasgow weather as they eyed the merchandise on offer. To the untrained eye, the place looked chaotic but in fact there was a degree of order to the whole place once you understood it. Not all the stalls were outside; quite a few were squeezed into a dimly-lit and draughty building for customers or traders who preferred not to have to dodge the rain. There were several secluded corners within the building and it was to one of these that Larry was headed to consult with Dixie Finnegan. He'd known Dixie on and off over the years, the way you do, and had bumped into him a while back when he was checking up on the guy who was selling his whisky.

He heard Dixie before he saw him, the rasping voice attempting to persuade a potential customer that the item he was examining was worth at least ten times the price that Dixie was asking.

'So why are you selling it so cheap?' the customer quite reasonably asked.

Dixie didn't miss a beat. 'I need to be out of here today, pack up, get on my bike. My ex and her brothers are after me. So everything's going at bargain basement prices.'

Larry had heard Dixie's story about the ex and her brothers before and knew it was a fairy tale. As he edged forward, he saw Dixie but he held back until the business was concluded. The customer was holding what appeared to be a miniature Japanese house. He was turning it this way and that, obviously not convinced of its worth. Larry saw an opportunity to get himself into favour with Dixie.

He edged forward, nodded to Dixie and started browsing through the items on display. After a minute he half turned and pretended to notice the other customer for the first time. He tapped the guy on the shoulder and pointed to the little house that he was holding. 'Excuse me, mate, are you buying that?'

The man looked up as if he'd been nipped. He gave Larry a hostile stare then turned back to Dixie. 'How much did you say it was again?'

'Twenty quid,' Dixie said.

'If he doesn't want it, I'll buy it.,' Larry said.

The man nodded. 'I'll take it.'

A minute later the money had changed hands and the customer had left with his miniature house.

Dixie gave Larry a wink. 'There might be something through the back that you'd be interested in.' He told his assistant, a purple-haired Goth named Kylie, to look after things for a few minutes, then gestured with his head for Larry to follow him.

'So what can I do you for?' Dixie said. 'Thanks for that, by the way. The guy had been humming and hawing over that wee house for ages.'

'No problem.' Larry took his phone out. 'One of my mates has a wee Buddha statue, I think it's jade and he wants to know if it's worth anything.'

Dixie's face was inscrutable. 'A Buddha? Any idea where he got it?'

Larry shook his head. 'But I've got a few photos that he sent me. I told him I knew somebody who might know something about it.'

273

Dixie frowned. 'Photos might not be any use. I'd really need to see the original.'

'I know, I told him that. I've seen it but he was a bit reluctant to bring it out of the house in case it was a wild goose chase. I told him if he wants a definite answer then he'll probably have to bring it in for you to eyeball it.' Larry opened the first photo and handed the phone to Dixie. 'There are about six photos, just scroll down. At least they'll give you some idea.'

Dixie hummed and hawed as he examined the images, enlarging some of them to home in on certain areas. He scrolled back and forth between the pictures for a few minutes then nodded his head slowly. 'Who's this friend?'

Larry grimaced. 'He's asked me not to say too much for the minute. He's trying to keep it on the lowdown. I think maybe he doesn't want his wife to know. How, is it worth something?' Larry was acutely aware that he had the original tucked into the inside pocket of his jacket.

Dixie rubbed his chin and gave Larry a searching look. 'Worth something? That depends.'

Larry felt the excitement bubbling up. 'On what?'

'Give me a minute.' Dixie went back to the stall and pulled a magazine from under the counter. He flicked through the pages until he found what he was looking for. 'Have a look,' he said, pointing to an article accompanied by a couple of photographs.

Larry had to read the headline twice before the words sank in. 'Priceless Buddha statuette is stolen,' he read aloud. Fucking hell. He glanced at Dixie then skimmed through the rest of the story. The thing had been stolen a number of years ago from a touring exhibition when it was in Glasgow's Art Gallery. Despite a massive investigation and a reward being offered no word ever emerged of its whereabouts. He had to stop himself from patting his jacket to make sure the object hadn't disappeared.

'Jesus Christ. Do you think this is the same one?' Larry could hardly get the words out.

'Well, that's the sixty-four thousand dollar question,' Dixie said. 'Though, in this case, that might be an under-estimate.'

Larry studied the pictures in the magazine and compared them to the ones on his phone. To his eyes they were identical. He was already dreaming of a new house and exotic holidays. He realised Dixie was speaking to him.

'Sorry, what did you say?'

Dixie sighed. 'What I'm saying is that if this is the same Buddha then '*your mate*', Larry could hear the scepticism and the speech marks in Dixie's voice, 'could be on to a fortune. That's if it's the same one. Even then, there are a couple of wee problems.'

'Problems? Like what?' Larry was in no mood to have his dreams shattered just yet.

'Surely I don't need to spell it out to you.' He lowered his voice. 'You've sold enough stolen gear over the years, though nothing in this league.'

He waited for Larry to respond but on seeing his blank look, he went on. 'The thing's nicked, right. So although it's worth a lot of dosh, how do you sell it without the cops and the museum and the insurance company finding out about it? I mean we're not talking about a few cases of malt here. '

Larry scratched his head. He hadn't thought that far.

'That wouldn't be your only problem.' Dixie waited for Larry to speak but there was no reply. 'Somebody nicked this from a museum. If it wasn't your '*mate*', again the speech marks, 'then how did he get it? Did he nick it from the original thief? If so, then the cops could be the least of his worries.'

Larry was starting to realise how simplistically he'd been looking at this. Then again, he hadn't been expecting anything like this. He'd had no idea how much the thing was worth. He'd probably have said a couple of hundred quid, tops. This was something else.

He realised Dixie was waiting for him to say something. 'You said if it's the same one. Do you think it is?'

Dixie shrugged. 'All I can say from these pictures is that it could be. But the only way to be sure is to see it.'

'How come you're not sure?'

'Well, these pictures on your phone are enough to give me a fairly good idea but they're not good enough resolution to see all the details and one detail in particular.' He paused, making the most of his story. 'There's a wee twist in the tale. Rumour at the time was that, a number of years ago, long before the thing went on tour the owners had an almost perfect copy made. Apparently it's not unusual for that to happen with these valuable pieces.'

Larry looked at the photos on his phone again. 'A copy? What would they do that for? I mean presumably experts would know the real thing.'

Dixie nodded. 'Aye, it's not like they were trying to pull a fast one, or anything like that. The original is a few hundred years old, the copy was made about thirty years ago. It was a sort of back-up, you know? They would use it to show people when they weren't happy about bringing the real one out. It was pretty valuable as well. Not in the same league as the original, but not to be sneezed at.'

'Who made the copy?' Larry asked.

'They kept that a secret. Remember it was never even confirmed that there was a copy. There was a story that it was maybe some sort of decoy as well. In case there was ever an attempt to steal it. So they didn't want to give too much away.'

'Larry looked up from his phone. 'But it was stolen, wasn't it?'

Dixie smiled. 'Well, there's the thing. There was also a rumour that the one that was in the museum, the one that got nicked, wasn't the genuine article but the replica.'

Larry caught up. 'So that would mean that it was the replica that was nicked?'

Dixie nodded. 'Exactly. But it was only a rumour. There was never anything official said about it.'

Larry shook his head, trying to follow the story. 'So if that was the case, then where's the original and who's got it?'

Dixie raised his eyebrows. 'Good question. Nobody knows the answer. Or if they do, they aren't telling. The story was that the replica had an almost invisible mark on the base, three tiny dots in the shape of a triangle, done deliberately, that could only be seen with a magnifying glass.' He tapped the photo where Larry had captured the base of the Buddha. 'That was a good idea, to take a picture of the base, but it's not clear enough. I would need to see that, in the flesh, then I would know, maybe.'

'What do you mean, maybe?'

'Well all of this is just stories that I hear from people in the business.' He looked at Larry. 'Tell you what. I might be willing to take it off your hands. I'm sure I could find a buyer for it.'

'For a fee, I suppose?'

Dixie shrugged. 'I've got to eat. So, what do you want to do?'

Larry had to stop himself from whipping the Buddha out and presenting it to Dixie. He had to think this through. 'I'll need to speak to my mate and let him know everything I've told you.'

'Maybe he already knows,' Dixie said.

Larry could see the man was trying to read clues in his face. He changed tack. 'So what happened after it got nicked?'

'The owners made a claim, for the genuine one, of course, and the insurance company paid out, eventually. 'One, million, quid,' he said pronouncing each word slowly and deliberately. 'So if the insurance company knew that somebody had found the original they would be very interested, and very happy.'

Chapter 43

Larry was in a state of shock as he made his way towards Glasgow Cross. He navigated his way through the crowds without seeing them and crossed the streets without noticing the traffic. All he could think of was that he might be carrying one million pounds in his jacket. He had wrapped the Buddha in a thin sheet of bubble wrap before fitting it into his pocket but now he was paranoid that he might have damaged it in some way or that somebody would bump into him and break it.

Dixie had offered him what he called 'some words of wisdom'. He suggested that there was no way Larry or his 'mate' could sell the statue without attracting unwelcome interest from the cops or the insurance company or the criminals who originally stole it. Of course, if it was the replica it would be easier, but still tricky and potentially dangerous.

So Dixie advised Larry to consider a safer option. Notify the insurance company and claim the reward. Even though they'd paid out, they would still want to get the original back as they could recoup at least part of their money. How much was the reward, Larry had asked? He couldn't believe it when Dixie said it could easily be about fifty thousand quid. Not exactly a million, but a small fortune for Larry. Dixie was right, it would definitely be an easier option than trying to sell it. But, Dixie had cautioned him, even then, the insurance company and the cops would probably want to know how he'd come into possession of the statue. Larry would need to think about that one.

The fact that the Buddha belonged to Arthur didn't trouble him. He'd already let Larry borrow it without too much fuss. In any case, there was no way that it legally belonged to Arthur. It was certainly in his possession, but how could he own it? Not legally anyway. He imagined the scenario. Arthur's mum was fencing stolen goods for the Glasgow criminal fraternity. Somehow, in one of those transactions, she had come into possession of something worth a million pounds.

Was she just watching it for someone? If so, why hadn't they come back for it? But it might be the replica, not the original, a voice kept nagging him. Even that was worth a reasonable amount, maybe twenty thousand, according to Dixie. So the same question applied, but, whatever claim Arthur had, Larry wanted to get a slice of any money that was going. He'd speak to Arthur. They'd work something out.

It was a pleasant afternoon so he walked the couple of miles home. He was keen to get back and find out if he was carrying the real thing. He was used to disappointments so he was trying to keep his hopes in check and part of his reason for walking was to keep the dream alive by postponing the moment of truth.

As he made his way across the bridge over The Clyde he saw the casino that Tina had mentioned, over to his left, near Glasgow Green. In a few days he could be in there with Tina and Arthur making a nice few quid. But first things first, he patted his pocket, if he was carrying a million quid in his jacket, he might not need to bother with the casino.

He let himself into the house. It was quiet; Sharon must be out with the kids. He remembered seeing a magnifying glass somewhere in the house. Kelly had got one with some science kit they'd bought her for Christmas one year. The tubes and their contents had soon been abandoned but she'd held on to the magnifying glass.

After a rummage through the drawers in the living-room and the kitchen he eventually found it in a basket beside the phone. He whipped out the Buddha and examined it with the glass. He couldn't see any marks. Christ, was this the genuine article? He needed more light. He went into the kitchen, switched on all the lights and stood near the window. He put the statue on the worktop and examined the base through the magnifying glass. It took him a minute to get the focus right and when he did, there they were, three tiny dots in the shape of a triangle, just like Dixie had described. He had the fucking copy.

He was sitting staring at the telly when Sharon and the kids appeared half an hour later.

'How did you get on?' Sharon asked.

It took him a minute to remember he'd told Sharon he'd been doing something for a customer. 'Aye, fine, I got it sorted. I'll speak to the guy later.'

He needed to change the subject. 'Where have you three been?'

Joe ran over to him. 'Mum took us to the pictures. We went to see 'The Incredibles.'

'The Incredibles, Two,' Kelly said, rolling her eyes.

'It was brilliant,' Joe said. 'The wee guy, Dash, could run like crazy.'

His children's infectious enthusiasm and excitement slowly brought Larry out of his depression as they told him about the film. At first he was responding on automatic pilot but soon he felt himself caught up in the story.

Maybe it wasn't such a bad thing after all that Arthur had the copy and not the original. After all, Dixie had explained the difficulties and dangers that the genuine article could bring with it. He'd said that the copy would be worth a few bob itself. He should probably take it and show it to Dixie, get a more accurate estimate of what they might be able to sell it for. Or they could go for the insurance reward of maybe a few thousand. Not quite the same as a million quid but almost no risk involved. Of course there was still the small problem that it wasn't actually Larry's to sell.

Would Arthur want to keep it? He obviously regarded it as his mother's. How would he react if Larry told him the thing had been nicked? He might not care. Or he might fancy getting some extra money. Larry would need to think carefully about how to raise this with him.

Chapter 44

Larry looked around, admiring the plush décor of the casino. There were a lot of people in the place but, although there was an undercurrent of noise, it felt quiet. Arthur was standing with his mouth hanging open, staring at the lights and looking like he was about to wet himself.

'What do you think, then? Not bad, is it?' Tina said. 'I mean, it is a Wednesday night so it's not as busy as the weekend. I've been to a few different casinos and this is my favourite.'

Larry had to admit it looked the business. He thought about asking Arthur but decided there was no point. The guy looked like he was in a daze. Was there any chance of this working, he wondered?

Tina nodded towards Arthur. 'He doesn't exactly look excited, does he?'

Larry shrugged. 'It'll take him a bit of time to get used to it, but it was his idea.'

He had confided in Tina to some extent. Told her about how Arthur was some sort of genius at numbers and that he'd always wanted to go to a casino with his mum but she had died before they could do it. He hadn't told her about his 'Rainman' idea.

Tina gave him a sceptical look. 'I'm not saying he didn't ask to come, but I can tell by the way you're acting that you're up to something. You're not trying to pull some 'Rainman' stunt, are you?'

Christ, he thought, this woman was a witch. He said nothing, pretending to be looking at someone on the far side of the room.

Tina laughed and shook her head. 'Christ, don't ever play poker.'

He thought he'd been getting good at lying but Tina could see right through him. 'I just wondered if it might be a way to make some easy money.'

'Look, do you realise how hard that would be. If you saw the film, then you know they get spotted quite soon. And that was even with Tom Cruise knowing what he was doing.'

She let the silence hang in the air for a minute then gave a sideways look at Arthur. 'Anyway, we're here now, so we may as well have a wee wander round and see if anything takes our fancy.'

Larry still couldn't believe he'd got this far. He'd swung it with Sharon by telling her that Arthur had loads of money and was thinking about opening up a small business in Glasgow. He'd told her that the man would need help and he'd taken a bit of a shine to Larry. She'd raised her eyebrows and made a few noises but she'd agreed, especially when he told her that he probably wouldn't even need to spend any money.

Now that he was here, he realised he had no real idea if this was going to work. Tina was probably right. He turned to ask Arthur what he thought about the casino but Arthur had disappeared. Tina saw his reaction and pointed him out.

'He's wandered away, over to the roulette table'

'Christ on a bike. We need to keep an eye on him. Otherwise somebody might try and take advantage of him.' Larry tried to convince himself that wasn't exactly what he was doing. 'Come on, we better grab him before he puts all his money on the first number that takes his fancy.'

They caught up with Arthur just as he reached the table. He was staring at the wheel as if he was hypnotised by it. Larry could see he was talking to himself under his breath, probably following the run of the numbers.

Tina took charge. 'Right, if you want to play any of these games, the first thing we need to do is buy some chips. They come in different denominations and I'd suggest you go for the smaller amounts cause that gives you more options. But there's a minimum stake.'

They went over to a quiet seat in the corner and discussed money. Larry was hoping to spend nothing at all. He knew that Arthur had brought money with him and his plan was to ride on the back of that.

Arthur reached into his inside pocket and started to pull out a huge bundle of notes. Larry nearly had a fit when he saw the size of it. 'Don't bring it all out at once. Just take some of it out and leave the rest just now.'

Tina suggested Arthur got a hundred pounds worth of chips and said she'd get twenty pounds to start with. Larry could feel her eyes on him and reluctantly agreed to do the same. She took the money and went over to the cashier's window.

A few minutes later she came back with a fair-sized bundle of chips. 'Right, let's get this party started,' she said, doing a little dance. She gave Larry his chips and then gave Arthur some of his and said she'd keep the rest for the moment.

As they walked over to the table again Larry realised he'd only ever seen roulette wheels in James Bond films and the like. They were always surrounded by well-dressed players with huge bundles of chips in front of them and the guy in charge would say something in French at the start of each game.

There were a couple of blokes here who looked well-off and had plenty of chips in front of them but most of the players seemed to be holding modest amounts of chips and, to Larry, the whole thing was a lot more low key than in the films. The croupier, Tina had told him that what the guy was called, didn't speak French and every time the wheel stopped spinning and the ball settled in its slot there was an air of anti-climax.

Tina suggested they watch the game for a few minutes to get the hang of it and then make a bet if they wanted. She explained the different ways you could place a bet and spoke about the odds. As far as Larry could see, Arthur didn't appear to take this in. Maybe he already knew how it worked but his attention was on the wheel and he was obviously raring to go.

As he listened to Tina and watched the bets being placed by the players and swept away by the croupier, the cold reality hit Larry. He had absolutely no idea how he was going to work this. It was true that Arthur had a gift for numbers but how was Larry actually going to turn that into a winning formula. He decided he'd just need to go with the flow and see what happened.

Eventually they decided it was time to place a bet. Larry and Tina, with their limited funds, held off but Arthur was keen to get started. He chose number thirteen and, on Tina's advice, placed a five-pound chip on the board. A minute later the wheel came to a stop and the ball bounced back and forth before settling nicely into the number thirteen slot. Larry couldn't believe it. Was it going to be as easy as that? If only they'd put a bigger stake on.

Arthur passed his winnings to Tina then put a chip on number twenty-nine and once more it came up a winner. Larry felt his heart racing and Tina gave a quiet cheer. Arthur and gave Larry a shy smile. Obviously, the man had somehow worked out a system while he was watching the earlier games. Larry felt his heart thumping as he started to plan how he would persuade Arthur to give him a share of the winnings.

For the next game Arthur chose thirty-one and put twenty-five pounds on it. Tina placed a tenner each for her and Larry on the same number. She explained this would get them three hundred and fifty pounds each and a lot more for Arthur. Larry couldn't quite believe it was this easy. Might as well take advantage. He noticed one or two other players doing the same, they'd obviously clocked Arthur's winning streak.

As soon as all the bets were placed the guy spun the wheel and dropped the ball in. As the wheel spun and the ball rolled, Larry imagined walking in to Sharon and showing her his winnings. The wheel slowed, the ball bounced and bumped its way round the wheel, a moment later the wheel came to a stop and the ball jumped into number thirty-one before jiggling out at the last minute and settling firmly in its neighbour, number one.

Larry had heard of your jaw dropping but had never experienced it until now. He stood there in disbelief, he glanced at Tina who just shook her head in annoyance and then he looked at Arthur who seemed to be on the verge of tears and was muttering something to himself. The croupier showed absolutely no reaction, just as in the previous games. He simply reached out and gathered in all the losing bets. A couple of the people who had followed Arthur's bet glowered at him.

Tina nudged Larry's shoulder. 'Right, we should move on, take stock and have a think about what we do next.'

Larry nodded, still not able to believe that his dreams had been popped as quickly and as mercilessly as they had. Plus, that was half his twenty quid gone. He tapped Arthur on the shoulder and, when there was no reaction, pulled him away and, in silence, they followed Tina over to a table and chairs in the corner.

Tina used some of Arthur's money to buy them all a drink, wine for herself, a lager for Larry and a coke for Arthur. Larry was now moving on from disbelief to anger. He knew it was completely illogical to blame Arthur, especially as he had lost more than Larry but, he couldn't help himself. His anger had to have some target.

The voice of reason came from Tina. 'It's not surprising. That's the way the game works. Roulette is completely unpredictable. Plus all the games favour the casino in the long run.'

'You mean they're rigged?' Larry asked.

She took a sip of wine and shook her head. 'No, well there might be some places where they are but generally no. It's just that the odds mean that over the piece the casino, or the bookies win.'

'So how come Arthur won his first two bets in a row?'

Arthur had been sitting staring into his coke and his head lifted on hearing his name and was obviously keen to hear what Tina had to say.

'It's just your luck, your Donald Duck. Nobody knows where the ball's going to stop. I mean, if we had jumped in with him on his first or second bet we'd be laughing. If he'd stopped after his second bet he would be as well. Mind you, he's still ahead.'

Arthur was still muttering to himself and then he spoke out. 'It was the turn of thirty-one.' He recited a list of about fifty numbers, finishing with thirty-one then looked at them as if that explained everything.

Tina looked puzzled for a moment then she turned to Larry. 'Was he memorising the winning numbers? How the hell did he manage that?'

Larry shrugged and took a drink of lager. 'I told you, he's got a gift for numbers and a great memory.'

'You really think you can beat the casino with Dustin here.'

Larry was confused. 'Dustin?'

'From the film, the wee guy, the genius, Dustin Hoffman played him.'

Larry glanced at 'Dustin', who seemed to be still reciting his list of numbers. 'I'm sorry, Tina. He genuinely wanted to come and I thought, why not try and make the most of it for everyone. I was going to share the winnings with you.'

Tina laughed. 'That's very generous of you, sharing Arthur's winnings.' She leant forward to speak quietly to both of them. 'Look, you can be a genius with numbers but that doesn't mean you can beat the casino, especially at roulette. If you were going to try anything it would be a card game, like Blackjack, where you could at least try and follow the run of cards. Even that's hard, and a bit risky.'

'Blackjack?' Larry asked.'

'You'd probably call it Pontoons.'

Arthur perked up at this. 'I want to play the cards now.'

'Right, I'll give you some more of your chips and you can have a go at the cards, but you need to be careful and there's still no guarantees.'

'What do you mean, careful?' Larry said.

291

Tina looked round to see if anyone was nearby. 'Casinos don't like people who try and keep count of the cards that have been played. Remember, they're here to make money. So you need to be subtle.'

A few minutes later they were standing at the Blackjack table. Larry had played Pontoons in his youth for pennies but he'd never been any good at it. Tina had given them a brief explanation of how it worked in a casino. It was mostly double Dutch to Larry but Arthur seemed to follow what she was saying. Time would tell.

Arthur took a seat and Tina stood at his shoulder. Larry stood back trying to follow the action. Everything seemed to happen so fast, a lot faster than Larry remembered from his childhood games. Again the dealer, a woman in her thirties, had the same monotone voice and emotionless expression as the guy at the roulette table. After all, it wasn't her money she was playing with.

At first Arthur lost money but after a few hands he started to win. Larry felt himself getting excited again. Tina had explained that, unlike roulette which was a game of pure chance, Blackjack had more skill attached to it and, if you could remember the run of the cards, you could get yourself a slight edge. So Larry's dreams of foreign holidays and a new car were on the table again.

The game fluctuated as Arthur won and lost but slowly he seemed to be building up his pile of chips. A few people came to watch the game and all the seats at the table were occupied. Larry looked around the room, the place was filling up, especially for a midweek night. Obviously, a lot of people had money to spend.

He noticed one group walking past the roulette wheel because people moved out of their way to let them past. Maybe some sort of VIP, he thought. Then his heart thumped when he recognised the big guy at the front of the group. It was one of Eddie Black's thugs, Shug Dunbar, the one who had battered the rabbit to a pulp. What the hell was he doing here? Larry started to turn away before the guy could spot him but just as he did so the group parted and right behind Dunbar he saw his worst nightmare, the man himself, Eddie fucking Black.

Larry turned to face the table and kept his head down, pretending to concentrate on what was happening in front of him. Fuck, fuck, fuck. Why now? Why here? Tina looked at him, puzzled. He was wary of saying anything for fear of breaking her concentration or Arthur's but he tried to do some sort of subtle mime with his eyebrows and his head to indicate that bad news was on its way. Tina shook her head and turned her attention back to the game where it looked like Arthur had built a respectable amount of chips. Larry sensed a nervousness in Tina's expression and a moment later he was proved right.

Larry felt a presence at the table and a hand tapped Arthur on the shoulder. One of the casino employees leaned in and whispered something to him. Arthur looked round in panic then stood up and Tina gave Larry a look that seemed to say 'the game's up'. As he turned to follow them he came face to face with Eddie Black, Shug Dunbar and Vinny Stuart, all three grinning coldly at him.

'Well, well, if it isn't dumb and dumber, the rabbit lovers and the wee lassie from the café. I think we need to have a quiet word in private.' He turned to Dunbar and Stuart. 'Bring this lot to the office.'

They were escorted to a room at the back of the casino and ushered inside. Black sat behind a huge desk playing with some sort of ornament with metal balls swinging back and forth against each other. There was an egg-timer on the desk and Black tilted it up so that the sands started to run.

'Right,' he growled, 'you've got three minutes to convince me not to have the guys break your legs.'

Tina screamed and Arthur looked as if he was about to cry. Larry had no idea what to say. He knew it wasn't an empty threat but he couldn't work out exactly what had happened and what, if anything, he could do about it.

'We were just playing Blackjack, or at least he was,' Larry tilted his head in the direction of Arthur.

'But he wasn't just playing, was he?' Black said. 'He was winning. And how was he winning? By cheating, by counting the cards. Taking my hard-earned money off me.'

Tina tried to intervene. 'He just hit a lucky streak. I mean he lost at roulette.'

Black directed an icy glare at her. 'Listen, darling. Never try and kid a kidder. Our people are trained to spot that sort of thing. Plus we've got cameras all over the place.'

He paused when there was a knock on the door and the man who had first spoken to Arthur at the table came in. Black raised a questioning eyebrow. 'How much?'

'Two thousand quid,' came the reply.

'How much did he lose at roulette?'

'He won a few hundred quid and then he lost his stake on his third spin.'

Black pulled a face. 'That's a shame, but that's how it goes. So if we give him back a few quid, we're all square?'

Black wasn't looking for an answer. Larry couldn't believe it. His plan was a disaster, a joke. Before he realised what he was doing he spoke out. 'Me and Tina both lost a tenner on the roulette.'

Black looked at his men then laughed. 'A tenner? Well maybe that'll teach you not to get involved in stuff you haven't got a fucking clue about. I'm feeling generous. You can cash in your original chips and...' he pulled three ten pound notes from his pocket and threw them onto his desk and looked at each of them in turn. '...take this as your winnings for the night and get the fuck out. I'm sure I don't need to tell you not to show your face here again.'

Larry took a step forward and picked up the money. As he turned towards the door to follow Arthur and Tina he almost froze on the spot.

There, in an alcove facing Black's desk was an exact copy of Arthur's Buddha statuette. He corrected himself. No, Arthur's was the copy. So that could only mean one thing.

Chapter 45

They decided to have a drink to drown their sorrows and Larry suggested 'The Scotia Bar' which was only a few minutes' walk from the casino.

'This is some place,' Tina said, looking around her. 'I've never been in here before.'

Larry's mind was buzzing with what he'd seen in Black's office. What, if anything, could he do about it? He wondered if Arthur had noticed the Buddha.

He took a drink of his pint before replying. 'It's meant to be the oldest pub in Glasgow, or at least one of them. It's a lot better than these new places with all those posers.'

Tina glanced at the clientele. 'Not a lot of posers in here,' she said.

'How are you feeling, Arthur?' Larry said. He was aware that the other man looked frightened and hadn't said anything.

'Those men were scary. I saw them before, when I came to buy the rabbit.' He looked as if he was expecting Black and his men to appear at any minute.

'I'm sorry about that, Arthur. Those guys are vicious.'

Arthur nodded his head vigorously. 'And they stole my money.'

Larry shrugged. 'I know. They're a law to themselves. Maybe we can try another casino at some point.'

Larry was aware of Tina giving him a look of disbelief but his comment brought a smile from Arthur. He doubted if they'd ever do it but he wanted to cheer the guy up. He felt vaguely responsible.

'I like it this place,' Arthur said. 'It's cosy.'

Larry nodded. 'It's quiet tonight, but quite often there's live music.' He took another drink and made an effort to think about something other than the Buddha statue. He looked at Tina. 'So, what happened back there?'

She shrugged. 'It was what I was warning you about. These places know that some people try and count the cards to get an advantage. It's not illegal but they don't like it, so the staff are trained to watch out for it. Like he said, they've got cameras all over the place.'

'How could they tell what he was up to?' Larry asked.

Tina glanced at Arthur before replying. 'Well, Arthur wasn't too subtle about it. He was more or less counting under his breath. I saw the warning signs and was about to call a halt when the heavy mob appeared.'

'Did you know that Black owned that casino?'

'Are you crazy? Do you think I'd take us in there if I knew? The guy's bad news. I suppose it doesn't really surprise me. That type will go wherever there's money to be made.'

Larry nodded. She was right. 'How do you know so much about it anyway?' he asked. 'I know you've been to the casinos a few times but you really seem like an expert.'

'I used to work for Tony, in the bookies. I was really good at calculating the odds and all of that stuff. My dad and my granddad were always into the horses. There was a bookies right next to our close and they were always in and out of there. I picked up a lot of the stuff from them over the years. Then I decided to learn about the gambling that went on in casinos. I read up on it and every time I went I studied it a bit more.'

Larry stared at her. There was obviously a lot more to Tina than he had realised. 'I never knew you'd worked for Tony. How come you stopped?'

She made a face and took a sip of her drink before responding. 'He was a bit free and easy with his hands, if you know what I mean.' She took another drink. 'I wasn't going to put up with that. So I told him where to get off. I managed to get a job in the café the next day and I told him I was leaving.'

'So that's how you think he might have been having an affair with somebody and got himself killed?' Larry said.

'Well, it would be in character, know what I mean?'

'Was it not a bit awkward still bumping into him most days?'

'No, I spoke to him straight. Told him I didn't care what he got up to but that he wasn't doing it with me.'

'And he just accepted it?'

Tina took another drink. 'Aye, it wasn't really a problem.'

On his way home Larry's thoughts returned to the statue in Black's office. How had he got hold of it? Was he the one that nicked it in the first place? Or had he acquired it later? Maybe somebody had given him it to satisfy a debt. Then he had a panicked, crazy thought. Had Black somehow found out about Arthur's Buddha and broken into Larry's house to steal it? As soon as he got into the house he hurried to the hiding place he'd found for it and checked. Of course it was there, safe and sound. So Eddie Black had the real McCoy. Could Larry somehow turn this to his advantage without ending up like that rabbit?

Chapter 46

Next morning he woke early after a restless night dreaming about roulette wheels, Buddhas and rabbits. He'd calmed down after the disastrous night at the casino. With hindsight he realised he never stood a chance of pulling it off. Tina had explained that it wasn't enough to have somebody that was a genius with numbers; you had to know what you were doing with the cards as well. If he'd confided in her up front they might have been able to work up a plan but even that would have been a long shot.

So, it looked like his main chance of getting some extra cash was the Buddha. Arthur had let him take it home and even hinted that it was a present to Larry for taking Arthur to the casino. That was good enough for Larry. Finders keepers. As soon as he got the chance, he'd speak to Dixie and then decide if he should sell it or hand it in for the reward.

The kids had some event on at school and Sharon had left early with them so he was spared her interrogation about last night. As he got ready for work, he realised he had something else he could tell the cops. Tony had been fond of chancing his arm with the ladies and that could have led to him being murdered. But he realised that, if he told them that and where the information had come from it would lead back to Tina. They might then suspect Tina of having killed Tony. Even though he knew that was ridiculous, the cops didn't think the same way as normal people and he didn't want to give Tina any grief.

The other piece of information he had for the cops, the big piece of news, was that Eddie Black was the proud owner of a Buddha statuette said to be worth a million quid. Larry was surprised that Black had the item out for anyone to see. Then again, he probably didn't let just anyone into his office and would hide it away if necessary. No doubt Black thought that it wouldn't mean anything to Larry, Arthur or Tina.

How could Larry benefit from it? He could report it and get the reward but Black might realise Larry was the one behind the tip-off. That was definitely not something he fancied. Anyway, one thing at a time. Right now he had to get to work, and pray he didn't get any hassle from Black or the cops today.

On his way to the bus stop he called McNally. He hadn't decided to tell him anything dangerous yet but he wanted to show willing and keep him off his back. McNally answered on the first ring.

'Well, Mr McAllister, I was wondering when I'd hear from you. You haven't exactly been overwhelming us with information.'

Larry fought to control his temper. Did this guy not know how dangerous it was to be around Eddie Black? 'I've been keeping my eyes and ears open but it's not easy. I don't see Black all that often and he's a careful sort of guy.'

McNally was silent for a moment. 'Well, that isn't my problem. Have you got anything for me?'

'I was at a casino last night, 'The Green Rooms', and Black and his heavies were there. It was pretty obvious that he owned the place.'

'I didn't have you down as a casino type of guy,' McNally said. 'You told us you weren't into gambling.'

Christ, did this guy remember every word you said? 'Aye, well it was actually only my second time.'

'Did he see you?'

'He saw me all right, and he made a point of letting me know I shouldn't come back.'

'How come?'

Larry cursed himself. He'd gone too far again. 'A guy I was with was doing well at the blackjack and Black wasn't too happy about it. So he gave us a warning and basically threw us out.'

'Well, we had heard rumours about him owning the casino, so that confirms it for us. That's something I suppose. Did you see anything that links him to Tony Hamilton's murder or even anything illegal?'

'No, sorry.' As he said it he saw, clearly, in his mind's eye the Buddha statuette standing proudly in the alcove in Black's office but he managed to stay silent. He needed to get things in order before he told them everything.

'Right, okay, I expect we'll be seeing you soon.'

Larry asked McNally what he meant by that but there was no answer, the line had already gone dead.

When he got to the shop the shutters were still down and the place was in darkness. Larry checked the time, nine o'clock. It wasn't like Casper to be late, especially if he hadn't contacted Larry. He opened up and started to get things ready.

A few minutes later Christine walked into the shop. Larry did a double-take. He'd never seen her anywhere near the shop before. It definitely wasn't her style, but his surprise at seeing her quickly gave way to curiosity when he saw that she was clearly upset.

She didn't waste time getting to the point. 'Do you know where he is?'

Even though it was obvious who she was talking about Larry couldn't help himself from asking. 'Casper? No, I've no idea.'

'He went out late last night, about eleven o'clock. Said he had to meet somebody but wouldn't tell me who.'

Larry was wary of saying too much. His first thought that it was something to do with Eddie Black. There was also the possibility that Casper was having an affair though he didn't really think that was the case. Casper didn't strike him as the type.

'Did it come out of the blue?' he asked.

Christine nodded, trying to hold back the tears. 'Somebody phoned him earlier, I don't know what it was about.'

Larry had never had much time for her. She was a bit of a snob as far as he was concerned and looked down her nose at him and Sharon, but he didn't like to see people upset.

'Come through to the back shop,' he said, 'I'll get you a cup of tea and we'll make some phone calls.'

Half an hour later they'd exhausted their ideas. They'd phoned Sharon first but she had no idea where he might be. She said she'd let them know if, by any chance, he got in touch with her and they promised to do likewise.

'Has he ever done this before?' Larry asked.

Christine shook her head. 'No. Well just once actually that I remember. He had to go out once because the police called to say that the shop had been broken into.'

Larry looked at her. He didn't remember that happening. It must have been before he'd started working in the shop.

Christine gave a bitter laugh. 'I mean, who in their right mind would want to break into a pet shop, especially this one.'

Larry agreed but decided not to comment. 'Talking about the police,' he said. 'Have you contacted them?'

'For a missing husband? No, they'd just say he was out boozing or something.' She got ready to leave. 'Anyway, thanks for trying. I'll let you know if I hear from him. You do the same.'

It was less than an hour later that Casper turned up, looking like shit. He limped into the shop in bare feet that were cut and bleeding. Larry stopped what he was doing. 'God almighty, what happened to you?'

Caser slumped onto a chair. 'That bastard, Black. He more or less fucking kidnapped me last night.'

'Kidnapped you?'

'Made me go out to meet him near his casino. Said it was urgent. When I got there, his heavies threw me into a car and took me to some godforsaken spot down the Clyde coast. Took my phone, money, cards, keys, everything, my shoes as well, then locked me up in some sort of shed or barn in the middle of nowhere.'

'They left you in there all night?'

Casper nodded. 'Came back this morning and let me out. They just laughed when I asked for my stuff. Said it would only take me a few hours to walk home.'

'Christ, you've walked all the way here?'

'No, after a while I managed to cadge a lift from this bloke who was coming up to Glasgow with a delivery. He dropped me round the corner.'

Larry shook his head. 'Well that was something. That Black's an evil bastard. What was he after this time?'

Casper didn't reply for a moment. He seemed to be remembering his ordeal. 'Same old story. More pressure to get me to sell him the property. He says that's my final warning. Next time it'll be Christine and me, and we won't be coming back.'

'Jesus fuck. I know it goes against the grain, but you either need to sell him the shop or tell the cops.'

'I can't go to the cops. He'd find out and then it would be even worse.'

Larry almost laughed. 'What could be worse than him killing you?'

Casper looked at him with a haunted stare. 'There are different ways of being killed.'

'You better phone Christine.'

'Did she call you?'

'No, she was in here, going frantic. I've never seen her like that before. I'll need to let Sharon know.' Larry looked Casper up and down. 'When Christine comes to get you, maybe you should go and see the doctor, get your feet looked at.'

Chapter 47

Larry had been wondering what to about the Buddha statues. He could ask Dixie for advice but the guy would be after a cut of the money so he didn't want to do that unless he had absolutely no other choice.

Dixie had said the insurance people would pay a hefty reward for the genuine one, so they were the ones to contact. He went over to the computer and opened Google. The first search gave him so many hits that it was useless. He thought back to what Dixie had told him and that article about the robbery. He keyed in a few extra words to narrow down the search, Sharon had shown him how to do that. After some trial and error he found what he was looking for. An entry that referred to the theft of the Buddha, a few years ago, when it was on display in Glasgow. At the very end of the item there were a few cross-references. One of them was for the police and one was for an insurance company. He saved the number into his mobile under Buddha, he hesitated for a moment, then hit the button.

The call was answered almost immediately. He launched into a convoluted explanation before he realised he was speaking to a machine. He was advised that the call would be recorded 'for training purposes' and then was asked to pick from a menu of numbers. He listened all the way through the menu but nothing seemed to fit what he was after. Because he took so long to make his mind up the call was automatically ended. He swore and dialled it again.

This time he knew he would need to pick one of the options even if it didn't seem like it fitted. He ignored the options for making a claim, renewing your premium, changing your payment details and a couple of others. Eventually he was offered the final option of 'speaking to one of our agents'. He didn't remember hearing that the first time.

He was on hold, listening to music when he remembered that the call would be recorded. A moment later a pleasant Welsh voice came on the line and asked him for his name. Larry panicked and said he'd rather not give his name at the moment. He was speaking in the Irish accent he sometimes he put on to make the kids laugh. His dad was Irish so he felt he was entitled.

'Yes, hello,' he said. 'I might have some information about an item that was stolen.'

'Does this relate to a claim that you've previously submitted sir?' the lilting voice asked.

He was getting agitated. 'No, it's about something famous that was stolen in Glasgow. A Buddha statue.'

'I'm sorry sir,' the woman said. 'Did you say a butter statue?'

'No, a Buddha statue.' He spelt it out.

'I see, and you have some information about it?'

'Aye, it was nicked from a museum in Glasgow.' He suddenly realised he was speaking in his own voice again. 'Glasgow,' he repeated quickly, in the Irish accent.

There was a pause on the other end of the call. No doubt the woman was alerting her supervisor that she had some madman on the phone talking about Buddha and who kept switching his accent.

'Can I ask why you called us, sir,' she said pleasantly.

'In the newspaper reports it said you were offering a reward for information that would help find it.' He was back to the Irish again.

Silence. A longer pause. 'Right, sir. I'm going to pass you over to one of my colleagues. He'll be able to help you with this.'

He had visions of the call being traced, the police already alerted, a squad being readied to come and get him, but he held his nerve and didn't hang up.

A minute later a hard-sounding man's voice came on the line. The accent was maybe Birmingham, Larry thought. 'This is Clive Wilson. I believe you might have some information relating to the Buddha statuette. Is that correct, sir?'

This guy sounded scary, Larry thought. He wanted to go back to the nice woman with the lilting Welsh accent. He swallowed. 'Yes, that's right.'

'Can I have your name, sir?'

'I don't want to give you my name just in case.'

'In case what, sir?'

'I don't know. In case there's trouble.'

'We're talking about a valuable item, sir. My colleague said you mentioned the possibility of a reward. If you're after a reward then, in the end, we'll need your details.'

'I know, but I want to check out the basics first before telling you my name and so on.' He was now on half Scottish, half Irish.

There was a brief pause. 'Fair enough. So what can you tell me? Have you seen the statue recently?'

Larry nodded even though the man couldn't see him. 'Yes, and I've seen the copy as well.' He cursed himself. He hadn't meant to mention the copy, but it was out now and maybe it would work for him.

There was a definite silence at that. 'Copy, I'm not sure what you're getting at.'

'A friend of mine, who knows a bit about these things, told me a copy was made, for security.'

'I see, well I can't comment on that.'

Arrogant bastard, Larry thought. 'So you wouldn't be interested in getting the copy back as well?'

Another brief pause, then a sigh. 'Maybe you could start by telling me what you know about the statuette. Where you saw it, how you know it's the same one we're offering a reward for and so on.'

Larry had a sudden moment of panic. What if it wasn't the same one? He'd only seen it for a brief moment, across the room. Maybe there was more than one copy. He gave a description of the statue, plus some further details of the circumstances, said that it might be difficult, even dangerous to retrieve it, without specifying where he'd seen it, or when, or even what city he was in.

He had absolutely no idea which accent he was using by now.

'Right, sir,' the man said, when Larry came to a halt. 'We would definitely be interested in learning more and we would want to keep in touch. Do you have an email?'

No way, Larry thought. 'Sorry, no, but I can call you back on this number.'

Wilson gave him a different number, one that he said would get directly through to him. 'Have you been in touch with the police, sir?' he asked.

'No, not yet.' At least, not about this, he said to himself.

'I would recommend you get in touch with them.' He gave Larry a reference number to quote if he spoke to the police. 'We will, of course, be informing them of this conversation.'

'So, if I speak to the police and let them know where it is and who has it, I'll get the reward?'

'We're getting ahead of ourselves, sir, but in theory, yes.'

'How much is the reward?'

The man hummed and hawed. 'That's hard to say at this stage. It depends on exactly how good your information is and what part it plays in securing the return of the item.'

'Give me some estimate,' Larry said.

'Ten thousand pounds, maybe more.'

'I was told it was a hundred thousand.'

'Well, as I say, it depends on the exact circumstances. If you were able to deliver the copy as well, then we might be able to consider a higher amount?'

'So there is a copy after all?'

'I really can't say more at this stage, sir.'

He knew he was snookered for the moment unless he was willing to give them his details and get some guarantee in writing. He didn't want to let them know who he was just yet. He thanked Wilson and said he'd call back tomorrow. As soon as he ended the call he realised that all his carry-on with accents had been a waste of time, they would have his mobile number and could trace him through that.

He was still thinking through the repercussions of this when the door was flung open, banging against its hinges and Black and his two men muscled their way in. Black wasted no time.

'Is he in the back office?'

Larry wasn't going to make the same mistake as last time. 'No, he's away home to get himself cleaned up and that, get his feet sorted.'

Black looked at his men and they all grinned. 'He needs to be more careful. A man of his age, losing his shoes and walking about in the middle of the night. It's not good for his health.'

Larry said nothing.

'Tell him I've got his phone. I'll be back later to have a wee chat with him. There's some interesting stuff on there. Isn't that right, boys?'

The 'boys' nodded and grinned. They reminded Larry of the evil twins from 'Hellraiser'.

Black turned to go and then stopped. 'I meant to ask. How did you enjoy your wee night out at the casino? That guy who was with you. He's been in here before hasn't he?'

'Aye, he came in to buy a rabbit.'

'Is that right? Well tell him if he ever thinks about counting cards in my casino again, I'll put the two of you and his rabbit into a couple of bin bags and dump you in the Clyde.' He leaned into Larry so that their faces were inches apart. 'Understand?'

Larry nodded frantically. 'Oh aye, definitely.'

Ten minutes after Black left, Tina turned up. 'I saw that evil bastard coming in earlier and I waited for him to leave.'

'Did he come into the café?'

'No, thank God. Did he say anything about last night?'

'Gave me a gentle reminder that if I ever try anything funny again or even go near his casino he'll make me suffer for it.'

'Well you'll not be going anywhere near that place anyway, will you? I don't think I'll be going back there again either. Not while he owns it anyway. Right, I better get back.'

Chapter 48

The next couple of hours were uneventful. Larry phoned Sharon and they talked about Casper. She'd already spoken to him but Larry didn't know what he'd have told her so he stuck to an edited version of events and played dumb when she tried to get more information out of him.

There were only a handful of customers over the course of the day and only one of them bought anything. Larry was wondering, yet again, how Casper made his money when McNally and Wallace arrived.

Christ, what a day this was turning out to be, he thought. First Christine, then Casper turning up like that, then Black doing his usual and now this lot. Probably wanting to know why he hadn't given them enough information to prove that Eddie Black had killed Tony. He grunted a hello.

McNally looked at his colleague, pretending to be offended. 'That isn't very nice, is it DC Wallace? I mean, here we are fighting to uphold law and order and that's the greeting we get. No offer of a cup of tea or anything.'

Wallace laughed on cue. 'Don't know if I fancy a cup of tea in here. The animals might have pissed in it.'

Larry was in no mood for their nonsense. 'If you want tea, there's a nice wee café just next door.'

He picked up a stock sheet trying to look busy. 'So, what can I do for you?'

McNally smiled, showing the gap in his teeth. 'That's more like it. Well, it's really Mr White we're looking for.' He jerked his head towards the back shop and started to move in that direction. 'Is he in?'

'No.' Larry hesitated, wondering how much to tell them. He decided to err on the side of caution. 'He's not well, phoned earlier to say he wouldn't be in today.'

McNally seemed to be weighing up if Larry was telling the truth. He looked towards the back of the shop as if he might see Casper there. Finally he nodded slowly. 'Okay, we'll find him at his house then.'

'Anything else?' Larry was keen to know why they wanted to speak to Casper but there was no way he was going to let them see that. 'I've got a lot to do here.'

'Oh aye, we can see that.' McNally made a show of surveying the shop. 'Run off your feet by the looks of it.' He moved in closer to Larry. 'The thing is, I'm a bit disappointed in you, Mr McAllister.'

'About what?' Larry swallowed. He knew what was coming.

McNally shook his head and laughed. 'About what?' He looked at Wallace for approval. 'Can you believe this guy?' He turned back to Larry. 'I'm still waiting for something useful on Eddie Black. You've not exactly been a mine of information, have you?'

316

'I phoned you this morning, first thing, didn't I.' Larry knew that what he'd told McNally that morning wasn't up to much but he wasn't going to admit to that.

'You did, you did, but you only told me stuff I already knew.'

Larry was genuinely angry, despite knowing he was in an impossible position. 'Look, how the fuck do you expect me to find out stuff about Eddie Black? Especially something that will prove he murdered Tony Hamilton?' He looked at both of them. 'I mean, you're the cops, for Christ's sake. You must know a lot more than I'll ever know.' He spread his arms, case closed.

McNally looked genuinely saddened by this outburst. 'You were at his casino last night, weren't you? If we had gone in there, the alarm bells would have been ringing. You were just another customer.'

'Aye, but only up until he threw me out.'

'You said the guy you were with was doing well at blackjack. What's this bloke's name?'

Larry was starting to feel nervous. 'His name? What do you want that for? He's just a guy.' Larry tried to tell himself it was no big deal. Arthur couldn't really tell them anything incriminating. Then again, you could never tell. Arthur wasn't street-wise. These guys would be able to get him to say anything. Then there was the fact that his house might be stuffed to the ceiling with stolen property.

McNally obviously had finely-attuned radar that could spot lies or evasiveness at a hundred yards. 'Is there something you're trying to hide?'

'No.' He could feel the sweat starting to trickle. 'The guy's a wee bit strange. He doesn't cope well with strangers. I only met him a wee while ago when he came in here to buy a rabbit.'

'So, what's his name, this new best friend of yours?'

Larry was thinking fast. He needed a diversion. 'Listen, I've just remembered. There was maybe something that you might be able to get Black for, but you need to keep me out of it, at least as far as police records go.'

McNally leaned in. 'I'm listening.'

Larry clicked on the computer and brought up the images of the Buddha. He angled the screen so that they could see it. 'This statue was nicked a few years ago while it was on display in a Glasgow museum.'

'So?' McNally didn't try to hide the boredom in his face and voice.

'So,' Larry continued, 'it's in Black's casino. On display on a shelf in his office.'

'How did you come to see it?' Wallace asked.

Larry turned to look at him, he'd almost forgotten the younger officer was there. 'When he hauled us in to warn us.'

'Warn you? 'McNally said. 'About what?'

'Not warn us, threaten us. Tell us he was throwing us out because my pal was doing too well at blackjack.' Larry realised he was opening that can of worms again so he quickly moved on.

318

'I saw this wee statue and the next day I happened to spot this article about it getting nicked from Kelvingrove Art Gallery. It says that it's worth a quarter of a million.'

Wallace was starting to look interested but McNally was still sceptical. 'You 'happened to spot this article'. A wee bit of a coincidence, wasn't it? You're taking the piss. How would you recognise something like that?'

Larry thought desperately. Suddenly inspiration hit him. 'My daughter.'

'Your daughter?'

'She's doing a project on the Art Gallery for school.' Where had that one come from? God, he was getting really good at pulling lies out of thin air.

He looked McNally straight in the eye. 'Black must have been the one that nicked it. Or at least he bought it from the guy that did.' He glanced from one to the other, looking for a reaction. 'You could definitely charge him for that.'

McNally looked thoughtful. 'I'd maybe need to speak to one of the people in the Art Theft section.' He leaned in close to Larry. 'If you're winding me up, I'll make your life hell.'

How would that be different from what you're doing now, Larry didn't say. 'You'd obviously need to catch him unawares. If he knew you were coming he'd put it out of sight.'

The two policemen looked at each other and laughed. 'Do you think so?' McNally said. 'I would never have thought of that.' He shook his head. 'Thanks for telling us how to do our job.'

Larry felt himself getting angry. 'Christ, I'm just trying to help you.'

'And help yourself, I assume,' Wallace said. 'There'll be a reward for this thing.'

'I've already been in touch with the insurance people. I told them I'd be talking to you today.'

'Did they give you a reference number and contact details?' McNally asked.

Larry passed on the information. Christ, it was actually going to happen. He was going to get the reward, but he had to make sure Black had no idea where the information came from. 'Listen, you need to go in to his place for some other reason. If he finds out I've shopped him, he'll kill me.'

McNally glared at him for a moment. 'We'll do what we need to do.' After a minute he finally nodded. 'No promises, but we'll try and think of something.'

They took a few more details before ending the conversation and Larry was left alone in the shop to think over what he'd done and daydream. Dixie had said it could be worth a million quid, so the reward might be a hundred thousand. No, no way. He couldn't believe that. He gave himself a shake. The guy on the phone had said ten thousand. What if the cops try and claim the reward? With that thought he called Wilson, the insurance man, on his direct number. He gave him his own details and said he was now willing to tell the police where they could find the statue. But first he wanted a better idea of how much reward he could expect.

'Well now that I have your name and so on I can email you a standard agreement form. It will show that the reward will be between five and ten per cent of the agreed value.' Wilson paused. 'Before you ask, the agreed value is not something I am prepared to discuss now, but you should be in for a tidy sum.'

'What about the copy statue?' Larry asked. He might as well get as much out of this as he could. A little voice reminded him that the copy belonged to Arthur. Then again, it was almost certainly nicked as well. He didn't want Arthur to get in trouble and Arthur had more or less given it to Larry.

'Well obviously the copy is much less valuable, but yes, we'd be keen to get it back and there would be a small reward.'

Larry told him he was going to speak to the police right now and would give them the information and Wilson's details.

He ended the call. Christ, he thought, I've done it. I've actually done it.

He spent the next few hours in a daze. Casper called to say he wouldn't be in the shop as he had business to take care of. Larry thought he sounded a bit odd but then again it wasn't surprising given what had happened to him last night. He was desperate to tell someone about the reward but there was no way. He had to be patient, but there was still the business of the copy statue. Should he try and sell it to Dixie? It was a bit riskier but he would get more than what he'd get from the insurance company. He decided to close the shop early and pay Arthur a visit.

'Have you recovered from last night's excitement?' Larry asked, as he settled himself in one of the armchairs.

'Excitement?' Arthur asked. 'What do you mean?'

He realised Arthur didn't get his attempt at a joke. 'Nothing. I just meant that the guy was pretty angry with us.'

'The shark man?'

'The shark man? Oh, right, Eddie Black. Good name for him. But did you enjoy your night? The roulette and the blackjack?'

Arthur shrugged, he didn't look too happy.

'What is it?' Larry asked.

'I thought it would have been easier. It was noisy and everything was a bit fast.'

'Aye, I know what you mean. It was a bit overwhelming. But, that's life sometimes.'

Larry could see Arthur was still shaken by what had happened and realised he felt responsible. It had been Arthur who had asked Larry to take him to the casino but even so, Larry knew he had taken advantage of the guy. But he'd done that sort of thing before so why did it bother him this time?

He gave himself a shake; it wouldn't do to get too upset about it. He sensed an opportunity so he pushed his feelings of guilt to one side.

'Listen, Arthur, there are some bad people out there. They just take what they want and don't care who gets hurt.'

He looked at the man to see if he was following what he was saying but Arthur stared blankly back at him.

Larry hesitated. He hadn't had the chance yet to speak to Arthur about the Buddha, but he couldn't put it off any longer. 'There's a problem and I need to explain something to you. You know your wee Buddha statue. Well I think it's stolen and it could get you in trouble.'

Arthur looked like he was going to cry. 'Stolen? Trouble? My mum got it from her friend.'

Larry did his best to look sympathetic. 'I know, but maybe your mum's friend wasn't completely honest with her. I think he stole it or else got it from someone who did steal it.'

Arthur was shaking his head frantically from side to side.

'Look, I know someone who would buy it from you. You could get some money for it and then you wouldn't be in danger.'

'I don't need money. Mum left me money.' Arthur waved his hand vaguely round the room as if the money was on display.

'Okay, but there's still the problem of the danger it could put you in. If you don't need the money you could always give it to charity, or to a friend,' Larry added, seemingly as an afterthought.

It took a while but eventually Arthur agreed to let Larry take care of his Buddha. The question of what would happen with any money was left vague. He had offered to share the money with Arthur but the other man wasn't interested and, for the moment, that was good enough for Larry.

He went over the conversation as he made his way home. He felt bad about scaring Arthur, but there was probably an element of truth in what he'd told him. If the cops ever did come calling to Arthur's house they would spot the Buddha and that would be that. Plus, he was sure that some of the other stuff was knocked-off so Arthur could be in even more trouble.

He felt just fine about the money side of things. Arthur didn't need the money, didn't want it in fact, he'd said so himself, and Larry did. He had the copy, which he could either try and sell to Dixie or return to the insurance company. Hopefully, very soon, the cops would raid Black's casino and Larry would be in for a nice reward. He'd treat the family to a five-star holiday, and who knows what else. Sharon would surely stop giving him such a hard time. His luck was definitely changing at last.

Chapter 49

'Run that past me again,' Flint said. She brushed her fingers through her short spiky hair. 'You lost me after the word Buddha.'

McNally and Wallace went over the story again to their boss. She didn't appear convinced.

'We only have the word of this McAllister guy that this is correct. Right?'

Her two officers nodded. 'Correct,' McNally said, 'but he's got no reason to lie.' He saw Flint giving him a sceptical look. 'Well, okay he does lie, a lot, but I can't see any reason for him to lie about this. He knows we'd go through him like a dose of salts, plus, he'd risk antagonising Black.'

'Then there's the fact that he's already been in touch with the insurance company asking about the reward,' Wallace said. 'We've spoken to them, a bloke called Wilson.'

'And he's convinced?' Flint asked.

'Well, he's obviously reserving final judgement until he sees the thing for himself, but he confirms that he spoke to McAllister. He says he was clearly serious and, from the description, it sounds like the real thing.'

'But you said there was a copy. What if this is the copy?'

McNally acknowledged the point. 'It still allows us a pretext for getting into Black's office and putting him into custody until we can verify if it's genuine.'

'Who did you speak to in the Arts section?'

Wallace checked his notes. 'A DS called Valerie Jackson. She knew all about the Buddha. It was a high profile case, still is to some extent. She would be happy to come with us when we go to the casino.'

Flint looked thoughtful, apparently trying to decide how much to tell her officers. 'I'm not happy about launching a raid on the basis of this guy McAllister. Even if he's being genuine, he could be wrong.'

She held up a hand to silence the protests. 'Plus, our case is the murder of Tony Hamilton. Okay, if we can use this Buddha to get some leverage on Black then fair enough. But, if we go out on a limb like that and it goes wrong, it could jeopardise the murder enquiry.'

McNally and Wallace waited to see which way their boss would go. 'Louise has told me the Serious Crime unit are planning a raid on Black's casino this evening. They've been holding off in case it messed up our murder enquiry.'

'Very decent of them,' McNally said.

'Anyway, since we've had no luck so far at tying Black or his men to Tony Hamilton's murder, they're going ahead.'

'So if we tell them about the statue that would give us a reason for joining them,' Wallace said.

Flint nodded. 'Okay, but this needs careful handling. I know McAllister is no angel but we can't put him or his family in danger. I'll speak to Louise.'

She stood up to show that the meeting was at an end. 'Get the search warrants done, word them carefully so they can cover the statue but without making it specific. Talk to this DS Jackson from the Art section and give the insurance guy an update. We'll meet back here as soon as everything's in place.'

Flint had checked the search warrant and briefed her team. She'd already spoken to Spencer's boss, Mick Aitken, and acknowledged that his Organised Crime Unit would head up the operation. He was happy to let Flint and her team deal with the statue and anything that might be of relevance to Tony Hamilton's murder.

DS Jackson from the Art theft section wasn't known to Black so she would go in early, and discreetly station herself near Black's office with one of her colleagues. Flint and the rest would follow as soon as Jackson let Flint know she was in position.

The Organised Crime team had a warrant to search for illegal immigrants and Flint had a separate warrant to look for stolen property or anything that might be a murder weapon, which gave her wide scope. Flint's priority was to tie Black to the murder of Tony Hamilton but she would take anything that might put Black out of action for a while and disrupt his activities or just give her leverage on him. So far, they hadn't been able to link him to the murder even though his prints and DNA were found in various parts of the bookies shop.

Her phone buzzed. 'Right, guys, that's it. They're in position.' She followed Mick Aitken into the casino flanked by Spencer, McNally, Wallace and several uniformed officers.

Black and his two heavies, Stuart and Dunbar, were near the centre of the room, beside one of the roulette tables. As soon as Black saw Flint and her team, he glanced towards his office but Jackson and her colleague quickly took up position in front of the door along with a couple of uniformed officers.

'Hello again, pet,' Flint said, smiling at Black.

Mick Aitken stepped forward. 'We've got warrants to search these premises.'

Black put on a brave face. 'On what grounds?'

Aitken pushed the warrants into Black's hand. 'Read them for yourself.'

As the Serious Crime officers were directed to various parts of the casino, Flint turned back to Black. 'We've had reports that you've got women working here against their will. Got them locked away in some of the rooms. That's not nice, pet.'

Black smirked at her.

She walked over to Black's office. 'What's in here?'

'Just my office. No women in there.'

'Well, we'll just take a wee look, if you don't mind. She tried the handle. 'Do you want to open it for us, pet, or are we going to have to break it down?'

After a moment, Black nodded to Shug Dunbar and he produced a key and opened the door. Flint and her team filed in, followed closely by Black, Dunbar and Stuart.

Once they were in the room, Black's demeanour changed. 'Okay, you can see there are no women in here. Can we move on?'

Flint was not so easily manipulated. 'Why don't we have a seat and you can tell me what you know about illegal immigrants and people trafficking.' Flint had spotted the statuette as she entered the room, exactly where McNally had said it would be. She sat with her back to it and focused on Black.

McNally and Wallace flanked Dunbar and Stuart while Jackson and her colleague began opening filing cabinets. She could see Black following them with his eyes. Presumably he was wondering if they would spot the statue and, if they did, whether it would mean anything to them.

Black glared at her. 'I know nothing about people trafficking or illegal immigrants, except what I read in the papers or see on the telly. It's a human tragedy, but nothing to do with me.'

She could sense him starting to relax as the conversation remained on that topic. A moment later an officer came into the room, right on cue, and whispered something to her. Black was intrigued, though not particularly worried-looking.

Flint stood up. 'Right, well I need to go and see what my colleague has to show me upstairs. I'll leave you to get on with your work here. The relief

329

from Black was almost tangible. He managed to stop himself glancing at the Buddha.

As Flint walked to the door she turned to speak to Wallace and her gaze passed over the statue. It was nicely done. She paused and approached the statue.

'This is nice, very nice. Do you mind if I have a look?' She was already lifting the item from its shelf. 'This looks like it cost a bob or two, pet. Business must be good.'

Jackson had been looking through a file of papers and looked up, appearing to notice the statue for the first time. She feigned surprise and walked over to Flint. 'Could I see that, please, boss?' she said. 'I'm sure I've seen that somewhere before.'

'Have you?' Flint turned to Black. 'Is this thing famous or what?'

Jackson keyed something into her phone and scrolled down to find what she was looking for. After a minute she held the phone out to Flint.

'I think we have a problem, pet.' Flint said. 'It looks like your little statue here was nicked from the Glasgow Art Gallery a few years back.'

Black pushed his chair back and clambered to his feet, a picture of indignation. 'Nicked? Well not by me. I paid for it fair and square.'

'I'm sure you did love,' Flint said. 'I'm sure you got a receipt and have all the paperwork to prove it was legitimate.'

'I'll have it somewhere, but I'll need time to lay my hands on it.'

Flint nodded sympathetically. 'I understand, pet. In the meantime we'll need to take this with us. We'll give you a receipt of course. I'm afraid you're under arrest for handling stolen goods.'

Black glared at her. 'Call the lawyer,' he said to Vinny Stuart.

Flint allowed Wallace and Jackson and a couple of uniformed officers to lead Black away. She and the rest of the officers continued with the search for any evidence of people trafficking or, if they were really lucky, anything that connected Black or his men to Tony Hamilton's murder.

Chapter 50

Larry was watching the telly with Sharon but he was thinking hard about what to do with the Buddha. McNally had called him to say they'd caught Black red-handed with the original exactly where Larry had said it was. The man sounded pleased. So, finally, Larry was in the cops' good books.

McNally had assured him Black didn't have a clue that they knew about the statue in advance. Flint and the others had played their roles well. They had now contacted the insurance guy, Wilson, and once he'd come up with the current estimate of its value Larry would know roughly how much of a reward to expect. He could hardly believe it.

But what should he do with the copy? It was worth a lot less, so the reward would obviously be smaller. Dixie had given him an idea of how much it would sell for and had indicated he'd be interested in buying it himself. Even on the black market he would get more by selling it than he would by handing it over to the insurance people for the reward. He nodded to himself, decision made. He went into the kitchen and called Dixie, arranging to meet him in Hielan Jessies, a pub on the Gallowgate, not far from the Barras. He told Sharon he was nipping out to the pub, strictly speaking it wasn't a lie.

As he crossed the street to the pub, Larry kept touching the statue in his inside pocket. He'd taken the precaution of agreeing a price of five thousand quid with Dixie on the phone. There was no way he was going to hand over the piece just for Dixie to go on about how it wasn't in quite as good condition as he thought.

The pub was one of the traditional ones in that part of the city. Not spit and sawdust but definitely not one of your flash, trendy places. As he pushed the door open, several heads swivelled round to check him out before turning back to their pints and whiskies.

He found Dixie sitting alone, at a table in the corner at the back of the room. When he saw Larry he gave him a cautious smile. There was no offer of a drink and that suited Larry just fine. He wanted to get the business over and done with and he didn't want to be sitting around in a place like this with five thousand quid in his pocket.

'Let's see it then,' Dixie said quietly, as Larry sat down.

Larry smiled. 'Cash first, that's what we agreed.'

Dixie hesitated and glanced around him. For a moment Larry thought he was going to try and pull a fast one. Then he reached into his pocket, produced a bulky envelope and slid it across the table to Larry. As he reached for the money Dixie seized his hand.

'Your turn now,' he said.

Larry snatched his hand free. 'I'm going to count it first.' He nodded towards the toilet, 'in there.'

Dixie didn't look too happy but obviously didn't want to stir up too much attention. Eventually he gave a brief nod. 'It's in fifties. I'll give you two minutes. If you're not back out by then I'll come in and rip you a new arsehole.' He tilted his head to dismiss him.

A few minutes later Larry was out. He sat down again and handed over the bag containing the statue. Dixie held it below the level of the table, opened it and glanced inside. He studied it for a minute. Then he produced some sort of magnifying glass that he pressed into his eye and quickly examined the base of the statue.

Larry waited for the verdict.

Dixie eventually nodded. 'Good,' he finally said. 'It's been a pleasure doing business with you.'

Larry nodded and got up to leave. 'I might be able to lay my hands on some other good stuff, if you're interested.'

Dixie gave a cautious nod. 'Aye, maybe. Give me a shout and we'll see what we can do. You know where to find me.'

Larry kept looking over his shoulder as he hurried back to his car. It was not a good place or a good time of day to be walking about with that amount of money on him. He felt that everybody he passed knew exactly what he'd been up to and how much he was carrying. He also suspected Dixie wouldn't be above doing a bit of double-dealing, arranging for somebody to mug him and steal back the money he'd just handed over.

He'd parked the car as close as he could to the pub but it seemed like miles away. He didn't breathe easy until he was on his way home with the car doors locked. Every ten seconds he put his hand on the package in his pocket, the money sitting in the same spot the statue had occupied just a short time earlier.

When he arrived home he realised he hadn't thought about what to do with the money. He couldn't risk leaving it in the car. He wanted to surprise Sharon but it had to be done in the right way, otherwise she'd know he'd been up to something dodgy.

Chapter 51

It had been a long day and Flint's dark mood matched the looks her team were giving her as she brought them up to speed on the results of the casino raid.

'Louise's people found no evidence of people trafficking or prostitution in that casino.'

McNally swore. 'The guy's too careful to leave any dirt at his own back door.'

Flint paced back and forth across the room. 'Not to mention that we've found nothing to prove that Black or any of his men were responsible for the murder of Tony Hamilton.'

McNally didn't like the way this was going. 'You're not saying we'll need to let that scumbag walk? What about the statue?'

Flint was clearly none too happy about it either and in no mood to placate her Sergeant. She looked round the room at her team. 'You know how these things go down as well as I do, Tom. Look, we both know that Eddie Black has got the best lawyers on his payroll. All we've got on him at the moment is handling stolen property and you can bet he'll wheel out a dozen witnesses who'll say that he paid good money for that wee statue and bought it in good faith.'

McNally ran his hand through his hair. 'If it's worth a million quid, then surely to God that counts for something.'

'Aye, it will, but we're waiting on the insurance guy for the formal verification. In the meantime, his lawyer's bending the ear of Superintendent Murrie and the Fiscal. Look, Black's not going anywhere, Glasgow is his place. We'll have him back in here before you know it.'

She paused while Wallace took a phone call. She could tell from the look on his face that it might, finally, be good news. He conferred quietly with McNally before nodding to Flint.

'Okay, Willie, it looks like you've got something interesting to tell us. Don't keep me in suspense.'

McNally spoke first. 'We've just had an update on the CCTV. You know we've been looking at the footage for the area near the bookies shop but that the images weren't much use to us.'

Flint nodded. 'There was nothing much from the cameras covering the front door of the bookies and what there was wasn't sharp enough.'

'That's right, boss. It was all of too poor quality to give us anything we could use.' He paused, then added. 'In fact, what we did get would, if anything, tend to rule Black out.'

'So you told us to widen the search radius,' Wallace said.

'Which you both said would take forever.' Flint smiled. 'I'm assuming you've found something.'

'As well as widening the radius, Willie also had the idea of specifically checking the CCTV near Black's house and near the casino,' McNally said. 'Even though he had an alibi of sorts, we knew it wasn't watertight so we thought it was worth a go.'

'So did you see Black or any of his heavies?' Flint asked. She was getting impatient with this piecemeal story.

'We've sent the footage to your email, boss,' Wallace said. 'If you call it up we'll talk you through it.'

A few minutes later Flint saw why they were all so excited. 'Excellent work, guys. So much for his alibi.' She looked up from the screen. 'Right, I think we need to have another word with him and organise some new search warrants.'

Chapter 52

Casper dropped into the chair in his office, slumped forward and rubbed his face with his hands. After a minute he looked up and gave Larry a weary stare. Larry had never seen him look so knackered.

'What the hell's going on?' Larry said.

'I might as well tell you the whole story. You'll find out soon enough and if I tell you now you might be able to do something with it.'

Larry shrugged his shoulders and perched on the corner of the desk. 'I've no idea what you're going on about, Casper.'

'Black's after me, for real this time, the cops will soon be here to arrest me and my wife wants my guts for garters.'

'Nothing new there,' Larry said, trying to make light of it, despite the look on Casper's face. 'I've been in that boat for a couple of weeks now.'

Casper shook his head. 'You can never take anything seriously, can you? I'm telling you, I'm in deep shit this time.'

Larry leaned forward. 'For Christ's sake tell me then. What the hell's going on? What have you done?'

He didn't say anything for a minute so Larry prompted him. 'Is it to do with how you make your money?'

Casper looked startled. 'How do you know about it?'

'I don't really know anything, but there's no way that the amount of money this shop brings in is paying for your lifestyle, the house, the fancy car and Christine's spa weekends.'

'You're not as daft as you look, are you?' Casper nodded his head as if answering a question only he could hear. 'Aye, you're right. This place has been a dead loss for years. I took it over from my dad. In his day it was a good wee earner. But nowadays,' he paused, 'people want something different. Plus there's so much fucking red tape.'

'What have you been doing then?'

'Same as every other bastard. Drugs.'

It was what Larry had been half expecting but it was still a shock to hear it out loud. 'And the cops know?'

Another weary shake of the head. 'Not yet.'

'So how come they're after for you?'

'I'm coming to that. But Black's found out about the drugs.'

'Fuck.' It was all Larry could think of to say. They both knew what that meant.

'Aye, fuck right enough.'

'But what drugs and where are you getting them?'

'That's the only thing this place has been any use for. Every time I got a shipment of exotic fish or snakes there was cocaine in the crates.'

Larry was puzzled. 'I don't remember them.'

'I've got a wee place in London Road. That's where they got delivered to. Once or twice they had to come here so I made sure you weren't about.'

That explained the occasional early finish Casper had given him, Larry realised.

'What about selling them on?'

'I made sure I didn't step on anybody's toes here, especially Black's. I moved them on to other guys like myself in towns away from the central belt. So it was always low-key, below the radar.'

'Something went wrong?'

'You can say that again.' He looked up as if he'd heard a noise but then continued. 'I think Black found something on my phone. Then somebody talked and now he's after my blood.'

The image of the rabbit battered to death jumped into Larry's mind. He looked round, half expecting Black to walk through the door.

Casper sighed, it was almost a sob. 'You know what he's like. He can smell things out. He was pressuring me to sell this place. He wants to develop the whole block into a spa centre. He wanted it for a knock-down price, said the shop was a loss-maker and that he was doing me a favour anyway.'

Larry was beginning to understand. 'But you needed the shop as the cover for getting the drugs in and moving them on?'

A nod. 'Exactly. With what he was offering me, I'd have had to sell the house.'

'What about the cops? If they don't know about the drugs how come they're on your case? Have you got evidence that Black killed Tony and they want you to go on the record?'

Casper shook his head and laughed. 'Not exactly.' He looked up at Larry. 'Me and Tony had agreed we'd both hold off on selling to Black to try and up the price.'

'Risky,' Larry said.

'Then Tony told me he'd changed his mind. Or at least Black changed it for him. '

Larry knew exactly when and how that had happened, but he wasn't going to jump in at this stage. He nodded for Casper to continue.

'That night you and Sharon and the kids were over for your dinner, the Sunday, Tony called me. He told me what had happened that Friday in his back shop. It was Black and his heavies.'

Larry shrugged. 'No surprise there.'

Casper nodded. 'They gave him a right doing, threatened his wife, said they'd burn his shop down. That was it. Tony told me he was selling out to Black.'

Larry remembered Casper arguing with someone on the phone that night. No wonder Casper had been angry.

'When you and Sharon left. I called Tony back, said I'd offer him a deal if he kept his nerve. We agreed to meet in his shop. I told Christine that I had to go to the shop, that the cops had called to say somebody had tried to break in. She didn't question me.'

Larry was suddenly sure he knew where this was going. 'What deal were you going to offer him?'

Casper waved the question aside. 'I don't know. I hadn't really thought it through. I suppose I was going to offer him a cut of the drugs money. The main thing was I needed to stop him accepting Black's offer.'

'When I got to his shop he took me through to the back. He was paranoid that Black was keeping tabs on him. Anyway, to cut a long story short, he wasn't interested. When I hinted at the drugs thing he suggested he might tell Black about it to get in his good books.'

Despite the circumstances, Larry was outraged at Tony's tactics. 'What a bastard.'

'I know. I went for him. He tried to get out the back door. There was a baseball bat propped up in the corner, I grabbed it and walloped him, just once. Just the once. He dropped straight down. Never made a sound.'

Larry thought back to the Monday morning when he'd first heard the news about Tony's murder. 'So that Monday when you turned up at my place as if you had just heard about Tony…'

'It was all an act. Well maybe not all. I mean I was shit scared. But aye, I was building up a picture in people's minds that it was a complete shock to me the same as everybody else.'

Larry's mind was whirring. All this time he was so sure that Black had killed Tony. All those visits to the police station, the photos, the threats. Jesus Christ. He'd been worrying himself senseless about having to testify that Eddie Black had killed Tony and all the time it was his own fucking brother-in-law, Casper.

343

'How have you managed to keep it quiet all this time?'

Casper looked at him. 'What do you mean? Who was I going to tell?'

'Why are you telling me now, then?'

'The cops know. They're coming for me. They're just putting the final pieces of the jigsaw together. They've asked me questions, and Christine, different questions from the first few times. These are questions where you know that they know the answers.'

'Like what?'

'Where was I on the Sunday night, the night that Tony was killed? Was I sure I didn't go out that night.'

Casper shrugged his shoulders as if to say the game was up. 'I had already told them that I had stayed in all night but Christine has just phoned me. They've been at the house, asking her if she wants to change her story, was she sure I didn't go out on the Sunday night, dropping in wee hints about having me on CCTV somewhere between my house and Tony's shop. They know I lied.'

Larry couldn't take it in. Everything was happening too fast. 'Christ, what's Sharon going to say? This will kill her.'

Casper didn't bother to reply.

'What did you do with the baseball bat? After…, you know?'

Casper walked to the back of the shop and rummaged about in the storage space. A minute later he came back swinging the bat.

'Christ, it's been here all this time? What if the cops had searched here and found it?'

Casper shrugged, past caring now. 'I panicked. After I hit him and realised he was dead, I ran out of the shop. I was halfway down the street and realised I was still holding this fucking thing. I thought about throwing it in the Clyde but I realised it might float. So I nipped in here and hid it behind those old bird cages. I sort of blanked it out, pretended it wasn't there.'

'When do you think the cops will get here?'

Before Casper could answer, the door was slammed open and Flint strode in, flanked by McNally and Wallace.

Chapter 53

The next few minutes were a blur. They arrested Casper, went through the formalities and hustled him out to the car.

McNally stayed to, as he put it, 'give Larry a wee update on the raid' and it wasn't good news.

Larry couldn't believe his ears. 'What do you mean Black's statue wasn't the original? It didn't have the three dots on the base did it? The one with the three dots is the copy.'

McNally was almost smiling. 'You had it the wrong way round. The one with the three dots is the genuine article. Black had the copy.'

'No way.' Larry's mind was racing. 'You're having me on.'

'We've had the word from the expert in the insurance company. Black's was the copy. In any case they've now had the original returned to them.'

'Returned to them? How? What do you mean?' Larry's mind was racing. It didn't make any sense.

'Just what I say. Somebody called them, they had the original and they'll get the reward.'

A sickening thought started to form in Larry's head. 'You're loving this aren't you?'

For a moment McNally looked like he might get angry. 'It's not that bad. You'll still get the reward for the copy, maybe a few thousand, the guy said. He'll be in touch.'

Larry shook his head, his brain trying to process what he'd just been told. He was desperate to deal with it but he pushed it aside for a moment to ask McNally a question. 'Tell me one thing. What made you suspect Casper for Tony's murder?'

McNally laughed. 'We never suspected him. We were searching CCTV footage from near where Eddie Black lived, and who did we see out and about on the Sunday night when he had told us he was tucked up in bed?'

Larry nodded. Casper had told him that Black lived quite near him. So Casper was caught by a complete fluke.

He watched McNally stroll out of the shop and saw his boss, DCI Flint, coming in.

'I just wanted to thank you for your help over the last couple of weeks,' she said.

Larry was taken aback. Unlike McNally, she seemed genuine. He shrugged. 'Aye, well, I tried my best.'

Flint nodded. 'People like Black always seem to get off scot free. It sickens me. I saw it all the time in Newcastle. But we'll keep after him. If you ever think of anything that might be useful give me a quiet word. If he's causing you trouble let me know and I'll see what I can do. No promises, mind.'

Larry was amazed. Maybe it was just her accent but the woman seemed genuine. 'Thanks, I appreciate it.'

Flint nodded and made to leave when a thought occurred to Larry and he called her back. 'Actually, there might be something.'

Larry tried to put Casper out of his mind for the moment. He gave Sharon a quick call but she'd already had a call from Christine and was expecting the worse. When Larry gave her the update she went silent and said she'd talk later.

With that out of the way, he needed to think about the Buddha. At first he was sure McNally had been winding him up but then the pieces fell into place and he realised it was true. He'd been conned, good and proper by that bastard, Dixie.

He called Dixie's number, but of course there was no answer. His only option was to try the Barras. He quickly closed the shop and ran along the Gallowgate as fast as he could. Dixie must have spotted his opportunity right from the outset when Larry had first asked him about the statue.

He'd kill him. If the bastard thought he could cheat Larry, he had another thought coming. When he reached the spot, Dixie was nowhere to be seen, his usual stuff wasn't on the stall and there was nobody minding the place. He looked around frantically and saw another stall holder. He ran over.

'Any idea where Dixie is today?'

The man laughed. 'Everybody seems to want to speak to him. 'Haven't you heard? He won the lottery. Him and that wee spiky-haired assistant of his have gone off to some Greek island.'

'The lottery?'

The man shrugged his shoulders. That's what he said anyway. He's obviously come into money of some sort.'

'How do you mean?'

'Well, he sold all his stuff in a job lot to some bloke, at a knock-down price from what I hear.'

Larry swore. The bastard had cheated him. He obviously knew all along which statue was the genuine one. He was about to turn away when something the man had said echoed in his mind.

'You said somebody else was looking after him.'

'Aye, that's right.'

'Who was it, do you know?'

'I don't know him to speak to and I wouldn't want to but I've seen him around. A right evil-looking bastard from all I've heard, especially with those two blokes he always has with him. I'd probably know the name if I heard it.'

Larry nodded. The pieces were falling into place. 'Eddie Black?'

'That's the one.'

'Did he say what he wanted Dixie for?'

'Something about Dixie having sold him a fake but charging him for the real thing. Christ, I wouldn't want to be Dixie if that guy ever catches up with him.'

As he headed back to the shop Larry was thinking it through. Dixie must have been involved in the theft of the Buddha, either directly or he knew the people involved. He had got hold of the copy and sold it to Black as the genuine article, either knowingly or otherwise.

When Larry approached him, Dixie had misled him about the markings. Then when Larry came back to sell the 'copy' to him, Dixie knew his trick had worked. He'd obviously contacted the insurance people and got the reward that should have been Larry's.

That was the story of his life. Every time he thought he was going to get a break, something buggered it up. Okay he was no angel himself but what Dixie had done to him was in a different class. Part of him hoped Black would catch up with Dixie.

He got back to the shop and opened up. He'd just slumped down on a chair when, for the second time that day, the door was slammed open.

'Where is the wee bastard?'

Larry had become used to Black storming in but he'd never seen the man looking so angry and dangerous. At first he thought it might be about the Buddha statue and that he was somehow going to blame Larry.

Before Larry could get a word out of his mouth Black was right in his face and seized him by the throat.

'Did you know about it?' He slapped Larry twice. 'Did you fucking know about it?'

Was he talking about the statue or Casper killing Tony or maybe even something else? Larry couldn't answer because Black was cutting off his air supply. He frantically pointed to his throat, trying to indicate that he was suffocating.

Eventually Black released his grip and threw Larry to the floor. He leaned over him. 'Did that wee bastard Casper tell you about it?'

Spittle from the man's mouth was spraying onto Larry's face but he didn't try and wipe it away.

Larry realised the 'it' in question had to be the drug deals that Casper had told him about a couple of hours ago. There was no way he was going to acknowledge that he'd known about it, even if it was only at the last minute. Black wasn't interested in such distinctions.

He needed to divert him. Larry thought frantically and a thought struck him. The first thing Black had asked was where Casper was. So that meant he didn't know that Casper had killed Tony and had been arrested by the police. As Casper had feared, Black knew about the drugs.

'He's been nicked by the cops. Just an hour or two ago.' Larry was fighting to get his breath back and his throat was killing him.

'Nicked? By those bastards?' Black's face looked like it was going to explode. 'So they know about the drugs?'

Larry was about to reassure him that they didn't know about the drugs but then he remembered he wasn't supposed to know anything about them either. He put on his best puzzled frown. 'Drugs? What do you mean?'

Another slap. Larry's ears were buzzing.

'If they don't know about the drugs then what the fuck have they arrested the wee shite for?'

Larry felt a strange sense of power, almost victory. For once he had the upper hand over Black. Even if it was just the fact that he knew something the other man didn't. He had to play it cool. If he so much as smiled he'd be picking his teeth up from the floor for the rest of the day.

'I thought you'd have heard. They've arrested him for Tony's murder.'

Black looked as if he was the victim of some practical joke. For a minute he didn't say anything, he didn't move. He continued to lean over Larry and seemed to stare right through him.

Finally he reacted. 'Murder? Tony? Casper? You have got to be fucking kidding me.'

'No. It's true.'

'What did he want to murder Tony for?'

Larry was getting on to dangerous territory again. He wasn't going to tell Black that his actions had, at least indirectly, driven Casper to kill Tony.

'I haven't got a clue. His wife phoned me to tell me.'

Black clenched his fist as if he was about to thump Larry but he turned away and spoke to Dunbar. 'Get on to our contact. Find out what the fuck is going on with that bastard, Casper. I want to talk to him.'

As Black left he turned back to Larry. 'By the way I'll be buying this place soon. I've got big plans. So your days playing with fucking rabbits are numbered.'

Tina almost ran into the shop, her eyes wide, her mouth hanging open and her arms spread out to the side.

'Are you kidding me?' she said, even though Larry hadn't said anything.

He gave a wry smile. 'So you've heard?'

'Of course I've heard. It's all over the street.' She wagged a finger at him. 'The question is, how come I had to hear it second or third-hand rather than straight from you? I thought we were mates.'

Mates, Larry thought. He liked the sound of that. He could do with a good mate. 'Sorry, but it's not that long since I heard myself and then I was tied up with the cops. They asked me all sorts of questions again. Then I had to tell Sharon, she's his sister.'

'What did she say?'

'Went mental. Couldn't believe it. I'm just off the phone to her and then I was going to come in and tell you.'

Tina made a face to show she didn't completely believe him. She parked herself in a chair. 'Right, give me the whole story.'

After Tina had left, Larry tried to absorb everything that had happened. He had suspected Casper was up to something dodgy but murder, that was something else. That female cop was a bit of a surprise. Hard as nails of course, but there was something different about her. Would she do anything about what Larry had asked her?

Then there was Dixie, he had cheated Larry out of a fortune. A little voice was niggling away at

Larry, even though he tried not to listen. Dixie had conned Larry big time, no doubt about it. But, Larry had been trying to con Arthur in the same way, hadn't he? Maybe he had been a wee bit ruthless with Arthur after all. Christ, what was happening to him? He wasn't suddenly going to become a saint, but he might need to be a wee bit more selective about who he took advantage of.

Chapter 54

Larry stood at the back door of the shop having his usual smoke. He didn't have to hide it from Casper any longer. He inhaled deeply, relishing the bitter taste.

Even when, if ever, Casper finally got back to the shop, it wouldn't be the same shop. Christine had told Larry she'd made a decision, partly influenced by Larry's own suggestions. Things were going to have to change. He'd told her how few customers there were, that the shop was a dead loss, had been for years. It seemed to come as no surprise to her. Maybe Casper had told her about the drug deals and that they were the only thing keeping them afloat.

Christine had been open with Larry, she was going to have to get used to having less money. She was clearly blaming Casper for everything but Larry wondered if she was as innocent as she was letting on. In any event she didn't seem to be the naïve wife Larry had taken her for. She was working out how she could salvage something from the mess Casper had left her in.

It turned out she wasn't particularly keen on animals either. So, with one thing and the other, it was an easy decision for her to make. The pet shop would be closing for business as soon as practically possible. They'd sell the stock on to another shop, somebody Casper had put

Christine in touch with. Larry would help her work out the details.

He took a last drag of his cigarette and threw it to the ground. He stepped back into the shop and looked around the place. He wouldn't miss it; that was for sure. Even better, he wouldn't be out of work for long.

Larry smiled as he remembered his conversation with Flint that day. She'd asked if there was anything she could do about Black. She obviously hated the way criminals like him could take over a city. So, taking her at face value, Larry told her there was maybe a way to scupper Black's plans for his spa development. It would depend on Flint and her superiors running with it. It was walking past the Art Gallery and the Kelvin Hall so many times on his way to Arthur's that had put the idea into Larry's head.

He had told her that if she could somehow persuade the council to have some of the properties in the street classed as listed buildings it might make the whole project too complicated and costly for Black. At first he thought she was going to reject it out of hand. She told Larry it wasn't that simple, it wasn't actually the council's decision and, in any case, it could take time. But then she had smiled as if remembering something and said she'd see what she could do, that somebody in the council owed her a favour and they might be able to pull some strings. Larry didn't really know if it would go anywhere, but, somehow, she'd pulled it off. He wasn't sure if the properties were actually listed yet but it seemed word had got out to Black that it was going to happen, and soon.

Black had dropped the planning application for his spa hotel idea. He decided he wouldn't be able to carry out the development he wanted at the price he wanted, so he was no longer interested in buying the pet shop or the bookies or any of the other properties. It turned out that the sale of the café hadn't actually been legally finalised and he had withdrawn his offer.

Christine had spoken to Rosa and they were going into partnership. It was Larry who gave her the idea and when she told him it was going ahead he had to admit he was excited. They'd knock through the adjoining wall and make one, large café-deli. The listed building status didn't impact on alterations like that. Christine knew he'd had previous experience in restaurants so they were offering Larry a job; that was that, a done deal.

If he had the choice, he would probably have chosen a life of idle riches but that wasn't on offer. He'd always fancied getting back into working in a restaurant or café. Then there was the bonus that he'd be working alongside Tina, his mate. She always made him laugh.

He thought back over the events of the last few weeks. He'd been battered and threatened by Eddie Black and put under the cosh by the cops. He'd come within touching distance of £100,000 but it had been snatched away by that thieving bastard, Dixie. At least he'd got a few grand from him for selling him the Buddha, the real one. Plus, he'd got a couple of grand from the insurance company for helping them get the copy back from Black.

The cops had stuck to their word about making sure Black didn't know that it was Larry that had tipped them off about the Buddha. He had to hope it stayed that way. The odd thing was that, in a way, he'd done Black a favour. It was only because of Larry that Black had discovered he'd been sold the copy. But somehow, he didn't think Black would see it that way.

He wondered where Dixie was. The guy must have acted fast to get the statue to the insurance people and then get out of the country. He'd be living it up on some Greek island. Then again, he'd be looking over his shoulder for the rest of his life.

Larry wasn't a religious person but somewhere deep inside himself, he knew he would never have been allowed to get that much money. God, or fate or whatever you wanted to call it, had stepped in. Some people were just unlucky. What would have happened if he'd got the money? He could never have handled it.

Another thought struck him. If Black's statue had been the real one then he would have been out for vengeance on whoever was responsible for him losing it. Even though the cops had kept it quiet, it would have been obvious to everyone that Larry had come into a lot of money. It wouldn't have taken Black long to join the dots. Maybe Larry had been lucky after all.

In any case, things could be worse, he wouldn't have to work in the pet shop any more, Black was no longer hassling him, and Sharon had stopped comparing him unfavourably to her wonderful brother. She never knew about the potential of the big money, she was delighted with the five grand that would get them a nice holiday and a new telly and washing machine. Her head was so messed up by Casper being charged with murder that she didn't question Larry too closely about the details of the reward money.

He was pulled out of his daydreaming by the door bell. It was Arthur. He looked about cautiously before stepping into the shop, presumably still scared of bumping into Eddie Black.

'Hi, Arthur, so, have you finally made a decision about buying a second rabbit?' Larry had let him know they were having a closing-down sale.

The man nodded and smiled, more relaxed now. 'I think Larry needs a friend.'

Larry was used to this by now and just laughed. 'Well, we can all do with friends.'

Arthur was gazing at the rabbit he had pointed out on a previous visit. 'I want this one,' he said.

Larry nodded. 'Good choice. I'll get it all sorted for you and bring it to your house tonight with all the bits and pieces.'

'The accessories,' Arthur said.

'Exactly.' As Larry looked at the man he thought about his recent conversation with him. After some soul-searching, he had tried to get

Arthur to take a share of the reward money but he wouldn't hear of it. Well, at least he had made the effort.

An idea suddenly struck him, he'd give Arthur his rabbit for free. It was the least he could do, a gesture; he would put the money into the till himself. It was already on sale, so it wouldn't cost him that much

In any case, Larry told himself, there was still more money to be made. The wee Buddha statue was just one among a whole load of stuff in Arthur's house. He was sure he could persuade Arthur to part with some of them and Larry was the man to help him sell them.

Was he taking advantage of Arthur again? No, this time he'd insist on splitting the proceeds. Fifty-fifty would be a fair way of doing it. But then again, he'd be doing all the work; no point in going crazy. On second thoughts, sixty-forty had a better ring to it.

Acknowledgements

I'd like to say a massive thank you to everyone who has helped or encouraged me with this book. The members of my two Writers' Groups, Strathkelvin and Kelvingrove, have read and commented on numerous extracts of the book and their input has been invaluable.

A sincere thank you also to my beta readers: Irene Lebiter, Patricia Hutchinson, Suze Clarke-Morris, Irene Paterson and Edna Carson. Their eagle eyes helped me avoid many mistakes. Any errors that remain are mine.

Thank you to all my family and friends, their enthusiasm and encouragement helped carry me through to the final full stop. They spread the word among their friends and colleagues by word of mouth and online. Moira, Jennifer, Kevin and Melissa also read all or part of the book and gave me lots of suggestions that helped improve it.

Steven Gladman designed the fabulous cover, thanks Steven.

Tom Carr won the 'Name a Character' auction at the annual dinner of the excellent JMA Trust. The trust does really worthwhile work and you can

read about it here on Facebook. (https://www.facebook.com/JMATrustCharity/).
Tom opted to use the name of his friend, Brian Murrie, so I 'recruited' Brian into Police Scotland as Detective Superintendent Brian Murrie.

Most of all, I thank my wife, Moira, and my children, Jennifer and Kevin. They've encouraged me so much in my writing from the start, giving me practical and moral support, providing endless suggestions and keeping me motivated and on track.

Most of the details about Glasgow are accurate but I have taken the occasional liberty with geography and the location of some businesses.

About the author

Pat Feehan is a native of Glasgow. 'Lucky Larry' is his second book. His first novel, 'Snap Judgement', is available from Amazon as an e-book or paperback; you can find it by following this link ('Pat Feehan - Snap Judgement').

Pat was recently shortlisted for The Scottish Arts Trust Short Story Award 2020 for his story, 'The Kill'. The story appears in the Scottish Arts Trust anthology, 'Life on the Margins and Other Stories' (www.storyawards.org).

You can get in touch with Pat on Facebook or on Twitter: @pat_feehan

Printed in Poland
by Amazon Fulfillment
Poland Sp. z o.o., Wrocław